PICKLED PINK IN PARIS

A JULIA FAIRCHILD MYSTERY

PJ PETERSON

FINNGIRL, LLC

Pickled Pink in Paris

Copyright © 2021 by PJ Peterson

This is a work of fiction. Names, characters, places, and incidents either are the product of the author's imagination or are used fictitiously. Any resemblance to actual persons, living or dead, events, or locales is entirely coincidental.

All rights reserved. No part of this book may be reproduced or used in any manner without written permission of the copyright owner except for the use of quotations in a book review. For more information, address: pj@pjpetersonauthor.com

Book design by 100 Covers

IngramSpark ISBN
978-1-7336575-6-5

www.pjpetersonauthor.com

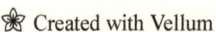 Created with Vellum

*To my sister Carleen Olsen.
She's the best little sister ever.*

FOREWORD

This is the third in a series of novels featuring Julia Fairchild, MD. She loves to travel and finds herself embroiled in mysteries despite her plans to limit her diagnostic skills to her medical practice.

BOOKS BY PJ PETERSON

Blind Fish Don't Talk

Rembrandt Rides a Bike

Pickled Pink in Paris

1
SUNDAY

"Where could he be?" Julia asked Carly. "Josh said he'd meet us after we cleared Customs." She again searched the crowd of hopeful faces in the waiting area of the Charles de Gaulle airport. Her heart dropped at not seeing him, then raced wildly in her chest as she had a moment of anxiety about making the decision to meet Josh in Paris at all.

She turned back to her sister. "Do you see him yet? Maybe I shouldn't have come. Maybe he'll be sorry he asked me to join him. Maybe he won't be here after all. Maybe…"

Carly rolled her eyes as she listened to her older sister. "You sure have a lot of doubts for someone who has to make split-second decisions regularly in your real life. Haven't you two been staying in touch regularly? Everything will be fine."

Dr. Julia Fairchild, now in her late thirties, had built a busy internal medicine practice in southwest Washington State over the ten years since she finished her residency. It was a challenge to take more than a week off at a time, but she had persuaded her new partner to cover for her while she made this big trip. She had met Josh Larson, a fortyish Washington D.C. corporate attorney who specialized in mergers, a few years earlier at an international hospital conference in

Monte Carlo. They had reconnected the previous fall, when he had shown up in Amsterdam while she and Carly were there on a tap-jazz dancing tour. She'd been thrilled when he had invited her to meet him in Paris the following spring, where he had scheduled business meetings. Josh had explained that he would be busy with his company's clients much of the time for the first several days of her trip, so Julia had suggested inviting her sister to keep her company. Now doubts clouded Julia's thoughts.

"What if you don't have a good time after I've talked you into coming?"

"Julia, calm down," said Carly. "I'm sure we'll both have a grand time here. How could someone come to Paris and *not* enjoy themselves?" She patted Julia's hand, which was resting on the fence separating the arriving passengers from the greeters. "Maybe we got through Customs faster than he could get through the airport traffic," she added. "Didn't he tell you the congestion here was horrendous?"

"Yes, but—hey, I see my name on a placard." Julia pointed to a line of livery drivers holding up signs identifying their intended passengers. "Follow me."

Julia and Carly dragged their luggage through the throng of travelers, saying "Pardon" several times as they moved slowly toward the uniformed man. He was of smallish build, with graying black hair, a cleft chin, and small dark eyes. He smiled as Julia and Carly approached him.

"Bonjour. I'm Julia Fairchild," she said, pointing to her name on his sign, "and this is my sister, Carly Pedersen. I don't see Josh. Isn't he here?"

"Welcome to Paris, mesdemoiselles," the chauffeur said with a slight bow. "My name is Vincent. Monsieur Larson is unable to be here. Please allow me to take you to your hotel and you will learn more." He took charge of their luggage and led the way to a gleaming black limousine.

Carly whistled. "Pretty fancy, sis. I should travel with you more often." Carly Pedersen, a homebody at heart with a golden mop of hair, hazel eyes, and an effervescent smile, didn't usually get the opportunity to travel to Europe and had jumped at the chance. Her husband, Rob, was quickly mollified by her promise to learn to prepare some French dishes at Le Cordon Bleu.

Julia flashed her a happy grin, pleased that Carly had agreed to come on this trip. As a physician dedicated to continuing medical education, Julia had traveled over the years to international conferences, but had not made it to Paris until now.

The chauffeur poured a flute of champagne for each of the sisters once they were settled in the limo. They toasted each other and Paris, then enjoyed the crisp bubbly drink in comfort as they motored through the city. Though disappointed that Josh hadn't met her at the airport with a bouquet of flowers and a kiss, Julia was too enthralled with the thrill of visiting Paris for the first time to dwell on it.

Carly sighed. "Pinch me, Julia. I'm not sure this is real yet."

"I don't recall the last time I was in a limousine," said Julia. "It wasn't the 'in' thing when I went to our high school prom."

"As if there even were any limos in our little town."

"That would be the other reason," Julia agreed. She pointed. "Look straight ahead, Carly. I can see the Eiffel Tower from here. It's so majestic. Let's plan to go to the top."

"I hope you mean by elevator." Carly had never been the athletic type but served as a cheerleader for Julia's efforts at running and tap dancing.

"Maybe we can walk partway up," Julia said, "and take the elevator the rest of the way."

The limousine stopped in front of an elegant older building, Hotel du Champs de Mars, which was nestled in the chic Gros-Caillou neighborhood of Paris. Julia had noticed a mix of embassies and other posh hotels and upscale restaurants lining the tranquil streets as Vincent drove through the area. She loved the welcoming "Old World" ambience of the entrance, where a debonair valet dressed in a gold-trimmed red and black uniform stood at the door, ready to help the new guests.

"Bonjour, mesdemoiselles. Welcome to Paris." He bowed gallantly, longish brown curls framing his young face, then helped Julia and Carly alight from the limo.

"Bonjour and merci, monsieur," Julia managed to say in her rusty high school French.

Julia and Carly grinned at each other and linked arms as they entered the foyer. Josh had told Julia he had arranged their stay at this hotel because of its location near the Eiffel Tower and other popular attractions. He had also told her that it was his favorite place to stay when he had business meetings in the city.

"Welcome to Hotel du Champs, Ms. Fairchild and Ms. Pedersen," said the desk clerk. "Mr. Larson left you a message, which you will find in your room. I hope you enjoy your stay with us." He motioned to the bellman, who had secured their bags on a cart, and who then led them to the elevators on his left, and on to their room on the fourth floor.

The bellman opened the door and stepped aside while Julia and Carly entered the suite. Julia stood still momentarily, gazing at the elegantly appointed room. A small settee and chair graced the main room. The bed looked inviting, with layers of pillows and a lush comforter. "I feel like a princess in here. This is my favorite shade of blue. Look at the detail, Carly." She plopped onto the bed. "I'm in love with Paris already."

Carly peered out the window, which opened onto the street below. "It's not far to the closest bistro either."

After tipping the young man, Julia eagerly tore open the envelope, which she saw was written on high-quality ecru paper.

"What's up with Josh?" Carly asked impatiently.

"His note says he has to entertain some important clients for dinner tonight. He says to meet him in the lobby here at four o'clock for a glass of wine." Julia checked her watch. "It's two now. We can wander around a little before we meet Josh and unpack later. Is that okay with you?"

"Sounds good to me," said Carly. "So does a warm cookie. I saw them downstairs in the lobby, but the bellman walked right on by before I could grab one."

Julia smiled, knowing Carly's fondness for sweets, especially fresh-baked cookies. "We can go down and get one on our way out the door." She headed back out the door and waited in the lobby while Carly nabbed their treats.

"How many museums on the list this time, sis?" Carly asked as they started walking down the street, cookies in hand.

"Six, I think. We can do more if you like."

"Six." Carly groaned. "You know how much I loathe musty old museums. I saw my share of them on the last trip with you—as well as their storage vaults, art, and forgeries. I don't want a repeat of *that* experience."

Julia grimaced. Too true. Neither did Julia. In fact, Carly had been kidnapped because of Julia's snooping around a murder in Amsterdam. Thankfully, with some help, Carly had been rescued. If anything, Julia owed her little sister a fabulous trip with no drama. "Agreed. Although you have to admit it was memorable." Julia ducked as Carly pretended to hit her with her bag. "Anyway, there are only a couple of absolute must-see museums here. We can't leave Paris without at least going to the Louvre and Notre Dame."

"I can tolerate visiting two of them."

"And maybe Versailles."

"That's three," said Carly.

"One museum, one cathedral, and one palace," Julia clarified as they negotiated crossing a busy street. "Think of them more as beautiful historical landmarks that happen to contain marvelous works of art."

"Very clever, Julia. Where are we going now?"

"I want to get my bearings around this area." Julia found their location on the map she'd accepted from the desk clerk. "The streets here are crazy, from what I saw in the guidebook. It reminds me of trying to find my way around St. Maarten." Although Paris was a full-sized city compared to the small towns of the Caribbean island, both locations perplexed visitors with their seemingly haphazard layout. Julia tried to shake off the thought of that island vacation, another trip that went awry. Julia felt herself scowl. She'd taken that trip to meet up with Tony—and that certainly went sour. And here she was again, this time to meet up with Josh. Would Josh also prove to be not what—

"Where are the street signs? They would be helpful right about now." Carly interrupted Julia's thoughts as they stopped at the street's end, and Carly looked right and left.

"Look on the corner of the building, about six or seven feet up." Julia pointed out a plaque bearing the street name. "We probably shouldn't wander too far away, since we're meeting Josh at four." She studied the map again, comparing it to her surroundings. "The Eiffel Tower is nearby," she said, pointing toward the park surrounding the famous structure. "We can walk around the grounds for maybe half an hour, then turn around and get back to the hotel to change and freshen up."

"Works for me. Lead the way."

The stately buildings gave way to lush greenery as they approached the Parc du Champs al Mars, which surrounded the Eiffel Tower itself. All cares melted away for Julia as she absorbed the Parisian beauty. Trees and shrubs and lush green lawns covered the acres and acres of parkland. Julia had read that three hundred workers had built the tower from eighteen thousand pieces in two years, two months, and two days, finishing in time for the opening of the World's Fair in Paris on May 15, 1889.

"Oh my. *C'est magnifique*," Julia said, snapping a few photos with her Nikon.

"It's worth the walk, I'd say. How many steps did you say it is to the top?" Carly asked.

"One thousand seven hundred ten. At the YMCA, there was a challenge to climb that many steps by doing one hundred eight round trips on the staircase."

"Wouldn't half of those be going downhill? That seems like cheating, kind of."

"But how else would you get back to the bottom of the stairs?" asked Julia, craning her neck to peer at the top of the tower. "Frankly, I agree that the elevator is a perfectly good option when we decide to go up. The website suggested going to the top in the late afternoon, and then staying to watch as the nighttime city lights turn on. That would be gorgeous, I'm sure." She sighed dreamily. "Then we could walk *down*."

After a few more minutes of admiring the lush ground-level scenery, it was time to leave to meet Josh. "Okay, Girl Scout," Carly teased. "Let's see how you do with your directions back to the hotel."

Julia turned the map upside down to help her retrace their steps. Then she raised her hand in the air, pointed her finger, and said, "That way."

They passed a few tourists and several people walking

dogs—not a French poodle among them. Several kiosks plastered with notices and handbills were scattered along the way. Julia suddenly stopped and grabbed Carly's arm.

"What is it? Why are you stopping?"

Tapping a handbill advertising tango lessons, Julia said, "Wouldn't that be fun?"

"Tango lessons? Not on my bucket list," Carly said, shaking her head.

"But we're in Paris. What better opportunity to learn the tango than right here?" Julia hummed a sultry tune as she danced solo on the sidewalk.

"Uh, Julia. People are staring at you, if you don't mind."

Julia giggled. "Oops. I got carried away."

Carly stood with her hands on her hips. "What would we do for partners if we went?"

"Josh, for me. Perhaps they have extra men who take these lessons." She tore off one of the stubs with the phone number. "Wouldn't hurt to call."

Carly shook her head more vigorously. "Not me. I'd almost rather go to a museum. Let's keep walking."

Five minutes later they were in the hotel lobby, where they found Josh waiting. Julia felt her breath quicken at the sight of the dark-haired, blue-eyed man with his trim athletic build. He returned her smile with a huge grin of his own, then enveloped Julia in a big hug, winking at Carly, who pretended to be embarrassed by the public display of affection. She was mollified by her own welcoming hug in turn. The trio chatted and laughed as they sauntered to the private patio, where a young, buff waiter seated them and took drink orders.

"Julia, let me explain what's happened since my last email to you," Josh said as he took Julia's hands in his own. "As you know, I was planning to stay at this same hotel so I would be close to you."

"You did say this was your favorite place. Where are you staying instead?"

"The Marriott on the Champs-Élysées. Roger Westover, one of my business partners, had arranged for us to stay in a suite of rooms because several of our clients are from out of town."

"I don't get it," said Julia. "Why do you have to stay together?"

"Here come our drinks. I'll explain in a minute."

Julia caught the waiter winking at Carly as he served the beverages. She smiled, recalling other moments when her adorable golden-haired younger sister had attracted a man's eye. Their Finnish heritage provided them both with striking high cheekbones, although Julia was bestowed brunette locks and sparkly blue eyes, in contrast to her sister's blonde curls and hazel eyes.

"First, a toast to two beautiful women who make Paris even more lovely." Josh raised his glass, with the sisters following suit. "Salud."

Julia tasted the delightful pinot grigio, which had been chilled to the perfect temperature, as Carly sipped her gimlet.

"Here's the story, Julia." Josh took a big breath. "Okay, normally we would meet our clients at local restaurants or in their own offices; but these men, except Pierre, came to Paris from other cities. It seemed easier to have our meetings in the hotel rather than trying to find a restaurant with a meeting room. Anyway, Roger told me a couple of clients had insisted that we stay at the hotel with them."

"Does that mean I won't be seeing you?" Julia asked.

"No, but it will be less of me for now," Josh replied. "That's why I'm glad you have Carly with you. I know you will find fun things to do. We'll catch up after these guys leave town in a couple of days."

Julia sighed and said, "I understand."

"In the meantime," said Josh, "I have instructed your concierge to take care of any tickets or excursions that you would like to do at my expense. And the limousine is at your disposal."

"You don't have to do all that," said Julia, disappointed that he had made arrangements as though he had known he wouldn't be joining them.

"Actually, my company can afford it, and they owe it to me, seeing as how they put us in this position in the first place."

Julia kissed Josh on the cheek. "Thank you, but I'd rather see you."

"You will in a couple of days. I promise."

Julia smiled hesitantly. "I knew we would have to entertain ourselves for the first couple of days anyway, so we have a Cordon Bleu course scheduled for tomorrow, and we can work in some sightseeing while we're waiting."

Carly piped up. "Julia is hoping you will want to take tango lessons with her while you're here."

"She is, huh?" Josh said, raising an eyebrow. "Sounds interesting. That might be safer than your tap dance adventures last year."

"I'm not planning to get involved in any murders this trip. Scout's promise." Julia raised her glass.

Carly snorted. "As if you could avoid them."

"A cooking class at Cordon Bleu sounds safe enough to me," Josh said as he finished his drink. "Just don't poison anyone."

2

MONDAY MORNING

Julia and Carly entered the main doors of Le Cordon Bleu, French for "The Blue Ribbon," and introduced themselves to a young woman who escorted them to meet their instructor. The modern building was a sharp contrast to what Julia had expected, knowing the school had existed since 1895. Their guide gave them a brief history as they traversed the hallways to the lecture room, where they would meet other students. She explained that the school's mission to teach culinary arts and hotel management had weathered one hundred twenty-five years, while the school itself had expanded to multiple campuses throughout the world.

Twenty men and women were gathered in the room, which was equipped with comfortable seating and a white board. They chattered amongst themselves in several languages as they waited for the instructor. After the introduction to the class, which was delivered in French, Julia and Carly were assigned to an English-speaking instructor, Francesca Caron, a short woman with a medium build and serious look who wore her hair pulled into a slicked back ponytail. Two other American women, Becca Taylor and Kate Opgrande, joined them.

Finally, Julia and Carly, freshly attired in their official Cordon Bleu *toques blanche*—white chef hats—and aprons, stood at the gleaming counter, ready to begin the hands-on part of the lesson on the "Secrets of Chocolates."

The four Americans listened carefully to Francesca for the next hour as she explained the origins of "chocolat." She described its unique qualities, such as heat sensitivity, which required "tempering," and other noteworthy facets of cooking with it. The varieties of chocolate went way beyond Hershey bars and powdered cocoa. When choosing the flavors to go in their truffles, Carly went for the raspberry filling and medium dark chocolate. But Julia went for Jamaican rum and the darkest of chocolate coverings, thinking it might meet American Heart Association guidelines about "healthy" chocolate.

During a short break, Julia and Carly learned that Kate and Becca were friends who hailed from Cape Cod, where Kate's parents owned a restaurant where both women worked. It was a ho-hum establishment, according to Kate. She had jumped at the chance to study at Le Cordon Bleu when Becca had suggested adding some French touches to the cuisine. Kate's parents agreed and were covering the cost of several classes and a two-week stay in Paris.

After two more hours of measuring, heating, stirring, and rolling, they had successfully created primitive truffles and bonbons. Their efforts sat like ugly cousins next to the professional delicacies formed by Francesca's experienced hands.

"Mine look more like footballs," Carly moaned, comparing her candies to the instructor's creations. Then she whispered, "But at least they look better than Kate's. Hers look like something a French poodle might have left behind."

Julia chuckled. "Who knew it would be that difficult to make something halfway presentable? As for Kate, I'm sure she and Becca will practice a lot more before they start serving them at the restaurant. Anyway, they'll taste divine, no matter what."

Francesca joined them as they cleaned their work area. "My little American chocolatiers did an excellent job today. You will take another class here, yes?"

"I would love to learn how to do fancy appetizers for special parties back home," Carly said, "but I didn't see that kind of class on your schedule."

"*Oui*, yes, I understand. We can do a special class for that. We require four students to sign up. I will check with Kate and Becca. It may be the perfect course for their restaurant."

"You have a smudge of chocolate on your nose, Carly." Julia picked up her mop rag as if to remove the gooey drop. "Or shall I lick if off instead?"

"Eww, gross." Carly backed away from Julia's annoying big sister behavior. "I can do it myself," she said, reverting to her own four-year-old inner child. She stuck out her tongue, then used it to lick off the offending bit of chocolate.

Julia made a face at Carly's trick. "Yuk."

"Yum. That made me hungry," Carly said, giggling at Julia's reaction.

Francesca was all smiles when she returned a few minutes later. "They would love to do the same thing, but it would have to be tomorrow morning. Is that okay?" She looked from one sister to the other expectantly.

Julia and Carly nodded at each other; then Julia turned back to Francesca. "Why not? It sounds like an offer we shouldn't refuse. I happen to know that our schedule is free."

Francesca beamed and clapped her hands. "It will be much fun. Can you all be here at nine o'clock?"

"Yes," Julia replied. "We'll be ready to go."

Julia and Carly left the building, proudly carrying their chocolate candies in the boxes labeled with the school's name. Bragging rights, Carly pointed out. They both figured that the chocolates would not last long, but they could keep the boxes as lifelong souvenirs. The sun had come out while they were inside and threw its golden light on the reflective windows of the buildings around them.

"Do you have any idea of where to eat?" asked Carly.

"How about we wander around here and pick one of the sidewalk cafés for lunch before we go back to the hotel? Maybe Josh will have left me a message by then." Julia spotted a row of teal blue umbrellas across the street and a few doors down. "There's my favorite color over there. Are you game?"

"Sure." Carly shrugged. "I don't know a better way to choose one café over another."

The limited lunch menu made it to easy to select a soup and sandwich combination, accompanied by a light rosé wine.

Carly sighed, enjoying her wine and the delectable soup, a creamy mushroom and leek bisque. "This is so nice, Julia. Makes me wish we had more of this kind of lunch option at home."

"It *is* delightful to get away from the routine of home now and then. A 'stay-cation' isn't nearly as appealing as going somewhere totally new, or at least out of town." Julia brushed her brunette bangs out of her face. "Plus, I don't have to cook."

Carly laughed. "We both got the travel gene from Mom and Dad. They hauled us to someplace fun every summer. I enjoyed those long car rides and tailgate picnics."

"Me, too." Julia gazed off into the distance. "Remember how we traded places in the backseat every time Dad stopped the car so the kid in the middle got to sit by the window too?"

Carly nodded, and both fell silent. Julia could guess what her sister, four years younger, was thinking. In a family of six siblings, compromises had been routine. They'd had another sister, a year younger than Julia, who had passed suddenly from a cerebral aneurysm. She was the one with whom they'd switched seats within the backseat of their station wagon. The one whose death had shaken the family, yet bonded Carly and Julia in their grief.

"And how Dad stopped at all those silly tourist traps when we begged, like the 'Longest Worm in Captivity,'" said Carly, brightening the moment. "Maybe he needed a rest stop and used those places as an excuse."

"Then we would have dinner at a truck stop, which always seemed to have a red-checkered tablecloth. And large servings of food at a good price. Those were great experiences, sis. We were lucky kids." Julia drained her glass and said a silent prayer of thanks for their dad.

JULIA'S FACE lit up when she learned she had a message from Josh waiting for her at the hotel reception desk. She ripped open the envelope while Carly took a couple of fresh madeleines from the cookie plate.

"Yum," said Carly, licking the crumbs from her fingers. "What does Josh say?"

"It says 'Meet me at the Marriott for dinner. Sending the limo at 7:30. J.' That makes it easy. Do you suppose we should dress up a little in case?"

"Probably," Carly replied. "I've noticed that women tend to dress up more here, even during the daytime. And we may end up meeting some of those business investors he mentioned."

"I'd rather visit with Josh," said Julia. "*You* can make friends with those business guys. Maybe they're rich Arabs. I've heard they like blondes."

15

"And how would I explain that to my husband?"

"Pretend it's business. It's not a commitment to a relationship, silly." Julia hugged her sister. "Let's check our wardrobes."

∽

"It's amazing what a curling iron and a little makeup can do," Julia whispered to Carly as they entered the lobby to wait for the limousine. Carly wore a short swirly skirt in a tropical floral pattern with a coordinating hot pink sweater set. Not to be outdone, Julia had donned a sleeveless knee-skimming black linen A-line dress with a wide white band near the hem and white piping. They couldn't help noticing a few heads turn as they strolled to the foyer. Julia walked a little taller. Carly beamed that electric smile of hers.

The limo driver was Vincent again, who had picked them up at the airport. He tilted his head and raised an eyebrow as he helped the ladies into his coach. Julia pretended to act like a movie star and said, "The Marriott please, Vincent," in a pseudo-haughty accent.

"Of course, mademoiselle," he replied, bowing, with a slight grin at her pretense. "You do realize there is more than one Marriott here."

"Oh," Julia said, deflated. "Then it would best if you drive the car, and I'll enjoy the view along the way." She and Carly chattered as they cruised through the streets on the short drive to the Marriott. Josh's hotel, the Paris Marriott Champs-Élysées, seemed immense compared to the smaller Hotel du Champs du Mars. The Arc de Triomphe rose majestically in the background, a short ten-minute walk away.

Vincent pulled up to the main entrance and opened the door. "Mesdemoiselles," he said. "Your host awaits you."

Julia spotted Josh standing outside the grand entry doors

and fairly ran to meet him, happy to feel his warm embrace and gentle kiss.

"Hi, Carly," he said as she caught up with Julia. "I hope you two are hungry. The chef has promised a feast." He wrapped one arm around each woman's waist, saying, "I have the honor of escorting the two most beautiful women in Paris tonight."

Julia again felt like her imaginary movie star as Josh gently guided her and Carly to the restaurant, where the maître d' awaited them. She admired the crystal chandeliers, the heavy brocade drapes, and the sheer number of tables in the elegantly appointed room. "This is fabulous, Josh," she said as he helped her with her chair. "I thought Paris was all about street cafés, the Eiffel Tower, and Notre Dame."

"I thought I'd show you a little Parisian hospitality, since I can't be with you as we originally planned," Josh explained, kissing her fingers as he bowed.

Josh looked up as Carly cleared her throat. "And I'm happy to see you too, Carly. You're a cool little sister."

Carly glowed and let her herself be flattered.

Josh took care of drink and appetizer orders while the sisters soaked in the magnificent décor. Turning suddenly, Julia whispered to Carly, "That server looks like Francesca. Near the entrance. Wearing black."

Carly swiveled her head, then whispered back, "You're right. Maybe she works here."

"Could be. She probably doesn't make enough money working as an assistant instructor and has to moonlight somewhere."

"And why are you two whispering?" Josh asked, looking at Julia with his deep blue eyes.

"I'm not sure," Julia admitted. "Habit, maybe?"

"And you are whispering about…?"

Flushing, Julia subtly inclined her chin toward the

entrance. "See the woman server near the entrance, wearing black, of course, with dark hair in a ponytail?"

"Yes. Pretty face, medium build. And?"

"It's Francesca from Le Cordon Bleu. She was our instructor today."

"Do you want to go over and say hello to her?" Josh asked.

"No, no. We're just surprised to see her here," Julia stammered.

"Paris is an expensive city. In addition to working at two jobs, she probably has a roommate to survive."

The waiter brought their drinks and appetizer course. Lifting his glass, Josh said, "I say we enjoy this wonderful food with my two favorite women."

"Salud," they chimed, glasses raised.

Julia's scampi Provençale was beautifully done, dripping with garlicky butter and presented with perfectly cooked young asparagus. Josh had chosen *blanquette de veau*—veal in cream sauce. Judging by the look on his face, Julia assumed it had to be delicious. Carly had been intimidated by the French names on the menu until the waiter helped her select *boeuf bourguignon*—beef burgundy. She was grinning as she tucked into the delicious meat and sauce.

"That was divine. I can't believe I ate every bite," Julia exclaimed as they finished dessert. "That crème brûlée was better than any I've ever eaten."

"You mean 'Miss Betty Homemaker of Tomorrow' didn't learn to make that in high school Home Economics?" Carly teased.

"They wouldn't let us use the torches to flame the top. Too dangerous, they said."

Carly snorted. "Knowing you, they were right about that."

Josh smiled at the sisters' bantering.

"Are you tied up with your clients all day again?" Julia asked Josh.

"I'm afraid so, but the day after will be free. I expect to complete our business transactions tomorrow afternoon and send them on their way. What about you and Carly?"

"We've arranged to do a three-hour appetizer class in the morning at Le Cordon Bleu with Francesca and two other ladies we met today," Julia explained. "Kate's parents own a restaurant on Cape Cod, and Becca works there. They want to add some upscale dishes for their catering business. Carly and I hope to get some fresh ideas for the next winetasting event at home."

"Sounds great," said Josh. He polished off the last of his glass of wine. "Say, would you want to share your skills with my guests tomorrow afternoon?"

"Skills?" Julia had a quick flashback of her misshapen bonbons of the morning. "We won't be very good by then," she replied, taken by surprise at the suggestion.

"It doesn't have to be fancy. A couple of items should be enough, I would think. I can arrange for a room and the beverages. What do you say?"

Carly could hardly contain herself. "Julia, say yes. It would be fun."

Julia furrowed her brow before acquiescing. "Okay. We'll come up with something."

A few moments later they reluctantly got up to leave. As they neared the hostess bar station, they heard a woman's voice. "Carly? Julia? What are you doing here?" Francesca asked, seeing the familiar faces.

"Hi, Francesca," said Julia. "Carly and I were here with my friend, Josh Larson, for dinner. Josh, this is Francesca Caron." They shook hands as Julia asked, "Do you work here?"

"Sort of. I am doing an internship to earn hours toward

my apprenticeship. It's something like what you Americans call 'work-study.'"

Julia laughed. "I remember it being a lot more work than study in my college years."

"Francesca," Josh interjected, "Julia and Carly told me you would teach them how to make some special appetizers tomorrow."

"Oui, Monsieur Larson," Francesca replied. "That is correct."

"Would they learn enough to do a small party for my business guests tomorrow afternoon?"

"But of course," she said. "Yes, I can teach them enough to do a fine party for you."

"That will be great. Merci, Francesca."

Josh escorted his dates to the entrance and called for Vincent, using the interlude to admonish them to have fun in their class and be careful otherwise. "No flaming torches," he joked.

Julia practically floated to the limo after Josh's sweet kiss. "Tomorrow should be fun," she said to Carly. Yet a part of her worried about serving Josh's clients. He certainly would want to impress them, and Julia wanted to impress Josh. Could she pull it off? But what could be the worst that could happen? Even if their appetizers turned out less than picture perfect, they should at least taste great.

3

TUESDAY MORNING

"Bonjour, Julia and Carly, Kate and Becca." Francesca greeted her students cheerfully in the modern kitchen of the school. "This will be much fun to learn to make special things for your parties and the restaurant."

Francesca had an impressive repertoire of delicious, but easy, hors d'oeuvres recipes. For Julia and Carly, she recommended simple items that wouldn't require cooking, such as buttery crackers with a selection of cheeses, simple saveur pâté, and fresh fruits and vegetables. She explained how to make even the simplest cheese and cracker platter look glamorous, and how to select the fresh fruit at its peak at the market. She kindly recommended a market near the hotel that would have everything Julia and Carly would need for a fabulous spread that afternoon.

For Kate and Becca, she shared several, more complex recipes that Julia and Carly could also use, although they wouldn't be able to create them for their Paris party. Julia was eager to try her hand making the elegant *escargots de Bourgogne* (snails with a garlic-butter-red-wine sauce) or a true French Vichyssoise (cold potato soup) for a formal dinner someday.

After tasting each other's creations and a round of applause, the newly minted hors d'oeuvres masters did double-kisses all around and bid each other adieu.

Julia and Carly chatted excitedly in the limo, eager to do their shopping. They were thrilled to find that the tiny French market had an enormous selection of cheeses and specialty crackers. Francesca's list of recommendations was right on target. They browsed the shop for other items to complement the cheese and fruit platter. Julia searched for pickles while Carly hunted down olives.

"Pink pickles?" Julia showed Carly a bottle containing said item. "Who's ever heard of pink pickles?"

Carly read the label. "It says 'Turnips and beets. A common Mediterranean delicacy.' They're certainly more colorful than dill pickles for the party. Let's get them."

"They're pretty," Julia agreed. "But would men object to eating pink pickles?"

"Men never object to food. Period. I found the olives. I could marinate them in vodka."

Julia chuckled. "I remember the time you did those for a family party. I wondered why they were so popular. I didn't know about the vodka till later."

"I believe you weren't an olive eater at the time."

"Still not my favorite, but I'm game." Julia scanned the store shelves as she asked, "Anything else we should buy?"

Carly checked the basket. "We've got enough here. There might even be enough olives for leftovers."

JULIA AND CARLY, elegantly dressed in cocktail attire and carrying their food in market bags, arrived at the Marriott at three. The maître d' showed them to the room where they would set up the party. Julia gazed appreciatively at the crystal chandeliers, the silver candelabras on the tables, and the mirrored walls that reflected the lights. She felt as if they were in a castle.

Serving staff came from nowhere, bringing the hotel's serving platters. The sisters got to work, and soon everything had been artfully arranged on the beautifully appointed tables. Josh had even arranged for a sommelier, who took a moment to explain the wine selection to the hostesses.

Julia and Carly smiled at each other and took their places at the room's entrance to greet Josh and his clients.

"Hi, Julia and Carly," said Josh, with quick a brush of his lips on Julia's cheek. "This is so special of you. Thank you."

"You're more than welcome," said Julia. "Carly and I had fun preparing a party." Carly's golden curls bounced merrily as she agreed.

Josh motioned to the men standing at the entrance. "Let me introduce you to Roger Westover, one of my partners in Washington, D.C. To his left is Pierre Dupont, who lives here in Paris. Alain Marchand, to his right, is from Calais. Clint Blackman," Josh motioned to the man standing by the wine, "hails from London. The three of them are considering a business deal with one of our clients back in the States." Handshakes and murmured "hellos" peppered the air.

"Welcome, Julia," said Roger, a husky blond built like a football tight end. "Josh has been talking about you ever since he got back from that trip to Amsterdam. You saved our bacon by figuring out what was happening with our client's security problem. Thanks."

"All in a day's work," Julia managed to say, as she felt herself turning red. "Would you like to try the wine?" She motioned to the wine table, where filled glasses awaited them. Everyone took a glass.

"Ladies, let me tell you a little more about these gentlemen," Roger continued. He pointed to the tall, dark-haired man on his left. "Pierre is a successful stockbroker who rode the upward rise of those technology companies. I wish I had done that. He brought the two other men here to the table."

Julia was flattered when Pierre, dressed in slacks and shirt with a navy V-neck sweater, bowed gallantly and kissed the back of her hand. His hazel eyes twinkled as she curtsied in response.

"And this is Alain, whose family owns a series of jewelry stores in the Caribbean. He lives in Calais, which is a bit south of Paris." Roger stood back as they acknowledged each other. Julia noticed that Alain's suit, impeccably tailored in a current style, was made of a faint pinstriped charcoal fabric that complemented his graying black hair and dark brown eyes.

"And last, but most British, is Clint, who made his money the old-fashioned way—manufacturing and warehousing," said Roger.

Julia smiled at the third gentleman, who seemed very relaxed in his slacks and tweed jacket. His red hair and green eyes gave him the appearance of a leprechaun, she thought, quietly amused.

"Gentlemen," Josh began. "My friends Julia Fairchild and her sister Carly Pedersen are visiting from the United States. They took a couple of classes at Le Cordon Bleu, and I convinced them to share some of what they've learned." He nodded at the sisters. "This seems like a good time to make a toast to thank you." Raising his glass, he said, "Salud."

The men raised their glasses to the hostesses, and everyone took a sip.

"To the rest of you, I say thank you for your energetic discussions and thoughtful questions. I trust we will be able to come to fruitful contracts as a result of these meetings." Josh raised his glass again.

After the formalities, Julia and Carly stood aside and

observed the interactions of the men as they enjoyed the appetizers and drinks. Julia whispered, "I feel like a nervous mom at a dance recital."

"At least there aren't any dance steps here," Carly replied.

"Not for us. But they're certainly dancing around the appetizer table. I think we have a hit!" Julia winked.

"This is great, Julia and Carly," said Josh as he joined them. "I owe you for this. It's a perfect way to end our sessions." He gave a little bow before returning to Roger.

Julia felt a little giddy with his praise. She was brought back to Earth when she heard her name being called from the doorway.

"Julia, my friend. I have one more item for your party," Francesca announced. "Can you make room?"

Julia oohed in admiration as Francesca approached the table bearing a platter of stuffed mushroom caps, perfectly arranged in concentric circles, with rose petals and parsley as accents. She moved a couple of serving dishes for the new appetizer offering.

"Francesca, they're beautiful. *Merci beaucoup.*" Julia clapped her hands together. "Thank you." She hugged Francesca and kissed her on the cheek.

"What brings you here?" Carly asked, tasting one of the delicacies.

"I enjoyed visiting with you and your sister and wanted to help you in a small way with your party." Francesca bowed her head slightly.

"That's so sweet of you," Julia said. "Did you make these yourself?" Julia sampled one of the mushrooms herself. "Delicious. Yum."

Francesca laughed in that special French way, demure and somehow sexy at the same time. "No, Julia. My friend in the kitchen here made them when I told him why I wanted them."

"Please tell him thank you from me."

"Of course," said Francesca as the ladies moved away from the appetizer table to allow the men to savor the mushrooms. "Now I must go to work. Will you be taking any more classes at Le Cordon Bleu?"

"Maybe, if we can work it into our sightseeing schedule. I'm interested in the class on bread-making," said Julia.

"Perhaps I will see you in two days then. Have fun seeing more of our beautiful city. Au revoir, my friends." She slowed her pace and hesitated as they drew near Roger, who turned away when he noticed Francesca looking at him, returning to his conversation with Pierre.

Half an hour later, with the guests finally gone, Julia and Carly stood by as Josh removed his jacket and talked with the headwaiter for a moment before joining them.

"What a terrific job on this shindig. You'll have to start a catering business when you get home." Josh hugged Julia and grinned at Carly. "Would you two care to join me upstairs and drink a toast to our successful soirée? I have a fantastic view of the city to share with you as well."

Carly scrunched her brows. "Isn't three a crowd?"

"Not today, Carly," said Josh. "I have a few details to take care of down here before I can join you." He checked the time. "Shall we meet near the elevator in about thirty minutes?"

Julia and Carly used the time to investigate the sumptuous shops in the hotel lobby. The elegant dresses and accessories were tempting, but too pricey for their travel budgets. Julia sketched one long black dress with a ruffled neckline that extended to an open back. She enjoyed sewing special-occasion outfits in her rare spare time. Carly found a souvenir version of the Eiffel Tower that she couldn't pass up.

Josh, true to his word, waited for them at the elevator, which whisked them to the sixth floor. He opened the door to his corner room and had his guests step inside ahead of him.

Floor-to-ceiling windows covered an entire wall of the grand sitting room. Julia did a slow 180-degree turn, stopping to admire the splendid view of the shimmering city below. She watched lights turning on like fireflies as the dusk darkened to the deep blue of night. She sensed Josh's presence behind her even before he put both arms around her. She melted into him as he did so. Their treats had been devoured with gusto, Josh had pleased his investors, and Julia was finally enjoying a great and romantic vacation where nothing had gone wrong.

"You two were amazing today," Josh said softly. "One of the investors, Alain, offered to be an escort for Carly if we need a fourth." He winked at Carly.

Julia shook her head, spinning around. "Carly, how do you do it?"

"Do what? What did I do now?"

Julia sighed. "Thing is, you don't do anything. You attract men with some powerful pheromones that I've never had."

Josh hugged Julia more tightly. He whispered, "I like your pheromones."

"Thank you, Josh. You're a keeper," said Julia. "Hey, may I use the restroom? I was too busy downstairs."

"Second door to the right. I haven't been here all day, so it should still be clean."

"I'll join you." Carly followed her down the hall. "I need to fix my lipstick."

Julia turned the handle and pushed on the door. "Hmm. It doesn't want to open." She tried again, using all her weight against it.

Carly gave her a little shove. "Move over, weakling. Let me get it."

The door still didn't budge. They shoved together. Still nothing. Carly peeked through the narrow crack. "I can't see what's keeping the door from opening."

Together they gave the door one more powerful shove and

it moved a couple of inches, exposing a finger under the bottom of the door.

Julia and Carly let out blood-curdling screams, prompting Josh to run in from the sitting room.

"What is it?"

Julia pointed to the finger, one hand over her mouth. And she'd thought nothing would go wrong this time....

4

TUESDAY EVENING

They pushed the door open with the help of Josh's physical strength and found Roger sprawled on the floor. He was unconscious but breathing. While Josh called for emergency help, Julia shifted immediately into "doctor" mode. She quickly assessed Roger's heart rate and rhythm, checked his head for signs of obvious injury, and gently palpated for broken bones. She didn't find anything in her cursory exam that might have caused him to collapse in the bathroom. When Josh returned from calling for help, she asked him if he knew whether Roger had any medical conditions. He didn't recall anything, other than Roger mentioning at one point that he was taking medication for high blood pressure.

Within a few minutes Josh's suite was swarming with emergency medical personnel and equipment. Julia gave the team a brief report of her findings as they began their own evaluation. She was impressed with their approach to assessment before preparing Roger for transfer to a nearby hospital, mentally comparing it to her own encounters with the first responders back home.

Alone at last, with Roger safely on his way, Julia asked

Josh, "Is there anything I can do to help? Does Roger have any family to contact?"

"His wife's name is Laura. I'll go to the hospital in a few minutes and call her from there, once I have more information."

"Good. She would know more of his medical background, which might be helpful."

Josh slumped on the settee, head cradled in his hands. "This might not go down well at the office."

"What do you mean?" Julia gently put a hand on his shoulder.

"Roger was the lead go-between with this group of men. It may take some time for them to trust me with finalizing the deal." Josh shook his head.

"Can you tell me what kind of deal you're talking about? Or is it a secret?" Flashbacks of an ex-boyfriend whose secrets had put Julia's life at risk brought an edge of skepticism to her question.

Josh sat up and wiped his forehead with the back of his hand. "I've never talked much about what I do, I guess. Roger and I work for a company called Blandings Incorporated, which is based in Washington, D.C. It's a huge corporation that does many things and has offices in several foreign cities, including Paris. Roger specializes in mergers between large companies. I am the so-called expert in our technology sector, which is why we're both here this time. One of his clients is in serious discussion with one of my clients about a potential joint venture."

"That sounds exciting."

"It is. Remember the security company I told you about in Amsterdam?"

Julia nodded. She had helped bring an art smuggling ring to justice six months earlier. "The security breaches in the museum's alarm system were a concern."

"Yes, and the bad guys are in jail, thanks to you. Since then, Alpha Gamma Security has beefed up their software, which is their signature product. They've been toying with the idea of a joint venture to enhance their market share and gain an influx of money for development of additional technology. Pulling off this deal would be a coup for both Roger and me. Now it may be in jeopardy."

"I'm assuming you can handle this as well as Roger," said Julia. "Why would you be worried, Josh?"

"Roger has done all the preliminary work, and now I can't ask him if there are any details that I should know about these companies—such as something that might derail the transaction. Alpha Gamma needs funding to gear up for this new system, and they have several potential major investors. They would love to form a joint venture with one of them, but their decision to invest hinges on this first sale being successful."

"I see," said Julia. "It's like a giant dominoes game being played by big corporations."

Josh smiled at another of Julia's attempts to understand complex corporate matters. "More or less. I also have a personal interest in having this deal go through after losing a big client earlier this year. Job security, you know." He ran his hands through his dark hair. "I don't mean to run you off, but I need to go to the hospital. It could be a late night." He clasped his hands on Julia's shoulders. "May I have a raincheck for the rest of the evening and touch base with you in the morning?"

Julia hugged him, noticing the pained look in his blue eyes. "Of course. Carly and I will keep each other company tonight and wait to hear from you. I do wish I could help you somehow though."

"My knowing that you're nearby is enough," Josh said. "I mean that." He kissed her on the forehead. "I'll have Vincent take you to your hotel while I grab a taxi to the hospital. I'll call you when I know something."

～

"Okay, Carly. Time for us to use those little gray cells in our brains, as Hercules Poirot would say."

"Are those the smart cells?" Carly looked up toward the ceiling, wrinkling her forehead. "I'm not sure mine are still awake tonight."

"Sure they are. We have a mystery to solve." Julia clapped her hands together and settled herself on the couch with a blanket over her shoulders. "Let's get started. What was Roger doing in Josh's bathroom? And what caused him to collapse?"

Carly plopped into a comfy chair. "The suites are adjoining. Maybe Roger was borrowing toothpaste."

Julia tilted her head. "Maybe. I was thinking more along the lines of whether he has a medical condition, like low blood sugar from taking medicine for diabetes, or a heart rhythm issue that caused him to collapse."

"The doctors at the hospital can figure that out."

Julia smiled, raising her eyebrows. "I'd love to be a fly on the wall and know what's going on. Sometimes I wish I had one of those handheld gadgets like the doctor used on *Star Trek* to scan a body and get an instant answer."

"I'm sure there's a team of smart scientists working on that very idea right now."

"Probably. And every one of my patients will want one. Maybe they won't even need a personal physician in a few years." Julia sighed as she tucked her feet under her knees, sitting cross-legged.

"Don't worry, sis. Your patients will still want a real person to explain the results and to listen to their heart and lungs—and to their life stories and complaints. A machine won't be able to do that." Carly reached across and patted her sister's knee.

Julia smiled weakly. "There's not anything we can do tonight, I guess. Hopefully Roger will be awake tomorrow when we go to the hospital."

Carly raised her eyebrows. "We're going to the hospital?"

"*Mais oui*—but of course!"

∼

WEDNESDAY MORNING

At nine the next morning, Julia hadn't yet heard from Josh. Carly had ordered room service breakfast to avoid missing a phone call to the room.

"Yum. These chocolate croissants are delicious." Carly licked every last crumb from her fingers. "I hope we learn how to make these in that breadmaking class."

"I'm surprised Josh hasn't called yet." Julia checked her watch, again. "I'd sure like to know what's going on with Roger," she said as she paced the room.

The hotel phone rang right on cue, interrupting Julia's walking. "That's got to be Josh." She picked up after one ring.

"Bonjour, ma chérie," said Josh. "Comment allez-vous?"

Julia smiled as she mouthed "Josh" to her sister. "And good morning to you too. Have you checked on Roger yet this morning?"

"Yes," Josh replied. "The nurse said he's stable and that I can go visit him at ten. Would you like to join me, please?"

"Of course, I'd love to. What did the doctor say about the cause of his collapse? Did they find anything specific?"

"They're waiting on test results for the most part, but nothing obvious like a heart attack or stroke."

"That's good. Hopefully the other tests will give them the answer. Are you coming by the hotel to pick me up? Is it okay if Carly comes too? You know how lonely she gets." Julia ignored Carly's vigorous head shaking. "She'd love to join us." More shaking of the head, now with dagger eyes. "And lunch afterwards at a sidewalk café?" Carly now nodded, grinning. "Sounds delightful. See you in thirty minutes."

"Okay, girlfriend," said Julia. "Let's get beautiful and go see what a French hospital looks like."

～

JULIA WAS RELIEVED to learn that Roger had been taken to the American Hospital, where English was spoken by the staff. It had been founded in 1906 to offer expatriates access to American-trained physicians and was now a modern facility offering a complete palette of medical care and cutting-edge technology.

Julia and Josh were directed to a private room while Carly remained in the waiting area. They found Roger resting, wired for everything imaginable, with intravenous drips in both arms. The registered nurse, though French, spoke excellent English. She gave them a brief narrative of his medical status, using medical terms once she learned that Julia was a physician.

"Merci, mademoiselle," Julia said as the nurse excused herself to take care of another patient. She turned to Josh. "Did you understand what she was saying?"

"I got that she was talking about seizures and blood pressure problems, but the rest was all Greek to me." Josh held his hands up in the air.

Julia smiled. "It was actually Latin. She also said that the lab tests may be pointing to the possibility of a toxin or poison. That doesn't make sense to me."

"Me neither," said Josh, looking back at Roger. "Hey, look. He's trying to talk."

Roger's eyes were open. He was mouthing something. Julia tried to read his lips. "Roger, are you saying 'bathroom'?" she asked.

He shook his head no.

"Is it some kind of 'room'?"

Roger nodded.

"A room in a house?"

More shaking his head.

"Please say it again."

Roger mouthed the letter "m."

"The word starts with an 'm'?"

He nodded. Then, "M-muh. . ."

"Mushroom? Is it about mushrooms?"

He nodded his head excitedly.

"Did you eat mushrooms?"

Roger suddenly started seizing, his face florid. Julia called for the nurse, who swooshed them out of the room as it filled with medical personnel.

"How would mushrooms hurt anybody?" Josh asked as he and Julia joined Carly in the waiting room.

"Normal mushrooms wouldn't, but there are plenty of poisonous ones out there. Mushroom pickers in the forests have to identify the species correctly, or they can end up with liver failure or worse."

What's going on with Roger, Julia?" Carly asked.

Julia sat in one of the uncomfortable waiting room chairs next to Carly's. "Roger started having seizures while we were visiting. The medical staff is working on him now. I hope he's going to be okay." She glanced at Josh who stood leaning against the wall.

35

Carly clapped a hand over her mouth. "Oh, no. That doesn't sound good at all."

Julia nodded grimly, then asked, "Are you okay out here? Did you find any English-language magazines?" She surveyed the reading material on the table.

"I'm okay," said Carly. "I met a friendly hospital volunteer named Simone. She'll be right back. She went to get us 'Americano' coffee."

The trio waited quietly while Roger was being attended to. As if on cue, Simone entered the room with two coffees and pastries. When she noticed that one person had become three, she stopped in her tracks. "Oh. I should go get more coffee. I'll be right back," she said, turning to leave.

"Simone, it's okay," said Carly. "We'll be going to lunch soon anyway. I'd like you to meet my sister, Dr. Julia Fairchild, and her friend, Josh Larson."

"Pleased to meet you both," Simone said, extending her hand.

"Julia and Josh, this is Simone Bouvier. She's an artist and volunteers here once a week. She's been keeping me company." Carly grinned at her new friend.

"Hello, Simone," said Julia. "How does an artist end up as a volunteer in a hospital?"

"Easy," said Simone. "My husband works in the laboratory department. We enjoy lunch together on days I am here. I also do art therapy classes for the children who end up in the hospital."

"That's wonderful. I bet they like that." Julia mused, "Maybe even I could learn to paint."

"Children are eager to learn something new," said Simone. "They don't have any preconceived notion of whether or not their work is good. To them it's pure fun. And I love to teach them." She ran her trim fingers through her long silver hair, which she had pulled into a ponytail. A colorful scarf tied loosely around her neck complemented her vibrant personality.

The nurse stood at the entrance to the waiting room and looked around before addressing Josh. "Mr. Larson?"

Josh turned. "Yes. Is Roger okay?"

"The doctor will come to talk to you in a few minutes."

Josh's face went ashen as he sat down, hands over his face. Julia and Carly hurried to his side, worried about what the doctor would say. Simone waited with them until Dr. Laennec arrived.

He explained that Roger had continued to have seizures, as well as a dangerously high temperature and blood pressure spikes. His heart had developed a rapid irregular rhythm that they were finally able to control with powerful medications. Roger was in critical condition and heavily sedated. He asked if Josh or Julia had any other information that might be helpful.

Julia spoke up. "Dr. Laennec, Roger was mouthing the word 'mushroom' before he started seizing. Do you suppose mushrooms could have played a role?"

"Perhaps, if they were one of the poisonous types," the doctor replied. "Do you know where he ate yesterday?"

"I'm not sure about breakfast," Josh replied, "but the luncheon and cocktail party were at the Marriott, where we're staying."

"There were stuffed mushrooms at the party," Julia added, "but they came from the Marriott kitchen as well. We all ate them, and no one else has become ill, as far as we know."

Dr. Laennec nodded. "Thank you for that information. I will order additional lab tests to see if anything unusual shows up. Do you have any other questions?"

"Were you able to contact his wife?" asked Josh.

"Yes, I have had a conversation with her. She's as

surprised as we are that he has taken ill," said Dr. Laennec. "Anything else?"

Josh and Julia looked at each other. "No, sir. Merci bien," Julia replied on Josh's behalf.

Carly, who had been silent in the doctor's presence, spoke up. "Wow, Julia. It's happened again."

"What's happened again?" Julia asked, perplexed.

"Another mystery."

"I'm not sure this qualifies as a 'mystery' yet," said Julia, hands on hips.

Simone, not knowing Julia's history of encountering mysteries and murders, asked Carly, "What do you mean by 'another mystery'?"

Carly rolled her eyes. "Julia seems to end up around dead people everywhere she goes."

"Roger's not dead," said Julia.

"There's still a mystery to solve about how he became ill. And you'll probably get in the middle of it."

"Okay, ladies," Josh said, "no mud wrestling here. Let's go find a sidewalk café and have that lunch I promised. Simone, you're welcome to join us."

"That's very kind of you. but I am teaching a class in a few minutes. Perhaps some other time." Simone reached into her pocket and found a business card. Handing it to Carly, she said with a big wink, "For you, when 'three's a crowd.'"

∼

BRIGHT RED TABLE umbrellas stood like silent beacons against the pale gray Parisian sky. Still somber, the threesome was relieved to be able to leave the hospital while the medical team took care of Roger.

"Aah," said Julia. "This is what I picture when I dream of

Paris. Baskets of fresh bread, wedges of cheese, and pitchers of French wine. I might be in heaven."

"That's the picture on the cover of the menu," Carly informed her.

"Don't spoil my dream, kiddo," Julia replied, opening the menu. "I've waited years to come here. This is picture-perfect."

Josh had signaled the waiter to bring a carafe of red table wine and poured three glasses. Raising his own, he said, "Here's to Paris and my lovely company. Let's keep Roger in mind as we enjoy a meal."

"Even the table wine here is delicious," Julia said after tasting the ruby drink. "Josh, does Pierre know that Roger ended up at the hospital?"

"Yes. I called him last night. I may have to reschedule our final negotiations."

"What a shock. Roger looked young and fit yesterday," said Julia. She propped an elbow on the table and rested her chin on her hand.

Carly shoved a menu in Julia's face. "Can we do food-talk instead of doctor-talk? Aren't we supposed to be on vacation?"

Julia smiled sweetly at her little sister. "Yes, you're right." She studied the offerings, each one enticing. "Everything looks good here."

The waiter had barely finished taking their orders when Josh's cellphone rang. "Excuse me, ladies. This is Pierre. I need to talk with him." He walked to a quiet place out of earshot.

Carly tapped on Julia's arm. "You aren't going to get involved with this, right?"

"Why would I?" Julia sipped her wine. She tried but failed to hear what Josh was saying.

39

Carly gave a little snort. "Because it's what you do. You solve problems. You figure things out. It's in your DNA."

"Not in Paris," Julia assured her.

Face grim, Josh returned. "I need to meet with Pierre after lunch. This could get messy."

"Why messy?" Julia asked.

"It's complicated, but Pierre told me that Roger recently talked with him about a competitor's product."

"So?"

"So that means Roger was having unsanctioned discussions behind my back."

"Oh, Josh." Julia sighed. "I'm sorry."

"I'm sure everything will be fine, but I need to talk with Pierre, then call my office in D.C. and talk to one of our other partners. I'm going to be tied up the rest of the day." Leaning down to hug Julia, he said, "I'm so sorry. I wanted to spend the day with you and Carly."

"It's okay," said Julia. "I totally understand. It'll work out."

"Look, anything you want to do here is on me," said Josh. "Please use the limo. Go to the Versailles Palace or Notre Dame. I'll catch up with you and Carly as soon as I get this straightened out." He turned and waved as he strode down the sidewalk, cellphone already at his ear.

Gloom hung in the air like a heavy black veil. Julia and Carly finished their lunch, delicious as it was, in silence.

"Well, Carly," Julia said after polishing off her wine, "we now have a free afternoon. What about doing a Seine River cruise? Or would you rather visit a museum?"

5

WEDNESDAY AFTERNOON

The morning clouds had lifted to reveal a brilliant April sky as Julia and Carly boarded the river cruise boat at the dock near the Eiffel Tower. The boat boasted an open upper deck, perfect for clear days like this one. A handful of cruisers headed down a ramp to the enclosed lower deck, which provided extra protection from the elements. The majority of the sixty or so passengers stayed up top and braved the light breeze. All of them cheered and toasted with the complimentary champagne as the boat pushed away and headed east up the Seine River.

"This was a great idea, Julia," said Carly, watching the buildings on the port side of the tour boat as they motored along. "Now, which bank is which? I know one is the 'Right Bank' and one is the 'Left Bank.' But wouldn't that be backwards if you're in a boat coming from the other direction?"

"Let's see what the web says," said Julia, scrolling down the page on her smartphone. "I found something. 'The history of the Right Bank dates to the Middle Ages. It was the first of the two banks to develop through trade. It has retained that status due to its commercial side, with the Halles district and its business area around the Opera House.'"

"So why isn't the other side the 'wrong' side instead of the 'left' side?"

Julia rolled her eyes and continued. "'Until the French Revolution of 1789-1799, it was called 'Outre-Grand-Pont,' or other side of the Grand Pont, which is the bridge of Notre Dame. For many years it was the only way to get from the Île de la Cité to the Right Bank.'"

"That still doesn't explain right from left, in my humble opinion," said Carly.

"There's more. According to this, 'the Right Bank is now very popular with partygoers and bon vivants. It is also fashionable and attractive, with the Avenue des Champs Élysée, the Louvre, Panthéon, Montmartre, and both of the city's opera houses.'"

"I'm still waiting to hear about the Left Bank. Look, Julia. We're almost to Notre Dame. It's beautiful."

"That it is." Julia took several photos with her Nikon as they neared the building. "It should be one of the 'wonders of the world.' We'll make time to go there in the next day or two." She resumed her search on her phone. "Here's the story of the Left Bank. This says that it's known for jazz, the Latin Quarter, and a long string of writers, artists, and philosophers. It's where they say Paris 'learned to think.'"

Carly sighed. "That explains everything, I'm sure. I'll just enjoy the scenery."

Passing by the small island in the middle of the Seine River where Notre Dame had stood for centuries, Julia pointed to the bridge connecting it to the mainland. "There's the Pont Neuf, the oldest bridge in Paris. Can you imagine all the millions of feet that have stepped on that bridge?"

"And it's still standing," said Carly.

"It's known as the 'Locks' Bridge because for years lovers have been putting padlocks on the rail as they declare their undying love to each other." Julia hugged herself and smiled to some unseen lover as she thought of the romanticism of that gesture.

Carly narrowed her eyes at Julia's silliness. "It's amazing to me that the builders of the day were able to build such a strong structure with the limited technology they had available. That bridge has stood for centuries. Our modern bridges probably won't last nearly that long."

Someone in the background began playing classical guitar, lending a romantic mood to the daytime setting. People took photos and videos of the city and its treasures as they cruised past the Musée de Orsay, the Musée du Louvre, and the Eiffel Tower, which loomed into view on the return half of the cruise.

Julia noticed that the other passengers were moving toward the boat's exit gate as they approached the dock, which she could see was still a good distance away. She wondered why they were in such a hurry to end the ride, but figured maybe they had another tour lined up or wanted to find a place for a drink. She felt grateful that she and Carly had the luxury of time to enjoy Paris at a more leisurely pace.

Carly held onto her shoulder as they navigated their way down the ramp, trailing most of the other passengers. "That was fabulous. I'm so glad we decided on this."

"Definitely a must-do. What do you want to do next, sis? Shall we find a spot for a glass of wine?" Julia checked the list of attractions on the webpage to see what would be nearby. "It would be smart to stay near the Eiffel Tower or the hotel, in case Josh decides to come our direction for dinner."

Carly put her hand over Julia's phone screen. "Look, there's one of Josh's investor group, on the platform waiting for the next cruise." She pointed toward the boat ramp.

"It looks like the guy from Paris with the dark curly hair. Alain, I believe," said Julia. "Could he be with somebody?"

Carly shaded her eyes from the sun as she tried to get a

better look. "He appears to be talking to the blond dude. That other guy could be a model."

"You're right." Julia squinted in the sun. "I don't recognize the blond. He is handsome, isn't he?"

"Must be a friend of Alain's or…"

Julia caught the same thought and finished her sister's idea. "Or maybe one of those competitors? I'll grab a photo to show Josh."

"He's waving at us. Alain is, I mean." Carly waved back. "The other guy has his back to us."

The blond guy managed to avoid turning his face toward Julia, but she was still able to get a passable photo of his profile. "It may be worth showing to Josh, although it's probably nothing significant."

The sisters sauntered past the Eiffel Tower toward their hotel, still another fifteen minutes away. A line for the next elevator was forming at the base of the tower. Julia gazed upward and said wistfully, "I can hardly wait to go the top and watch the night lights of the city come on."

"I'm sure Josh would agree," Carly said, "but that might be a 'three's a crowd' kind of thing."

"We'll figure something out. Maybe your new friend, Simone, would like to join us. Then we'd each have company."

Carly brightened. "I can ask her when we have something definite set up."

"Unfortunately, it's going to depend on when Josh gets things cleared up with his company. That's Josh now," Julia said as her cellphone rang. "Hi. Carly and I were just talking about you. Are you a free man yet? Have you heard anything new about Roger's condition?"

"No change. As you might imagine, the doctors were interested in Roger's mushroom comment. I checked with the kitchen, but there weren't any appetizers left from yesterday's party, so unfortunately they can't test those for poison."

Julia frowned. "Maybe he had mushrooms somewhere else? Soup? Fresh mushrooms on a salad?"

"Good ideas. Roger had been hanging out with Alain earlier in the day, before the meeting started. He may be helpful on that point. Maybe they ate something beforehand."

"Ah, Alain," said Julia. "Carly and I saw him a little earlier at the dock, waiting for a Seine river cruise. He was with a good-looking blond dude."

"You're sure it was Alain?"

"Not a hundred percent, but he waved at us and I have a photo on my camera. I'll show it to you later."

"Perfect," said Josh. "How about we meet for an early dinner somewhere? There's a great bistro near your hotel with wonderful food."

"We'd love it. We sent the limo back your way earlier."

"Thanks. Can I meet you at six-thirty at your hotel? I can hardly wait to see you, Julia."

Julia's heart lifted. "We'll be ready. But you haven't answered my question about Roger. Any more news?"

"When I called, the nurse said he was stable but still unconscious. No point in going to see him right now. His wife is flying in tomorrow."

Julia took a big breath. "That's a relief. Thanks for the update, Josh. See you soon."

"Well?" Carly asked, all ears, eager to hear what Julia had learned.

"Nothing substantial yet. Roger's stable but still not awake. I sure hope he comes out of this."

"Me too. Especially for Josh's sake."

"Hopefully it'll turn out to be nothing serious, and Roger wakes up so he and Josh can carry on with the business."

"In the meantime," said Carly, checking her watch, "we

can have a glass of wine in the hotel bar before we get dressed for dinner."

⁓

JULIA AND CARLY dressed a little more casually for the neighborhood bistro. Wary of looking too much like a tourist, Julia donned a navy-blue sundress with a lightweight white jacket. Evening chill settled in during the dinner hour at this time of the year. Carly found a black-and-white long-sleeved tunic to wear with her white jeans. She looked smashing, according to the bellman, who held the door for them when Josh arrived in the limo.

The atmosphere at the dinner table was almost morbid, despite the cheerful place settings of blue-and-white cloth napkins atop a crisp yellow tablecloth. A small, dark blue vase of daisies at the center of the table completed the look. Josh ordered a carafe of chilled pinot grigio for the occasion.

Julia surveyed the faces of her companions. Josh looked downcast, worried about how this event would affect the investment deal. Carly, usually bubbly and happy, seemed to absorb the worry in the air. Even Julia couldn't shake the sense of something sinister in the background.

"This food is delicious, Josh," she ventured. "I absolutely adore French onion soup made like this—dripping with cheese and with a sturdy French bread that doesn't fall apart in the soup. I wasn't quite ready to try pigs' knuckles. Maybe next time."

Josh chuckled despite his gloom. "I'm glad you approve. I discovered this place my first or second trip here. I'm in love with their prawns."

Carly poured second glasses of wine. "Julia, what about that photo you were going to show Josh?"

"Oh, yes. Thanks for the reminder." Julia pulled out her

phone and found the photo of Alain and his friend. "Here it is. Is that Alain?"

"What's *he* doing here?" Josh asked.

"Alain? He's one of your clients." Julia rechecked the photo in case she had shown him the wrong one.

"No, the guy he's talking to," said Josh. "He's a former client, Troy Ainsworth. He manages a major investment company in London. He's the one I was referring to earlier, when I said I'd lost a major client. I wonder what's going on."

Julia's antennae twitched. "Do you suppose they're up to something?"

Josh nodded. "It certainly seems like a possibility. I'll have a chat with Alain. Maybe there's a simple explanation."

"Are we having dessert?" Carly asked. "I'm still hungry."

"What about stuffed mushrooms?" Julia braced herself for a punch from her sister.

"Very funny. Not." Carly made a face at Julia. "I was thinking more like ice cream. I can't pronounce some of those other dessert names."

"I'm in," said Julia. "Josh? Do you have time?"

"Sure, but then I'll have to track down Alain. Do you and Carly want to join me? The photo is on your camera, after all."

Julia winked at Carly, who shrugged and said, "Why not? I love a good mystery."

~

ALAIN, drink in hand, was waiting for them in the lobby at the Marriott. He stood to greet them, a little unsteadily, thought Julia, though he still managed to look elegant.

"Hi, Josh," Alain said, extending his free hand. "And Julia and Carly, isn't it, from the party yesterday?"

"Right. Thanks for meeting with me."

"Of course. What's going on?" Alain signaled the waiter to bring three glasses of wine.

Josh sat down next to him on the long sofa. "Is there any chance Roger ate anything with mushrooms in it when you were together before the meeting? Soup or a salad? An omelet or quiche, maybe?"

Alain shook his head. "We had wine, that's all—we didn't eat because we knew there would be food at the cocktail party. And it was delicious," he added, nodding to Julia and Carly.

Josh took a deep breath. "One more question. Alain, how do you know Troy Ainsworth?"

Alain shrugged. "Not sure that I do."

"Really? Does he have a twin brother?" Josh opened Julia's smartphone and held it so Alain could see the photo. "He's here in the photo with you, Alain. What's going on?"

Alain drained his glass. "College friend. He's considering investing in my company. That's all."

"It seems odd that you would be talking to him while negotiating with Roger," said Josh. "A conflict of interest, perhaps?"

"Nothing there, Josh," Alain replied, slurring his words. "Roger introduced us. He thought Troy might be interested in investing in our jewelry stores in the Caribbean. Especially if they can install better security software," he added, rising to leave.

"Good to know." Josh stood to shake hands. "How about I get back to you in a few days and talk numbers on that system?"

"Sure," said Alain. "I'm sorry about Roger. I hope he recovers. Give me a call when you get back to your office."

Once they were alone again, Josh, Julia, and Carly sat quietly, sipping their drinks.

"I don't understand why Roger would want to jeopardize this deal," Josh finally said. "It could be worth millions of dollars to the investors."

"Maybe he was trying to woo Troy back to your company," said Julia. "Perhaps he thought the improvements in the security software would entice Troy to bring his business back."

Carly had experience in finance from her job in the pulp and paper industry and understood the ripple effect from major investments. "Wouldn't the partners of your firm also benefit?"

"Yes, they would. We help broker a lot of these deals with consortiums. It can take months of phone conferences, meetings, and trust-building to get the investors to the table."

Julia asked, "Could Roger have been doing something on the side?"

"I honestly don't know," Josh answered, elbows on his knees. "But why would Alain pretend he didn't know Troy at first? I wish I could ask Roger about this myself; but I'll let my other partners take care of that question."

Julia eyed Josh over the rim of her glass. "Does this mean that you're done with the business part of being in Paris? Are you going to have a few days to enjoy the city?"

"Yes and no, Julia. I'll have to do some major scrambling to keep this deal from falling through. It would mean a lot to my company financially, and to me personally. But I want to go to the Eiffel Tower with you tomorrow afternoon and watch the city lights come on at nightfall."

Julia and Carly laughed together. "How did you know Carly and I were discussing that very idea earlier today?"

"ESP?" Josh winked.

"We'd love to," said Julia. "We've even thought of a fourth person to go with us. Even numbers, you know."

"I'll call my office this evening to take care of some

details," said Josh. "The police want me to check with them tomorrow morning, which I'll do after checking on Roger. Then I should be able to show you the Paris I love."

Josh draped his arm around Julia's shoulders as they walked through the lobby. Carly, a few steps behind, almost ran into Francesca, who had entered the lobby from a side door.

"Carly. Julia. And Monsieur Larson!" Francesca gushed. "We meet again."

"Hi, Francesca." Carly and Francesca did the double kiss thing. "Are you working here again?"

"Oui, mes amies," said Francesca. "It pays the rent. Are you taking another cooking class soon?"

"Maybe." Carly glanced at Julia. "We want to see more of Paris while we can, so it depends on how much free time we have left over."

"Well, you can call me at the school anytime you like. Ciao." Francesca exited the lobby through the same door.

"Carly," Julia said, "maybe Francesca would like to go up the Eiffel Tower with us tomorrow?"

Carly thought for a moment. "Maybe, but I'd rather ask Simone. I enjoyed her company."

"Maybe Simone could guide us in a 'sip and paint' party at the top of the Eiffel Tower. Like the one we did last winter at the gallery back home."

Josh cleared his throat. "I'll stick to sipping, thank you."

6

THURSDAY MORNING

Julia sat on pins and needles the next morning, following the encounter with Alain. She wanted to know more about how he and Troy were connected to Josh and Roger. She was deep in thought when her phone rang. She smiled when she saw that it was Josh. "Good morning. I was hoping you'd call. What's the latest on Roger? Is he getting better?"

"Nothing new. I called the hospital first thing to check on him. He's still in critical care and hasn't yet awakened. I plan to meet his wife, Laura, at the hospital later today when she gets in. And a moment ago the hotel housekeeping manager called to tell me that his room has been trashed. It's the adjoining room to mine, but I didn't hear anything, so it must have happened some time while I was out. The hotel manager has already called the police to investigate, and I'm going there now to meet them."

"Carly and I aren't doing anything this morning. Would you like us to join you?"

"Why not? I'll send Vincent over with the limo and meet you in the lobby in about twenty minutes. The manager wants me to remove Roger's things from his room anyway, so you could help me with that."

~

Julia and Carly sat quietly on Roger's settee while Josh and the policemen searched the suite and its contents. The only item obviously missing was the well-worn leather satchel that Josh said Roger typically used for his files. They also discovered that the room safe was open and empty. After dusting for fingerprints and collecting additional forensic evidence, the police prepared to leave, having completed their visit.

"Thank you for your cooperation, Mr. Larson," said the taller of the two policemen. "We will check with the hotel security manager to review any video footage from the hallway security camera. Good day."

Josh collapsed into the chair next to the settee. He wiped his brow with the sleeve of his tailored shirt.

Julia waited a couple of minutes before quietly asking, "Are you ready for us to help you pack up Roger's belongings?"

"Sure. I'll get his suitcase from the closet." Josh glanced around the room as he went to retrieve it. "I don't see much here. He travels pretty light."

"Men have it easy compared to women, in my opinion," said Julia. "You guys can get by with a pair of pants, three shirts, and a jacket. I would need twice that."

Josh chuckled. "I'll take care of his clothes. How about you two taking care of the sitting room and the bathroom?"

Julia busied herself with opening dresser drawers and doors and collecting the few personal items she found, while Carly tackled the bathroom.

"Hey, guys," Carly called. "Here's a receipt of some kind

that I found in the bathroom wastebasket. It looks like a deposit slip for something."

Julia examined the crumpled paper. "It's from this hotel. Do you suppose Roger put something in the main hotel safe?"

Josh was already at the door. "Let's check it out, ladies."

Julia's stomach felt like it was full of butterflies as they waited for the reception clerk to check the vault. After several long minutes, he returned empty-handed.

He announced gravely, "That item was claimed two days ago, I am afraid."

In full detective mode, Julia asked, "Does your system identify who picked it up?"

"I'm sorry, mademoiselle," he replied, wincing. "It is quite an antiquated system."

Josh asked, "Is there any way to tell what the item was?"

The clerk shook his head. "I'm sorry. The client would have to note it on his ticket."

"What about *your* records?" asked Julia. "Wouldn't you identify the item somewhere?"

"We simply tape the deposit slip to the item, then remove it again once it's been claimed," he explained.

Julia thought for a moment. "Does that mean anyone with the receipt could have picked up this item? No ID required?"

The clerk reddened, then brightened. "We do require a signature. Let me get our register."

He returned a moment later, smiling, the record book in hand. Julia and Josh looked up the receipt number in question.

Josh examined the signature. "*R Wxxxx*. Roger had lousy handwriting, but that's not how he usually wrote his 'R.'" He met Julia's eyes. "It could have been anybody pretending to be Roger." Sighing, he closed the book and handed it to the clerk. "Thank you, sir."

Julia led the way to the high-back chairs in the lobby, where Carly was holding court.

"Roger could have picked up whatever he had in the vault," said Julia, "and given it to someone already."

"Or," suggested Josh, "whoever trashed his room could have found the receipt and claimed it. I'm betting Alain or Pierre or even Clint, I suppose."

"But why would they return the receipt to the room, if that were the case?" asked Julia.

"It would be helpful," said Carly, "to know what we're supposed to be looking for. You know—animal, vegetable, or mineral?"

Julia said solemnly, "Small enough to fit in the hotel safe and valuable enough to—"

Josh answered his phone, then gasped. "Yes, of course. I'll be right there." Turning to Julia, ashen-faced, he said, "Roger's dead. Will the two of you go to the hospital with me?"

"—kill for," Julia finished quietly.

7

THURSDAY MORNING, A LITTLE LATER

Julia and Josh waited outside Roger's room for a few minutes as Laura, his widow, cried softly at his bedside.

"I'm so sorry, honey," they heard her say to Roger as they entered the room.

Josh walked the few steps to her side and hugged her gently, offering a few words of solace. Then he turned and nodded toward Julia. "Laura, this is my friend Julia Fairchild."

The women acknowledged each other, as Laura wiped tears from her mascara-stained eyes. Medium height with an athletic body, she had long, wheat-colored hair with blonde highlights masterfully applied. Her green eyes were set in a pretty face with a narrow nose and cupid lips, and her fair coloring was accented by the soft mint of her twinset sweater. Her pale ecru linen pants looked barely wrinkled, despite the long cross-Atlantic flight.

Laura sniffled, then said to Julia, "Roger told me Josh had a friend coming to meet him here. I'm sure visiting hospitals wasn't on your vacation to-do list." She managed a weak smile.

Julia smiled back, offering her hand. "That's my day job. I'm a physician in the real world back home."

"Oh," said Laura. "Roger didn't mention that."

Josh interceded. "He wouldn't have known until he met Julia a couple of days ago. I don't recall having a reason to tell him."

"Of course not," Laura said absently, turning back to gaze at Roger.

"I overhead you telling Roger that you were sorry as we walked in," said Josh. "Is that something relevant?"

Laura blanched. "Oh, it was a...a... We had a fight before he left home. You know, a money thing, and I hadn't had a chance to apologize for my part."

Josh nodded sympathetically. "I understand that's the number one cause of fights in marriages. I'm sure Roger would forgive you." He paused. "Laura, if you need any help taking care of details, like getting Roger home, you should call the office. The firm's secretary will take care of you."

"Thank you, Josh," said Laura. "I will do that. Thank you for coming."

Josh started to leave, then paused. "One more thing. How long are you staying in Paris?"

"Just long enough to take care of this business. That's all," she replied. "Why?"

"Roger's room may still be available at the Marriott."

"Thank you," she said. "I'll look into that."

Julia and Josh left the room silently, gestured to Carly, who had been sitting in the waiting room, to join them, then took the elevator to the main lobby.

"Well?" asked Carly. "What gives? You look puzzled. Both of you."

Julia grimaced. "Something doesn't feel right, Josh."

"Roger did mention money being a little tight a couple of

times recently," said Josh. "I don't understand that. I'm sure he makes at least as much as I do."

"You don't have a wife with expensive tastes," Julia pointed out.

"Yet," Carly blurted out, then quickly clamped her hand over her mouth.

"We're jumping to conclusions," said Julia. "Let's have lunch at that cute bistro near our hotel and talk about it over food."

∼

THE WAITER BROUGHT a platter of crackers, cheeses, and fresh fruit with three bowls of the day's special soup—vichyssoise—as well as a carafe of chilled pinot grigio. He brought a small cup of kidney soup as well for them to taste because Carly had mentioned wanting to try something "really French."

Julia and Carly filled their small luncheon plates and began nibbling and trying the soups. Josh sat quietly with his head down. "I can't believe Roger is dead. He was a really good guy, and we worked well together."

Julia reached out to touch his arm. "It is certainly a shock."

"We weren't exactly social friends, but we had several clients in common. This is definitely going to impact the team at the office." He propped his head on his hand, elbow on the table. "And our boss is going to expect me to salvage this deal."

"You mentioned that Roger had been working on this business prospect for some time," said Julia. "Do you have enough information to carry it out?"

"I'm not sure. It doesn't make sense that someone ransacked his room—for what?"

"It could come down to money, I'm afraid," said Julia. "Roger apparently had something in his possession that was valuable enough to store in the vault, and someone else knew and wanted it badly. Josh, who would you add to our suspect list?"

Josh shook his head. "I still can't believe this has happened. But okay. Pierre, Alain, and Clint. Or someone else Roger knew who had nothing to do with this investor group."

"What about Laura?" asked Julia. "Could she have been the one with the money problem?"

Josh pursed his lips. "She struck me as a typical trophy wife. Roger occasionally mentioned her expensive tastes in clothes and cars. He joked that he should make her find a job."

"Good point," said Julia. "Laura stays on the list. Even if she just got into town. We also know Roger had been talking with Pierre about a competitor. Maybe you can ask him for more detail on that. What about Alain? Could he be doing a side deal with that Troy guy?"

"Possibly," Josh admitted, "but I would expect him to work *through* Roger, not steal whatever it might have been that Roger had with him."

"What would Roger have that could be that valuable?" asked Julia.

"Pierre and Alain were both interested in the newest security technology that Alpha Gamma had recently improved," Josh replied. "The newest software upgrade solves the problem that allowed those art heists last year, as well as adding some new features."

Julia frowned skeptically. "But would he have been carrying the actual software with him? I wouldn't expect him to have access to that proprietary information."

"You're right," said Josh. "He wouldn't have it with him.

Roger's not a techy guy at all. I doubt he could even begin to explain anything that technical." He shook his head again and sighed deeply.

"Maybe he wouldn't have to explain it—just get hold of it," Carly suggested. "There's a black market for everything, I'm sure, as we learned last year in Amsterdam with that art smuggling ring."

Josh nodded. "And plenty of scumbags who are willing to spend a lot of money to get something the wrong way." He slammed his fist into his other hand.

"What about that Troy guy?" Julia asked. "He intrigues me. What's his background?"

Josh's face fell. "He had been a joint client of mine and Roger's, but I was his primary contact in the technology sector. He bailed when he thought Alpha Gamma might have financial problems after that series of museum heists. His company didn't want to take any additional risk with their investment."

"That's a pretty short list, Josh," said Julia. "A wife and two potential business investors—Clint and Troy. I suppose we should include Pierre and Alain while we're at it. And we have no leads."

"Unless you count Roger saying 'mushroom' as a clue," said Carly. "It's got to mean something."

Julia nodded. "I doubt he was describing his last meal, although it may have turned out that way. I didn't notice if he even ate any of them at the party." She checked with Carly and Josh, who were both shaking their heads. "Let's start by finding out more about those mushrooms at the Marriott."

∽

GETTING permission to enter the kitchen, let alone talk with the chef at the Marriott, had been harder than Julia anticipated. She had to promise not to steal any recipes or share any information about food she might observe being prepared, and practically signed away her future firstborn child before she and Carly were allowed behind the swinging doors.

Now, Julia and Carly sat nervously in the sterile office of Tomas Lafayette, the head chef, as he shuffled through some papers on his desk. He struck an imposing figure. Julia guessed he was at least six feet three inches tall and had strong hands, close-cut black hair tinged with gray, and was impeccably garbed in his white chef's coat and black slacks.

"Mesdemoiselles," he finally said, "I understand that you believe someone on my kitchen staff prepared a tray of stuffed mushrooms for a private party of yours. And a person has been taken ill? Is that correct?"

"Yes, sir," said Julia, purposely failing to mention that Roger had died—the man seemed defensive enough already. "But we didn't request them. One of our friends, Francesca Caron, who is an instructor at Le Cordon Bleu and one of your apprentices here, surprised us with them. And it wasn't exactly *our* party. It was organized by one of the hotel guests, Josh Larson."

"I see. I do not know this 'Francesca,'" he said, glaring at Julia. "Are you sure of her name?"

"Yes, Francesca Caron," said Carly, stiffening in her chair. "We took two classes from her at the school."

The chef thumbed through his papers again. "All special requests are recorded on this list," he said, holding up a clipboard. "As you can see, there is no such order here."

"Perhaps you will have to check with Francesca," said Julia. She thought maybe Francesca had made them in the kitchen on her own, not listing it as a special order. That was likely against the rules, and she hated to get Francesca in trouble, but they had to figure out if the mushrooms had killed Roger or not. "The serving staff at the party might remember the mushroom tray. She brought it in toward the end of our cocktail hour. It was very lovely." Julia smiled as she recalled the platter. "Perfect circles of stuffed mushrooms with rose petal decorations."

"Rose petals?" he replied. The chef waved an imperious hand. "Who would use rose petals on a mushroom tray?" He shook his head. "I will check with the staff about that tray. I can assure you, however, that there are no poisonous mushrooms in this kitchen. That is all."

∽

JULIA AND CARLY found a sunny table in the hotel's outdoor café. Julia breathed in the heady fragrance of the roses and peonies and lilacs blooming in the garden surrounding the patio. "They smell lovely, unlike the perfumes of some of my older patients, who apply too much. Their noses can't smell it very well, but I sure can. It makes me a strong supporter of fragrance-free zones in the workplace."

Carly chuckled. "I work with a couple of women like that. I know exactly what you mean."

Julia ordered a couple of glasses of pinot grigio as she and Carly perused the menu. "Now what?" she said. "It's odd that the head chef doesn't seem to know Francesca, although I suppose there could be quite a few apprentices around the kitchen. Maybe they come and go too quickly for Mr. Lafayette to learn their names. Or there may be several midlevel managers between her and the head chef. She probably reports to some assistant person."

Carly nodded. "Yeah, like a manager who is in charge of that specific program."

"We should have thought of that question while we were in the kitchen."

"Or," said Carly, "we could go to the school and ask Francesca."

"That's a good idea. Let's finish our drinks and check that out. I hope Josh is having better luck than we are so far."

～

"How are things back at the office?" Josh asked Sharon White, Roger's personal assistant. "It's so terrible about Roger. Things are crazy here in Paris. I talked with his wife this morning. Laura seems to be holding up okay, considering the situation."

"Not how you planned to spend your time in Paris, I'm sure, Mr. Larson," Sharon replied. "It's been a shock to us here too. I can't believe I'm never going to see his face again. Did you know he always remembered my birthday? Every year he gave me a gift certificate for a restaurant that I wouldn't normally be able to afford. What a sweetheart." She sniffled. "Enough of that for now. How can I help you today?"

"It's certainly a huge loss all around. We'll all miss him. Here's why I called. Roger and I had a client named Troy Ainsworth a year or so back. Do you have his contact information in the files?"

"Let me check for you," she said. "I remember the name because of his British accent. He was always snippy when he called. Like I was beneath him."

"Little did he know how much power you have, Sharon," said Josh. "A good administrative assistant is worth her weight in gold." Josh looked around the lobby as he waited for Sharon to find the information. He didn't see anyone familiar at first but then caught a glimpse of Alain and a well-dressed woman walking on the far side of the foyer.

"Here it is, Mr. Larson. I'll read it to you and text it as

well." Sharon gave him Troy's cell number and email address. "Good luck. I hope you find out what happened."

"Thanks, Sharon. I hope so too." Josh ended the call and hurried across the foyer to see if he could locate Alain and his companion. They were nowhere in sight, but they had been walking in the direction of the main door, as if to go outside. The other option would be the lounge located just inside the lobby door. Josh scanned the sparsely populated lounge, where one couple sat with their drinks. Then he headed outside and looked up and down the street. A taxi had just the left the curb. He described Alain and the woman to the valet, who confirmed they had just driven away.

"They mentioned going to the Eiffel Tower, sir."

∼

JULIA AND CARLY were ready to call for the limo to take them back to their hotel when Julia's phone rang.

"Is this a good evening to take that ride up the Eiffel Tower?" Josh asked. "Where are you, anyway?"

"Carly and I enjoyed a glass of wine in the patio café at the Marriott. We were heading over to the cooking school to talk with Francesca. Where are *you?*"

"In the lobby, heading your way," said Josh. "I'll call the limo and we'll go to the tower now, if that's okay. I have another reason."

"Its fine. I'll have Carly call Simone and see if she can join us there—as a fourth, you know. We'll see Francesca at the school tomorrow." She checked her watch. "It's probably closed for today anyway, since it's already after four."

Carly dialed Simone, who was delighted to meet them at the tower. Her husband, she said, was working the late shift in the lab.

"What's going on?" Julia asked Josh as the trio waited for the limo. "You sounded worried."

"I'm not sure if it's anything, but I saw Alain and a woman in the lobby," he replied. "The valet said they were going to the Eiffel Tower. It seemed like a good idea to run into them there." He grinned mischievously.

"Uh huh," said Julia. "And ask him more questions about that guy from London, maybe?"

"Yeah, something like that," he admitted. "And he said he was going right back to Calais when I spoke with him at the party, so why is he still here?"

Simone was waiting for them at the entrance and greeted each of them with a double-kiss. With the long line of people waiting for the elevator, they decided to troop up the stairs, all three hundred sixty of them, to the first level. There, they took a poll and voted to ride the elevator to the top, then make their way down the stairs for dinner.

Josh was anxious to check the restaurants for Alain but agreed to stay at the top of the tower to watch the city lights turn on as dusk deepened to night. Within fifteen minutes the city below shimmered with thousands of lights.

"Ah. The 'City of Lights,'" Julia exclaimed, as Josh hugged her close. "Now I understand that expression. It's more beautiful than I imagined."

Carly and Simone took photos of everyone against the city backdrop, as well as a few selfies.

With the wind picking up, Josh proposed that they head down and decide on a restaurant. "I'd like to treat you all to dinner, but Julia has a different plan it seems. Julia?"

"Why don't we split up and scout out two different restaurants?" said Julia. "Carly knows what Alain looks like. If she sees him, she can call Josh or me. Is that okay with you, sis?"

"We'll call if we see him or if he starts to leave before

we're done eating," Carly replied. "Simone said we should check out the shops also, in case they went there first."

"Good idea," said Josh. "We can all meet up after dinner and compare notes. Whether or not we see Alain."

Julia hugged Carly and added, "And stay out of trouble," as the two women started down the stairs to the restaurant on the next lower level.

Josh turned to Julia. "Okay, beautiful. I finally have you all to myself." He kissed her sweetly and sighed. "I've always wanted to have dinner at the restaurant up here and see the lights for myself. I've heard it's very romantic."

"Another first," said Julia.

"For both of us this time," Josh agreed.

The hostess led Julia and Josh to a table next to the outside window, where the view of the city was fantastic. Sipping on a delicious French cabernet sauvignon, Julia turned her thoughts back to Roger and the problem at hand.

"What's the latest on Troy?" she asked. "Were you able to get what you wanted from Roger's secretary?"

"I got Troy's contact information, but he hasn't responded to my email yet," said Josh. "My phone call went to his voicemail."

"What about the police? Anything new there?"

Josh stiffened. "They seem to think I'm innocent of any wrongdoing, but until they have the break-in figured out, they told me I'm not going anywhere. No one is saying Roger's death was anything other than an accident, but . . ."

"What possible motive could there be for someone, especially you, to kill Roger?" Julia asked. "On another note, how would Alain fit into this?"

"Alain is the CEO for the largest insurance company in Calais. They have recommended our client's security system to museums and banks in his territory. His family, as you may remember, owns a chain of jewelry stores in the Caribbean. They use this system as well."

Julia nodded. "That sounds normal."

"Yes, but he told me that they had recently been hearing reports of software failures. Isolated instances, it appears, but it's raising concerns of professionals hacking into the system."

"That wouldn't be good."

"Right. Alpha Gamma Security had sent some of their own experts to check it out."

"And?"

"You're like a straight man in a comedy routine," said Josh, smiling. "And so far they haven't found any definite issue in the software itself."

"That's good, at least for your client," said Julia.

"But what's *not* good is that Alain said a couple of the businesses are making noise about switching to one of Alpha Gamma's competitors. That would mean more lost business for our company."

"Didn't you mention that the security company had improved their software after the museum incidents last year?" asked Julia.

"Yes. That's why it's surprising that there are new failures. Alpha Gamma is suspicious of tampering somewhere along the way," said Josh.

"Sabotage?" Julia raised an eyebrow. "Not good."

"Julia, you're like an 'emoji' with your comments." Josh reached across the table and took her hands. "This doesn't seem nearly so bad with you here with me, sharing our thoughts."

Julia felt her face flush. "Is there anything specific I can do to help?"

"There's something bigger going on that doesn't make

sense. Pierre reported a couple of software glitches, and Clint, the guy you met from London, is saying the same thing."

"Is this the first you've heard about these issues?"

"Yes, but remember," said Josh, "these are Roger's clients, not mine. I don't know if Roger knew any of this. But I would expect that he did."

Julia thought for a moment. "Is it possible that Roger was hiding something? What if he was holding back information from the security company?"

"I'm not ready to go that far. It is a concern, though, that these failures are happening in a system that has been foolproof for the last eight years."

"What about the problems last year in the museums in Germany and Amsterdam?"

"Alpha Gamma has programmed additional firewalls to prevent that from recurring," he explained. "Those were caused by human intervention on the user's part, not by software failures."

Julia nodded. "I see. So the experts haven't found any common thread in this series?"

"Not in the software itself. They suspect human interference."

"Like an inside job?"

"Yes, but it's occurring in multiple locations, which makes it difficult to track down the common denominator."

"Computers aren't my area of expertise," Julia said, shaking her head.

"The company is working on possible technology issues from their end," said Josh.

"Thank heavens. On another note, one thing that bugs me is that Roger was in *your* bathroom. Why? And how did he get into your suite?"

"Our suites had a connecting door and either of us could

unlock it with our room key, so that's the 'how,'" said Josh. "I'm not sure of the 'why.' That *is* a good question."

"Could Roger have hidden something in your bathroom? After all, it's not very likely that he was there to borrow shaving cream, is it?"

"Good point. I'll check the drawers when I get back to the room later, although I'll be surprised if I find anything."

"Humor me, sir." Julia giggled. "Have the police said if they found anything when they checked the hotel security tapes?"

"Not that I've heard. I'll ask them about that tomorrow, when I touch base with them."

"Another missing puzzle piece is Roger's briefcase. Could he have left it in one of your meeting rooms?" Julia asked.

Josh closed his eyes as he thought. "I'm quite sure he had his brown leather case with him when we left after the last meeting. I remember thinking it was so scuffed up that he should probably buy a new one."

"We didn't find it in his room," said Julia. "So where is it?"

"And what was in it?" added Josh.

8

THURSDAY EVENING

Leaving Julia and Josh at the entrance to the Jules Verne Restaurant, Carly and Simone strolled along the second level of the Eiffel Tower and admired the views of the city. They peeked into the boutique shops while keeping an eye out for Alain and marveled at the many opportunities to buy souvenir versions of the tower.

"This is cute, and it might even be useful," said Carly, admiring a small hand-mirror shaped like the tower and bedecked with rhinestones.

"It's more original than some of these other options," said Simone.

"And more expensive," Carly said after checking the price tag. "Those are pretty valuable rhinestones."

"I don't understand why we are supposed to be looking for this man…Alain," said Simone as they walked to the stairway entrance.

"He's one of Josh and Roger's business clients that Julia and I met at that social at the Marriott. Josh thought he had already left Paris, but he saw Alain a short while ago at the hotel. The valet said he was headed here." Carly shrugged a shoulder. "Josh wants to talk to him."

"So we're stalking him, *non*?"

Carly chuckled. "I guess that's what you could call it. If we happen to see him, we'll tell Josh, but mostly I plan to enjoy our dinner."

The descent down three hundred sixty steps to the first level took a mere five minutes—much less time than the walk up from the ground level. There, they checked out the new glass floor outside the tower—with some trepidation, given it was as high as the eighteenth floor of a skyscraper. Carly and Simone walked cautiously across the open expanse to the rail, where Carly posed for a photograph, pretending that she might fall over. The view of the surrounding city was spectacular even from this lower level. She and Simone felt braver after a couple of minutes and twirled their way back to the entrance door. Carly was glad she had pants on instead of a skirt, though she thought it unlikely that her underwear would be visible from any observers on the ground two hundred feet below her.

Simone had suggesting eating at the 58 Eiffel Tower restaurant to cap the evening. Carly thought they were lucky to get a table near the window without having made a reservation, although Simone's flirting with the host may have helped. The night sky was a shimmering backdrop to the sleek modern décor, complemented by a view of the Champ-de-Mars. Even the cover of the menu was beautiful.

"This is wonderful, Simone," said Carly. "I'm so glad you suggested this. I thought we would end up eating at some ground level kiosk."

Simone raised her glass. "It's out of my usual budget, but your sister offered to pay so I thought we should take her up on it. This is such a lovely way to enjoy this beautiful place. And we'll remember it always. Salud."

"That we will," said Carly, raising her own glass. "Salud!" She clinked Simone's glass and took a sip of her wine, as did Simone. She glanced around the beautifully appointed room at her fellow diners. "Simone—don't be too obvious about it but take a peek to your right."

Simone casually tossed her mane of long hair in that direction, sweeping it off her neck. "Which table? I see three of them."

"The middle one. Check out the couple with the blonde lady in a short black lacy cocktail dress and a curly-brown-haired guy wearing a charcoal gray pin-striped suit. I'm pretty sure that's Alain, the guy Josh is looking for."

"I see them," said Simone. She pretended to admire the view. "I've seen that man before. At the hospital."

"Really? When?" Carly glanced at Alain one last time, keeping her face partially obscured by her glass.

Simone furrowed her brows. "I'm sure he went into Roger's room the morning I met you in the waiting room."

"And?"

"He seemed to be nervous. He didn't stay long, and he looked both ways down the hall when he left the room."

"Wouldn't he do that to look for the elevator? I know that's what I would do."

Simone shook her head. "It was more like he was checking to see if anyone saw him. I can't explain why I thought that. It was something about the look on his face. Or maybe it was that I sensed something sinister about him."

"We need to tell Julia and Josh," said Carly. "That could be important information to share with the police."

"Of course. But they wouldn't talk to the police until tomorrow, so I say we tell them after dinner." Simone raised her glass. "Bon appetit."

Carly shook her blonde curls. "No. I need to call her. I promised. Julia can decide for herself what she wants to do."

Julia answered immediately. "Hi," she said. "How's your dinner?"

"We just ordered so I don't know yet, but the drinks are good. We're in the 58 Eiffel Tower restaurant on the next level down from you. Alain is here with the lady Josh saw. I don't think they've noticed us."

"Okay. How far along in their dinner are they? Can you tell?"

Carly turned and casually looked across the room. "He's got a salad in front of him. And there's a basket of bread on the table."

Julia relayed the information to Josh then said to Carly, "We're halfway through our entrée. We'll come down when we're done and find you. If they start to leave before we get there, stall them. And call me. I'll count on you to sweet talk them for a few minutes."

~

TWENTY MINUTES later Julia and Josh approached Carly's table. They were careful to stand with their backs to Alain and his lady friend. "Hi. How's the food?" asked Julia.

"I would need a month of classes at the Cordon Bleu to cook like this," said Carly.

Simone nodded her approval, dabbing at her lips with her napkin.

Carly kept her voice low. "Simone recognized Alain. She saw him go into Roger's room at the hospital."

"No way," said Josh. "Tell me more."

Simone told him what she had observed.

"Josh, you're going to want to tell the police," said Julia.

"Yes. But it was probably totally innocent. I mean, I hate to point fingers without knowing more. Besides, there's no urgency to talking with the police this evening, is there?" he said to Julia. "It wouldn't hurt to chat with Alain now and ask about that visit." He offered her his arm. "Will you join me, Beautiful?"

Carly and Simone watched as Julia and Josh approached Alain's table. The conversation between the four of them started with smiles, then became animated, with gesturing of hands, nodding of heads, and a napkin tossed onto the table as it ended.

"Well?" asked Carly as her sister and Josh returned.

Josh answered. "He admitted that he had been to the hospital, but he said he was paying his respects. That makes sense. I doubt there's anything to be gained from going to the police."

"Back to square one, I'm afraid," said Julia.

∽

FRIDAY MORNING

Waking up to a glorious morning the day after Roger's death, Julia and Carly headed off for their next adventure. Josh had insisted they try to enjoy the day while he dealt with police and his ongoing office business priorities.

"Paris in springtime is as beautiful as the song says it is," Julia remarked as they waited in line to enter Notre Dame. She and Carly, armed with comfortable shoes, cameras, and lightweight jackets to suit the early April weather, planned to climb all four hundred twenty-two steps to the top.

Julia felt a sense of awe build in her chest as they started the climb. She imagined the thousands of monks of centuries past doing the very same thing as they carried out their duties within the cathedral.

The first stop they made along the stairway was to admire the Salle Haute, or "high room," known for its amazing Gothic architecture featuring intricate ribbed vaults. The craftsmanship was especially impressive considering it had all been done with relatively primitive tools.

Further up the stairs they encountered the gargoyles in the Galerie des Chimères. Julia and Carly made faces at the famous Styrge, then at each other. Tourists near them did the same thing as they all laughed. Julia recalled seeing an advertising poster depicting that same gargoyle holding a glass of wine. "Too bad we didn't bring a canteen of wine with us. Next time, Carly."

A few steps from the top they stopped to marvel at the cavernous belfry, with its ancient church bells, and the thirteen-ton bell named "Emmanuel." Julia paused a moment, catching her breath. "Why would you name a bell? Do you suppose they had a contest to name it?"

Carly shook her head and rolled her eyes as she gazed at the gigantic bell.

"This view is absolutely magnificent. There isn't a word that adequately describes the incredible awe-inspiring vista from here." Julia inhaled deeply as she tried to take it all in. "Think about it, Carly. Millions of people have been here before us. Artists have spent lifetimes painting its beauty. Poets have woven tapestries of words trying to tell others what it did to their souls. Hundreds of books have been written about Notre Dame and love and romance. My heart is simply full of—something—like magic, ready to explode." She turned to her sister. "Do you feel anything?"

"Besides hungry?"

"Carly…we're at the center of Paris, the center of France. It touches my soul to be here."

"I get that, but have you thought about the hard labor of the people who built this? I bet it wasn't uncommon for them to have serious injuries, or even die, during the construction."

"Of course. There was no OSHA in the twelfth century,

when they started building this. Your background would certainly make you consider work safety."

"You see work-related injuries in your office, Julia."

"Neither of us can change what may have happened back then," Julia said softly, "but we can keep them in mind and appreciate the work they did to create this beautiful monument."

Julia and Carly smiled at each other, a silent truce between them. They moved down the stairs much more quickly than they had climbed up. Around the corner to their left was the main facade, where the Rose Window was centered majestically above the entrance. They walked past a statue of an early bishop of Paris, St. Denis, who held his amputated head in his hands, then past the carving of the Last Judgment above the central doorway before entering the cathedral through the Portal of St. Anne.

The sisters strolled slowly through the beautiful church, starting at the Nave and moving toward the Altar along the long middle aisle, then back to the Choir and the Ambulatory before exiting next to St. Denis.

"I want to soak up all that majesty," said Julia, "and etch it in my brain, seeing as I can't paint a lick, and words don't begin to do it justice."

"Here's the Point Zero stone that is supposed to mark the exact center of Paris," said Carly. "I'll take your picture first; then you can take mine. I've always wanted to be at the center of something."

After a fellow tourist took a photo of the two of them standing on the stone, Carly again mentioned that she was more than hungry. "How about finding a café nearby? Our driver probably knows a good place."

Shortly thereafter the two found themselves on a sun-dappled patio, enjoying a delightful meal, sipping crisp pinot grigio, and watching the river traffic on the Seine. "I'm not going to want to go home," said Julia. "This is so divine—sitting in the sun, inhaling the wonderful fragrance of the flowers, watching the world go by. Not a care in the world."

Julia's cellphone rang, interrupting her reverie. "It's Josh," she announced as she answered. "What's up?"

"Do you have time to go with me to the police station? They want to ask some more questions related to Roger's death. One of them isn't so sure I'm innocent."

"Oh, no!" Julia gasped. "What's happened?"

"They won't tell me anything yet. I need you to vouch for me about the food at the cocktail party."

"I can do that. We're finishing lunch in a café near Notre Dame. I'll have Vincent bring us to the Marriott."

"That's great. See you soon. Thank you, Julia."

Carly, having noticed Julia's face go pale, asked quietly, "What's wrong?"

"Josh has to go to the police station. He wants us to tell them about the food at the party."

"That doesn't sound good. We both know that our food was poison-free. Right?"

"As far as I know."

∽

THE TRIO WAS ESCORTED into the police detective's office. They entered a stark room with gray metal chairs and desk, a gray filing cabinet, and a tired ceiling lamp trying to light up the dingy space. Julia felt as though she'd been sent back to the nineteen-fifties.

A detective with a dour expression invited them to be seated as he turned the page of a legal-sized pad. He wrote a few words before addressing them. "It has come to my attention that Mr. Larson arranged for a cocktail party for his clients at his hotel." He looked up as they all nodded.

"You two ladies were in charge of the food, I am told."

Julia and Carly nodded again.

"Can you tell me exactly what you served and where it came from, please?"

"Yes, sir," said Julia. "All the food came from a market near the Cordon Bleu school. We purchased several kinds of cheese, crackers, a pâté, and pink pickles."

"Don't forget the olives," Carly added.

"Pink pickles?" The detective scowled. "What about the mushrooms that were served?"

"We didn't supply those," Julia explained. "They came from the kitchen at the Marriott. Francesca, one of our Cordon Bleu instructors, brought them. It was a surprise for the party."

"So you know nothing more about the mushrooms?" He glared at them.

"No, sir," said Julia. "Except that they were delicious. Carly and I each tasted one. May I ask why you're asking about the mushrooms?"

"Normally I wouldn't reveal this detail, but this is an unusual case." He stood, hands behind his back, then started pacing as if trying to decide what to share. "The autopsy found poison in Mr. Westover's stomach. The pathologist believes it may have come from mushrooms he had eaten."

Julia leaned back in the hard chair. "Roger did mouth the word 'mushroom' when we saw him at the hospital and nodded his head when I asked if that was the word he was trying to say. Then he started seizing before he could answer my question as to whether he'd eaten some. I'd like to point out that no one else got sick from eating anything at the party, as far as I know."

"That is a puzzle, Dr. Fairchild, isn't it? Your friend Mr. Larson explained that you are a physician and that you have solved a couple of mysterious deaths in the past."

"They certainly didn't involve mushrooms," Julia replied.

"Understood," he said, narrowing his eyes at her. "Well, if you have any ideas, you are welcome to offer them to this office. We will continue the investigation, and you are free to go today, but I ask that the three of you stay in Paris. Mr. Larson is on my short list of suspects."

9

FRIDAY AFTERNOON

Julia sipped her cabernet as she sat with Carly and Josh in front of the fireplace at the Marriott.

Thinking out loud, she said, "Where could Roger have possibly eaten poisoned mushrooms? It doesn't seem likely that the kitchen would have them on hand. The chef was certain they didn't come from there."

"Maybe it wasn't the mushrooms that were poisoned.," said Carly. "The detective said they found poison in his stomach and they assumed it was the mushrooms. It could have been something else."

Julia nodded. "That's true. The chef was surprised about the rose petals. Do you suppose they were the culprit?"

"Would anyone actually eat those decorations?" asked Josh.

Julia and Carly snickered. "Some flowers are edible and sometimes used for decorations—like nasturtiums or chrysanthemums," Julia explained. "Other cultures eat them in salads, like in Japan."

Josh grinned. "Maybe that's the real meaning of the term 'flower power.'"

Julia shook her head as she pulled out her phone. "I doubt

that, but I'll look up 'poisonous roses' and see if that's a possibility. Let's see—the web says rose petals are generally nontoxic. One comment here even says that they're very good dipped in chocolate."

"Probably better than grasshoppers," teased Carly.

Josh looked at Carly. "Grasshoppers? In chocolate?"

"You don't want to know, Josh," Julia said. "Trust me on that." She and her country-raised siblings had eaten a few live grasshoppers as children, specifically the small green ones that were easy to catch in the long grass in the pasture. They had swallowed them quickly without chewing because the 'juice' was too gross.

"If the poison didn't come from roses or mushrooms," said Josh, "then what could have been the source?"

"I wonder if Alain gave something to Roger when he was in the hospital room," offered Carly.

"With a nurse watching?" asked Julia. "Doesn't seem very likely. Besides, he had already collapsed by then, and he wasn't ready to eat anything when we saw him. I say we wait for the toxicology results before we spend too much time following this angle."

"One of us, probably you, Julia, should talk with Laura, his widow," said Josh. "Maybe he has some medical history that plays a role here."

"Yeah," said Carly. "And you should ask her more specifically what she meant about money issues."

Julia nodded as she considered how to approach Laura. "Josh, why don't you see if Laura will meet me for lunch tomorrow? I'll keep it friendly." She grinned slyly.

"I could find out more about Roger's finances, maybe," said Josh. "I know a couple of his close friends who might know something useful."

"Could he have been playing the market? Or gambling?"

asked Carly. "I know even smart guys can lose their shirts in those games."

"Josh, you still haven't heard about the security videos, have you? Maybe Roger's intruder got caught on video."

Josh nodded. "I'll check with the security manager right after we finish our drinks. It's also possible Roger knew his visitor and let him in. We don't know when his room was trashed, exactly."

"True," said Julia. "But if we assume his room was straightened up by housekeeping on Tuesday morning, it had to have occurred sometime after that. It may even have been after our party but before Roger went to the hospital on Tuesday evening. We don't know what his room looked like because he was taken to the hospital from *your* room, Josh, not his own. That could even be why he was in your room, Josh. Maybe he found his own room trashed while we were all still at the party and went into your room to hide something the intruder didn't find."

"The room could have been ransacked any time between Tuesday evening and Thursday morning," said Carly. "If housekeeping did routine service in his room Wednesday morning as I would expect, the intruder could still have gone in later that day."

Julia nodded. "It looks like we should talk to the maids. Whoever cleaned his room will know if it had already been trashed when they went in on Wednesday, but they just didn't report it until Thursday. That would allow us to pinpoint an approximate time."

"And then what?" asked Josh.

"Let's talk with housekeeping first," said Julia. "That will narrow down the window of opportunity. You can check with security while Carly and I are doing that. They can also tell us if a key card was used for entry. And if so, *whose* key card."

81

JULIA AND CARLY waited impatiently in the bland office of the Director of Housekeeping. They noticed that several awards for "Excellence in Housekeeping" and "Employee of the Month" hung on the otherwise blank wall. The desktop was immaculate. No cleaning supplies in sight anywhere.

"I should take some lessons on how to keep my desk this clean," said Julia.

"Me too," chimed in Carly. "If I could only figure out how to do everything without writing things down. Sometimes I need more than my computer, but it would be great to go paper-free."

"Sounds funny coming from someone who works for a company that makes paper," said Julia. "Better not say that out loud at work."

A tall black male dressed in an off-the-rack suit tapped lightly on the door and entered the room, which suddenly seemed smaller with his presence. He smiled as he extended a hand. "Bonjour, mesdemoiselles. I am Jonathon Taylor. I understand you want to talk about one of our rooms. Is that correct?"

"Yes, sir," said Julia. She introduced herself and Carly. "Our question is about suite number 668, where Mr. Westover was staying, which adjoins our friend Mr. Larson's suite."

Mr. Taylor entered the number on his electronic table and looked up at Julia. "What do you need to know?"

"We hope you can tell us when your housekeeping staff first discovered that it had been trashed. Knowing the time frame could help us find the guilty party."

"Ms. Fairchild, this has already been covered with the police."

"Oh, I'm not trying to interfere with the investigation." Julia held her hands up. "This is unofficial. I am helping Mr.

Westover's colleague, Mr. Larson, make some inquiries. Would it hurt to tell me when his room was checked? Or if he had called for extra service of any kind sometime on Tuesday, the day that he collapsed?"

"Julia is an amateur detective," added Carly. "She might be able to figure out who trashed the room."

The housekeeping manager looked over the top of his rimless glasses. "You are aware, are you not, that our hotel has our internal security staff, as well as the Paris police detectives, working on this?"

Julia nodded, replying, "Yes, of course. We're trying to find out if Mr. Westover's briefcase was noticed in his room when they serviced it. That's all."

Mr. Taylor appeared to be satisfied with her explanation. "I see." He entered some data and checked the screen again. "There is no record of housekeeping entering his room until six forty-five on Tuesday, which would have been for evening service and bed turn-down. Nothing was reported to be out of the ordinary, but I wouldn't expect there to be a comment about a briefcase. Many businessmen have one but they don't always leave it in their room."

"Okay," said Julia. "What about morning room service?"

"There was no response when the housekeeper knocked at eight-thirty in the morning, according to the notes here. The maid entered and took care of normal servicing. The next morning, Thursday, she found the room in complete disarray and reported it to me. Because it was an adjoining suite with Mr. Larson, I reported the information to him as a courtesy."

Julia ventured another thought. "I don't suppose your staff notes things like food or beverages in the room."

"Not typically, and there's no comment here of that nature," he replied. "What would that have to do with personal articles?"

"It wouldn't," said Julia. "I was just curious."

"Is there anything else?" Taylor asked. "I have a staff meeting to run in a few minutes."

Julia looked at Carly who shrugged her shoulders. "No, sir. Thank you very much for your time."

Out of earshot, Carly asked, "Why did you ask about food in the room?"

"I was wondering if Roger had mushrooms in his room later, after the party. But that looks like a dead end for now."

"Maybe Josh is having better luck with security," said Carly.

∽

"How can I help you, Mr. Larson?" asked Howard Berg, Director of Hotel Security. His deep voice was inconsistent with his small stature. Josh had expected to see a taller man with bulging muscles, based on his telephone voice. This guy looked like he should stick to cybersecurity.

Josh phrased his question benignly, he hoped. "Would it be possible to check my partner's suite to find out who accessed his room between Tuesday morning and Thursday?"

"I can tell whether or not someone has used a keycard to enter that suite, but that doesn't necessarily tell me who used the card," Mr. Berg replied. "What are you looking for, might I ask?"

"One of his personal items, his briefcase to be specific, is missing," said Josh. "I'd like to locate it because it contains private business information. My company is obviously concerned about the security of its contents."

"Of course, Mr. Larson," he replied. "The hotel takes the utmost care in securing its clients and their possessions." Mr. Berg consulted his tablet. "There are two entries of the room, other than by the housekeeping staff, between ten a.m. Tuesday and noon on Thursday. Mr. Westover's key card was used at one thirty-five p.m. and again at four twenty-seven p.m., both on Tuesday."

"No room service calls?"

"None listed, although that wouldn't require the use of a key card, as Mr. Westover would have opened the door from the inside," Mr. Berg explained.

Josh nodded. "Makes sense. The first of those would be Roger going to his room after we finished our meeting. The second time would fit with going back to the room after the appetizer party ended."

"Is there anything else? You do realize that we have been fully cooperative with the police."

"Of course, Mr. Berg. I'm just trying to locate the briefcase." Josh leaned forward in his chair. "What about checking security cameras in that hallway?"

"I was already asked to review the tapes for the police." He ran his fingers down a yellow legal pad. "Unfortunately, his room is out of range of the cameras that are installed at the elevator and stairwell doors on that floor, so I'm afraid they did not record any visitors to Mr. Westover's room during that time period."

Josh frowned. "So no help there."

"No, sir. I'm sorry."

∼

"WE COULD CHECK with Francesca while Josh is busy with the security guy," said Julia. "At this time of day, she should be at Le Cordon Bleu."

"Good idea," said Carly. "We can also tell her we won't have time for any more classes after all."

"Not unless we get stuck here in Paris with this Roger business." Julia sighed. "I do want to know what killed Roger and who's responsible."

"Do I have to remind you that you're on vacation?" asked Carly. "The fine Paris police are already working on it, you know."

"Yes, but they have lots of cases to solve," said Julia. "How do I know they'll give this case their full attention?"

"We can at least talk with Francesca," Carly said, acquiescing. "And get the final skinny on the mushrooms."

~

JULIA AND CARLY were happy that Josh's limo driver, Vincent, was available to take them over to the cooking school. Leaving them at the front entrance, he informed them that he would have the rest of the day free, courtesy of Mr. Larson, as it was his seventieth birthday. He pointed out the closest Metro station, should they choose that route instead of a taxi.

"Merci, and happy birthday, Vincent," said Julia. "We'll try the Metro. Mr. Larson will be impressed that we can do it by ourselves."

"Speak for yourself, sis," said Carly. "I don't want to get lost trying to use the subway here. Remember how we got turned around in New York City?"

"Yeah, yeah, yeah. I remember. And people helped us get going the right way."

"They spoke English," said Carly. "This is Paris."

Julia made a face at her sister. "Don't worry. We'll figure it out."

"Famous last words."

Julia tossed her brunette bob as she walked up to the receptionist.

"Bonjour. My sister and I took a couple of classes here earlier this week. We're hoping to talk with our instructor, Francesca Caron."

"One moment, please," the young woman said as she dialed an extension. She spoke in rapid French, occasionally turning to glance at the sisters. Finished, she smiled graciously and said, "I am so sorry. Francesca is no longer here."

"What?" Julia and Carly exclaimed in unison.

"What happened to her?" asked Julia.

"I'm sorry, mesdemoiselles," the receptionist said. "I do not have any more to tell you."

"It's important that we talk with her," said Julia. "Do you have her contact information?"

The receptionist shook her head. "We have no phone number for her on file."

"An address perhaps?" asked Julia.

"Again, no," she replied, less patiently. "I wish you luck in finding her."

Julia and Carly looked at each other. "How will we find Francesca?" asked Carly.

Julia thought for a moment, then asked, "What about a phone number for Kate Opgrande or Becca Taylor? They were in our class and might know how to reach her."

"One moment, please."

"Good idea, Julia," said Carly.

"Ms. Opgrande has a telephone number listed. But I would need her permission to share it with you. I will call and see if she will allow that and notify you. May I have your phone number?" The receptionist handed Julia a pad with the school's logo on it. Julia quickly jotted down her name and number.

"Merci bien," said Julia. "It's important that we talk to her."

10

STILL FRIDAY AFTERNOON

"Another dead end," said Carly as they exited the Cordon Bleu building. "What do we do now, Miss Amateur Detective? What if the receptionist can't reach Kate, or maybe Kate won't give permission to share her phone number?"

"There's always another way to get information." Julia stopped mid-stride and held up a finger. "Kate's parents own a restaurant in Cape Cod. She told us the name. Now what was it?"

Carly scrunched up her face. "I remember thinking about the movie *Jaws* when she said it."

"Yes. It had to do with sharks. Something unexpected. And it was clever."

"And I thought it was a strange name for wanting to add French cuisine," said Carly. "It sounded more like a good name for a bar."

"Sharks . . .bars…drunks—Drunken Shark. That's what it was called!" Julia squealed and grabbed Carly's hands. They did a little jig on the sidewalk as passers-by steered clear of them. "Let's call the restaurant and get Kate's number that way."

Julia did an internet search, found the number, and left a message for a return call. "I forgot that they would be five hours behind us in time. It's ten a.m. there, and they don't open till eleven."

"Maybe someone will check for messages before opening time and call you back sooner," said Carly. "Where are we going now? Do you want to brave the Metro?"

Julia consulted the map from the hotel concierge. "It's not that far from here back to our hotel. Do you feel like walking?"

Carly looked at the beautiful sky before answering. "It's a gorgeous day for it. If you have your Girl Scout compass with you, we might even get there without getting lost."

Julia started walking down the street. "Ha, ha. No compass, but I can read a map. Plus we'll get more steps this way." She showed Carly her step tracker.

"That one looks different than your old one. Is it new?"

"I got it a couple of weeks before we left on this trip. It has some cool features, like being able to track my walks on this exercise icon," Julia said as she tapped the clock face. "And it lets me know when I have a message on my phone, although I haven't been able to figure out how to use it to reply." She opened the corresponding app on her smartphone. "Here's the walk from yesterday."

"Hmm. That does look interesting. I don't remember to wear mine most of the time. I figure I easily get my ten thousand steps a day anyway, with all the walking around the huge buildings at work."

Julia smiled as they crossed another street. "I needed the extra incentive of the watch to keep me honest about my steps."

"On another note, has Josh seen Pierre at all since the cocktail party?" asked Carly.

Julia shrugged. "There may not be any reason for Pierre

to interact with Josh at this point. I mean, Roger was his agent for this venture, not Josh. I don't know how their firm replaces someone when something like this happens." She stopped and looked at Carly. "Although Josh did mention that he would be expected to complete the deal with Roger gone."

"So why is Alain still here?" asked Carly. "His business is in Calais. Why is he hanging out in Paris?"

Julia shook her head. "He doesn't seem to be offering moral support for Josh, based on the interactions I've seen. Maybe it's because of the lady he had dinner with, or perhaps he set up other business meetings since he was already going to be here for Josh and Roger's meetings."

"Makes sense," said Carly.

"What still doesn't make sense is why Roger collapsed, and why was he in Josh's room in the first place," said Julia. "Was he hiding something? Looking for something? But why would he be looking in the bathroom?"

"Could he have been hiding himself?" asked Carly.

"But why?" asked Julia. "He wouldn't have to answer his door at the hotel if someone knocked. He would more likely wait them out—unless they were entering with a keycard and he didn't want to be seen in the room."

"Maybe he heard someone knock, didn't answer, and then he heard them using a key card, so he slipped into Josh's room to hide," said Carly. "And the intruder could have taken the briefcase while Roger was in Josh's room."

Julia sighed. "But why would he be in the bathroom? We may never know. Oh. I forgot to ask Josh if he checked his bathroom drawers when he got back to his room last night. Would you remind me later so I don't forget again?"

Julia held her face to the sun as they sauntered down Rue Champfleury, then along Avenue Charles Risler, through the beautiful grounds surrounding the Eiffel Tower. They emerged from the park on Rue de Grenelle and walked the last few blocks to the hotel, where they saw a tall man leaning against a car: Pierre Dupont.

"Speak of the devil—what's Pierre doing here?" Julia wondered aloud. "Let's go talk to him." She waved to Pierre as they neared his car.

"Bonjour, Julia and Carly," said Pierre. "Lovely day today, *non*?"

"Yes, it is," replied Julia. "We decided to walk from the Cordon Bleu school instead of taking the Metro when we realized how close we were. We wanted to take advantage of this beautiful weather. What brings you here?"

"I wasn't sure how Josh was taking this thing about Roger dying and all," said Pierre, shoving his hands into his pockets.

"I'm not sure I know what you mean, Pierre," said Julia. "He's devastated, of course, and has been busy talking with the police and the hotel staff to try to figure out what happened. And he's scrambling to salvage the deal he and Roger were working on for his company. I'm sure he will be talking with you, and you can certainly ask him yourself."

"Yes, yes, of course, but I feel so badly," Pierre said. "Happening in Paris and all, you know. Have the police discovered anything?"

"The police are looking at food poisoning," said Julia. "They've mentioned the mushrooms as a possibility."

"Mushrooms?" he scoffed. "That's a crazy idea. We all ate them, *non*?"

Julia glanced at Carly, then asked, "Do you remember if Roger had a briefcase with him at the meetings?"

"Not really," Pierre replied. "He had a laptop with him, but…" He shrugged. "Why do you ask?"

"His briefcase seems to be missing," Julia said casually.

"Josh was pretty sure Roger had one earlier, but we didn't find one in his suite later when we checked his room."

"Perhaps he was mistaken?" asked Pierre. "I rarely use one myself."

"Possibly. As a doctor, I never use one either. Seems we do everything on a laptop or phone these days." She paused. "Um, I'll be seeing Josh later. Is there something you want me to say to him?"

"Oh, no, Julia," he answered. "I'll touch base with him tomorrow. We need to finish some discussion about the investments anyway. But thanks."

Pierre nodded a goodbye as he climbed back into his car —a sleek, late model black Audi, Julia noted.

The sisters watched him drive off and shrugged simultaneously as they looked at each other.

"I wonder what he wanted," said Julia. "I bet he had something else in mind."

"Yeah. He could have asked Josh directly," said Carly.

"Although in my experience," said Julia, "guys don't talk with each other about this kind of stuff. Pierre stays on my list of suspects."

"How about seeing if Josh has a line on Laura for lunch tomorrow?" Carly glanced at her watch. "My stomach and watch are both telling me it's time for dinner soon, as long as you're touching base with Josh."

Josh was waiting for them in the lobby of Hotel du Champs.

"Hi, Josh," said Julia, reaching out to hug him. "What a nice surprise."

Carly accepted a brief hug as she said, "At least *you* haven't disappeared."

"Huh?" asked Josh. "What does that mean?"

Julia chuckled. "Francesca is no longer at the cooking school."

"And the head chef at the Marriott didn't know who she was," added Carly.

"Oh, by the way, Pierre was just here," said Julia. "He seemed to be waiting for us. Did you see him standing by his car at the curb?"

Josh shook his head and asked, "What did he want?"

"He wanted to know how you were handling Roger's death," said Julia. "I wondered why he wouldn't have asked you himself."

Josh angled his head. "Maybe he's avoiding me because he doesn't want to tell me any details about the private conversations he and Roger had been having about forming a new business liaison."

"Why not, now that Roger is dead?" Julia asked, eyebrows raised.

"Maybe that means the deals are dead too. I'm guessing Roger was looking for some new business opportunities for Pierre," Josh explained. "He would get a commission if he was able to sign a contract with any of them. On behalf of his clients, of course."

"That doesn't sound like a big deal," said Julia.

"These are mega-buck deals. I'm talking six-figure commissions."

"Oh, I see." Julia nodded. "More than my salary, I guess."

"*Way* more than mine," said Carly.

"But why would it matter if Roger and Pierre were talking to each other?" asked Julia.

"Even attorneys have ethics," said Josh, blue eyes glaring. "Roger and I work together in the same legal merger firm. Pierre was already his client, so there was no reason to hide any potential new ventures with one of his clients from one of his colleagues. We might vie for new clients, but we don't interfere with another partner's existing collaboration. Yet this new venture was all hush-hush. Trust me. This is not how we normally do things."

"Okay," said Julia. "I don't quite understand, but I believe you. What about arranging lunch with Laura for tomorrow? Were you able to reach her?"

"Yes, finally. She's not staying at the Marriott. Said it was too painful."

"I can understand that," said Julia.

"She said she'd meet you at Au Bougnat. It's a nice lunch spot about a block away from Notre Dame."

"Give me an address and I can find anything."

"You haven't found that briefcase," said Carly. "And now we have to find Francesca."

Julia waved a hand. "Details."

"How about finding a nice place for tonight's dinner?" suggested Josh. "We can plan our moves for tomorrow and do some people-watching at the same time."

Carly beamed. "Did you hear my stomach growling?"

"I thought it was mine," said Josh. "There are several lovely cafés nearby, or we can venture away from here."

Julia pushed the door open. "Follow me. Let's walk to one somewhere close by. We'll be further afield tomorrow when we meet Laura."

∼

JULIA, Josh, and Carly were delighted to snag a table downstairs at the Café Constant, which was a scant few blocks away. The atmosphere was more like a small bistro-wine bar than a café. Julia reveled in the choices for her favorite red wine, cabernet sauvignon. She was surprised at the reasonable dinner prices compared to what she was used to seeing in similar restaurants in Portland or Seattle.

"Okay, Josh and Carly," she said after finishing the delicious shrimp scampi, "what do we know and not know about Roger getting sick, a missing briefcase, and now a missing person?"

"Hotel security didn't have any useful information about other keycards being used to access Roger's room," said Josh. "They did suggest that Roger could have let someone into his room that he knew. Unfortunately, the door to his room wasn't visible from the security cameras."

"The police don't seem to be very concerned about this being anything but an accidental death," said Julia. "Is that what you're getting from them, Josh? Although the detective did mention you could still be a suspect."

Josh chuckled. "They don't have any real leads. This isn't like 'NCIS' or 'CSI' in the States."

"I keep getting vibes about it being connected to Francesca and mushrooms," said Julia.

"Logical, considering Roger said 'mushroom,' or so you said, at the hospital," said Carly. "Maybe he meant something else?"

"Maybe, but what?" said Julia. "His briefcase seems to be important. What could have been in it? Josh, any ideas?"

"Most of what we talked about at the meetings was business strategy that I had already loaded into a Power Point on my laptop. I used a projector in one of the conference rooms. Roger didn't even need to bring a laptop. I don't know what else he would have had."

"Pierre told us he thought Roger did have a laptop, but he didn't remember seeing Roger using a briefcase," said Carly. "But is he telling the truth?"

"Like I said earlier, I'm pretty sure he had the briefcase with him at some point," Josh reiterated.

"Let's assume he did have it with him, and someone else

now has possession of it," said Julia. "Who would that be? Pierre, Alain, and Clint all had opportunity to snatch it at some point."

"Do you mean like at the meeting?" asked Carly. "I suppose one of them could have nonchalantly taken it, as though it belonged to him."

"Roger might not have noticed it right away," said Josh. "Especially if he was distracted by something or someone."

Julia nodded. "That's certainly happened to me when I'm with a group of people at a meeting, especially if I've been chatting with someone at the end. I've walked off without my binder, or maybe a coat, without realizing it."

"Pierre denies having seen it, but that doesn't mean he isn't guilty," said Josh. "I can ask Alain and Clint if they recall seeing it."

"Okay, Josh," said Julia. "That's your assignment."

"What about your plan to call Kate?" asked Carly.

Julia noted Josh's puzzled look. "Kate and Becca from our classes at the school might know where Francesca lives," she explained. "They spent more time with her than we did. We want to ask her about the special mushrooms at the party."

"We don't have to do anything more, Julia," said Josh. "The police are handling this like an accidental death. My office hasn't noticed anything unusual related to Roger's untimely demise. Laura will get our standard widow's package. End of story."

Julia frowned. "I doubt this was totally accidental, Josh. Someone wants something that Roger had. Why else would his room be turned upside down? Why is Francesca suddenly absent? Why did Pierre show up at *our* hotel?"

"Oh, yeah," said Carly. "How did he know where we were staying? Did you tell him, Josh?"

"No," Josh said, scowling. "He didn't get that from me."

"Did you remember to check your bathroom drawers? Did you find anything?"

"Nothing but my own toiletries."

"So we're no closer to solving Roger's death," said Julia. "This puzzle has too many missing pieces."

11

SATURDAY MORNING

Julia's phone rang early the next morning. Carly pulled the covers over her head to avoid the sun streaming in through the window.

"Hi, Josh. Is there something new?"

"Good morning, *ma cherie,*" he said. "The police detective called. He's asked me to meet him in about an hour. I'm not sure what it's about."

"Maybe he has good news, like they've found the briefcase," said Julia.

"Wishful thinking, I'm sure, but that would be nice."

"Is there something else? It sounds like you have something else on your mind."

"I had planned to meet you at your lunch with Laura, but I'm not sure I'll be free. Depends on how long this police thing takes. And I still have to talk to Pierre about this joint venture." Josh sighed audibly. "This certainly isn't how I planned this week to go, Julia. I'm so sorry."

"Hey. None of this is your fault. Carly and I will chat with Laura and tell you what we found out when we see you later today. I will see you later—right?"

"Of course. Thanks for understanding."

"Oh—one more thing. Did you ever follow up with Troy?" Julia asked. "That other guy we saw with Alain on the boat cruise."

Josh groaned. "I totally forgot about him in this mess. I promise I'll track him down today."

"See you later then. Ciao." Julia placed a call to room service for coffee and croissants while Carly pretended to be asleep.

"Double chocolate for me," Carly croaked, sitting up while rubbing her eyes. "What did Josh say?"

"The detective asked him to go in for some more questioning."

"That might not be good."

"And he mentioned meeting with Pierre about the business deal."

"Hm. I hope that goes okay for him."

"And he's going to skip our lunch with Laura."

∼

JULIA EXPECTED to find crushing crowds at the café, considering it was both a Saturday and the location was near Notre Dame. She was pleasantly surprised to find a modest dining crowd. She spotted Laura in a booth near the front, despite her "disguise" of sunglasses and a scarf à la Audrey Hepburn.

"Hello, Laura," said Julia, extending her hand. "I'm Julia Fairchild and this is my sister, Carly Pedersen. We met you at the hospital. We are so sorry about Roger."

"Yes, of course," Laura replied, removing her sunglasses to reveal teary, red-rimmed eyes. "Josh said you might be able to help clear up this mess."

"We'll try," said Julia. "Has something new happened?"

Laura nodded grimly. "Maybe you can help me with this."

She handed Julia a small scrap of paper. It had been folded several times.

Julia opened it carefully, noting that it was on the same type of notepaper she had seen on Josh's desk at the Marriott. She read it aloud for Carly's sake. "'Francesca 01 42 72 64 04.' That's almost certainly a telephone number."

"Who's Francesca?" asked Laura.

"Francesca is an instructor at the Cordon Bleu cooking school here in Paris," Julia said. "She also works in the restaurant at the Marriott where Roger and Josh have been staying during this business trip, and she brought the mushroom appetizer to the cocktail party."

"Okay," said Laura, calmly. "I assume Roger met her at the Marriott, but why would he have her telephone number in his pants pocket?" She looked up at the sisters.

"How about calling this phone number?" Julia suggested. "Before we jump to wrong conclusions."

She pulled out her phone and dialed. She held her breath while waiting for someone to answer.

"*Café Hugo. C'est Aimée. Comment puis-je vous aider?*"

"Bonjour, Aimée. *Parlez-vous Anglais?*" asked Julia. She nodded at Carly and Laura.

Aimée replied cheerfully, "*Mais oui.* Yes, mademoiselle. How can I help you?"

"I'm calling to ask for Francesca. Is she available?"

"Francesca Caron?"

"Yes, that's correct."

"No, not today," Aimée replied. "The schedule says she works on Monday for the evening meal. Shall I tell her you called?"

"Thank you, but no. I can call her at home. Merci bien." Julia sighed as she ended the call. "I suppose you figured out that the number is for a restaurant. If she works there, she has at least three jobs. That's a complicated schedule to juggle."

"It also means that Roger may have been planning to meet her there," Laura said with a touch of sadness. She downed the rest of her glass of wine, elbows on the table. She sighed. "I wish we hadn't had that fight before he left for Paris."

"You should have asked for her home number," said Carly.

"Oh, you're right. I'll call back after lunch and ask," said Julia.

"Why do you need her number?" asked Laura.

"We wanted to know more about the mushrooms she brought to the party, and the school wouldn't give us her number." Julia signaled the waiter for a second round of drinks. "What was the fight about, Laura?"

Laura poked her fork into what was left of her salad before answering. "We've gotten into financial difficulty due to Roger's gambling. He had a crazy idea about borrowing money from one his clients, a major banker, in exchange for a special deal."

"Do you know which bank?" Julia asked, excited about a possible lead.

"He didn't say, but Sharon would know who his clients are, and maybe Josh, too."

"That's a place to start," said Julia. "He didn't mention a specific bank or client, then?"

Laura shook her head. "No. Not that I can recall."

"What about checking his calendar at work?" suggested Julia. "Maybe he put something helpful on his schedule."

"And check his cellphone," said Carly. "I put all my appointments on both my work and personal schedules."

"By the way," said Julia. "Did the police give you Roger's cellphone? We didn't find it, and the police haven't mentioned it."

"It wasn't with his belongings," Laura said. "I didn't think to ask them about it."

"If the police don't have it, we can ask them to try the GPS locator to find it," said Julia.

"Maybe Josh or Laura should be asking them instead of us," said Carly.

Julia nodded. "One more question, Laura. Did Roger have any medical problems that might explain why he collapsed in the first place? Was he on any medication, like for diabetes or high blood pressure?"

"Nothing like that, but he had been on a strong antidepressant for several months," said Laura. "I'm not sure it was helping very much. I explained all that to the doctors when they first contacted me."

"Do you know the name of the antidepressant?" Julia asked.

"It's a funny name," said Laura. "Always makes me think of dogs."

Julia frowned. "What kind of dogs?"

"Weiner dogs. Dachshunds."

"Doxepin?"

"Yes, that's it," said Laura. "Is that important?"

"Maybe," said Julia. "I don't have enough information yet."

"What else do you need to know?" Laura asked.

"The little bit that we know doesn't hang together nicely," said Julia. "I wish I knew more about the possible motive to kill Roger. That would help with the 'who' or 'why,' although the financial issue could still be the underlying trigger."

Laura dropped her fork dropped on the table. "Did you say that someone tried to kill Roger? As in murder? I thought he died accidentally. The police have just been investigating the ransacking of his hotel room."

"We're not certain," said Julia, realizing she had been

indiscreet. "An accident just seems less likely, considering that someone was looking for something in his room. Any ideas, Laura?"

She shook her head, visibly pale. "No clue. But I can't imagine that anyone would want to kill Roger."

"I have an idea," said Carly, who had been unusually quiet to this point. "It's Saturday afternoon. The banks will be closed, so Josh can't pursue that idea today. But he *could* ask the police to do that GPS locator thing. And Julia and I can talk to Francesca, once we get her number."

"And we can all meet for dinner and debrief," said Julia.

"Um, I already have plans for this evening," said Laura. "Will you call me in the morning instead?"

∽

JULIA CALLED the Drunken Shark again and was pleased to talk to a human, who happened to be Kate's mother. Mrs. Opgrande offered her daughter's number and asked that Julia tell Kate to "Please call home." Julia chuckled as she promised to do so.

"Got it," Julia announced to Carly, who was busy composing an email to her husband. "Wish me luck." She tapped in the newly acquired number.

"Hello?" Kate's voice was hesitant.

"Kate. This is Julia from the cooking class. I got your number from your mom. She'd like you to call her, by the way."

"Really? You spoke to my mom? To find me? What's so important that you tracked me down?"

"I'm trying to find Francesca. She's not at the school any longer, and the receptionist didn't have her cell number. I thought maybe you would have it, since you and Becca seemed to be so chummy with her."

"Sure. I'm sure she wouldn't mind if you called her. Just a sec."

Julia heard paper rustling in the background.

"Sorry. I hadn't entered it into my list of contacts, so I had to find my class notes where I'd written it down. You might need an address too." She recited the information, ending with "Tell her 'hi' for me."

"Sure thing. Thanks a lot."

Carly looked up from her email messages. "Didn't she ask why you wanted the number? *I* would have."

"You're more suspicious maybe, but no, she didn't ask," said Julia as she dialed. She hung up after ten rings, no answer, and no voicemail. "Drat," she said. "I suppose we could go by her apartment. Kate gave me the address."

"With all her jobs, she could be anywhere right now," said Carly.

Julia held her phone up for her sister. "I found it on the map," she said. "It's not too far from that Café Hugo."

Carly scrunched her forehead. "That could explain why she gave Roger that telephone number."

"Maybe," said Julia. "In the meantime, do you feel like visiting the Orsay Museum on the way back to the hotel? It's a small one and has some fabulous artwork that would be worth a look."

"I suppose your artist friend Paula recommended it," said Carly, "like all those museums last year in Germany and Amsterdam."

Julia grinned. "How did you guess? We can take a taxi or walk forty-five minutes."

"Taxi, please. We won't have all that much time to see anything at the museum if we walk."

"You're a good sport, Carly," said Julia, hugging her little sister.

Josh entered the now-familiar police station in the 8th arrondissement, the most upscale district of Paris. He was directed to Martin Durand, the detective in charge, who reviewed the case material on his computer.

"We still view this death as accidental, although a homicide isn't out of the question, Mr. Larson," said Officer Durand. "Why do you think Mr. Westover may have been murdered? And remember, sir, that you are still on our suspect list for the break-in at the hotel."

Josh explained the missing briefcase, cellphone, and the mysterious Francesca. "And I understand the possibility of poisoning was raised by the autopsy?"

"That theory is being discounted without additional evidence," said Durand.

"What about using a GPS locator to find his phone?" asked Josh, following up on Julia's suggestion. "Can you do that? We've tried calling the number, but I suspect his battery is dead by now."

"Not until Monday, I'm afraid. I don't have the staff this late on a Saturday."

"Well, then, that's all I have. Thank you, officer," said Josh, rising from the industrial chair.

"Actually, I have a few more questions for you, Mr. Larson. Please sit down. It has been brought to our attention that you may have a motive for murdering Mr. Westover. We are under the impression that the business enterprise in which you were partners involves millions of dollars. Is that correct?" He stared at Josh over the top of the computer.

"Yes, but—"

"And if you were able to complete this deal in Mr. Westover's absence, you would potentially benefit?"

"Yes, but—"

"It appears that you could have a financial motive to arrange the demise of your partner, does it not?" The detective swung slightly in his swivel chair.

Josh sat forward in the uncomfortable chair and slammed his hand on the desk. "I swear I didn't kill Roger. Has someone accused me?"

"I can't tell you at this time."

"As to a monetary motive—I would get a commission or maybe a bonus, but the company I work for would be making the millions of dollars—not me."

"I would like to believe you, Mr. Larson, and at this point there is no direct evidence that a murder has occurred. I am not at liberty to divulge my sources, but you must agree that you could have a motive after all."

"I wouldn't be here asking you to investigate a potential murder if I were the killer, would I?" Josh demanded, feeling his pulse race. "What do you want me to do? How can I help you find the actual murderer?"

"If we determine a murder has occurred, that is *our* job. I ask that you stay in Paris and keep us apprised of your whereabouts should you check out of the Marriott." The detective stood and waited for Josh to accompany him to the door. "That is all."

∞

"What did Paula suggest you see here?" asked Carly, Musée d'Orsay brochure in hand.

"Absolutely the Impressionists," said Julia. "I know you've heard of the most famous of them—Monet, Renoir, Degas, Cezanne, and Manet."

"Why are they so important in the art world?" asked Carly. "I don't get it."

"They used color in a new, different way," said Julia.

"The artists of the classical tradition before them drew outlines of their subjects, then filled them in with color. Like 'staying in the lines' in our childhood coloring books."

"Yes, and…"

"These guys didn't bother with drawing outlines," Julia continued. "They used dabs of paint and created a figure or an object with a general shape that the eye recognized as a human or vase or tree and so on. They were the artistic rebels of the time, using more color, playing with light, and painting easygoing outdoor scenes, instead of painting stiff people in drawing rooms."

"Sounds more fun to me," said Carly. "I always hated having to stay inside the lines."

"Exactly," replied Julia. "Paula said they also used color differently in another way. Instead of bothering to mix red and green and blue to make brown, for example, they would dab those colors next to each other on the canvas. From a distance our eye sees the color brown, but close up the eye distinguishes all three colors."

They meandered through the exhibit, appreciating the beauty of Monet's many paintings of his own garden in Giverny, Degas's famous "The Dance Class," several paintings by Van Gogh, and many other pieces of artwork.

They paused in front of Renoir's "Dance at Le Moulin de la Galette."

"The people seem happy," said Julia. "Not dark and serious."

"I can see another reason for this kind of painting," said Carly.

"Like what?" asked Julia.

"If they didn't have to stay inside the lines, they could probably finish a painting a lot faster." Carly grinned as she added, "So they didn't have to starve quite so many years."

Julia rolled her eyes, but admitted to herself that her sister might have come to the correct conclusion.

"Have you seen the movie *Monument Men*?" Julia asked as they continued their walk through the museum.

"Not that I recall," said Carly. "Tell me what it's about in case I've seen it but don't remember the name."

"During World War II, Adolph Hitler became obsessed with creating a 'Fuhrermuseum' he planned as a showcase in Linz, Austria. He had been rejected by the Academy of Fine Arts in Vienna as a young man, which quashed his ambition of becoming a successful artist. Now that he was in power, he decided to steal art instead. The Nazis stole hundreds of thousands of priceless works of art and hid them in deep chambers of several mines, like the salt mine at Altaussee, as well as in deserted castles. I read that there were over a thousand hiding places in southern Germany alone."

"So who were these 'monument men'?" asked Carly.

"They were men and women who volunteered to try to recover and protect the artwork that had disappeared. It's mind-boggling that they were able to locate the hiding places and rescue some of it in the nick of time. Paula told me this museum has some art that had been recovered, but she didn't remember the specific pieces."

"That's amazing," said Carly. "I'll bet it was a huge job tracking down ownership in a lot of cases."

"Yes; it's still going on today." Julia admired the painting in front of her for another moment before walking to the next exhibit. "The movie highlighted one woman who documented thousands of pieces of art on her own as part of her job under the Nazis. She listed where they had come from and where they were stored. That information helped to find them and return the art to their proper owners."

"Wow," said Carly. "I might have to watch the movie."

"Or read one of the books about them. There's a foundation that is still tracing missing art and establishing proper ownership." Julia sighed. She'd enjoyed this reprieve from the mysteries of Roger's death, but Josh's freedom and career were still on the line. "I wish we could trace the missing briefcase and had the kinds of resources those art foundations have to help them."

"It's okay, sis," said Carly, patting her big sister's arm. "We'll figure it out. Now…enough art history for today. Maybe Josh has some good news."

12

SATURDAY EVENING

Julia, Josh, and Carly shared their findings of the day over a light early dinner at a small bistro near the sisters' hotel. The highlight of their meal was the dessert, "Blacker Berry Galette," that Julia was eager to try making once she got home. She was sure it would be beyond delicious when made with wild blackberries.

Josh had been ready to be done with investigating until his conversation with the police earlier, which he shared with the sisters. Now that it seemed someone was trying to implicate Josh, Julia was more certain than ever that Roger's death was no accident. And she felt even more determined to identify the 'who' and 'how' of Roger's murder, with Josh now considered a prime suspect with motive and opportunity.

"Carly and I have only the rest of this week in Paris." Julia took a swallow of the ruby red table wine and sighed. "I wish we could enjoy the rest of our time as tourists instead of detectives."

Carly raised her glass. "I'll drink to that."

"But we can't." Julia looked at Josh, her expression grim. "I'm beginning to think that you were set up, Josh. Somebody knew you and Roger had adjoining rooms and might have lured him into your bathroom to implicate you somehow. I can imagine the police theorizing that *you* ransacked Roger's room looking for something, whatever it is. You wouldn't have needed a keycard to get in."

"I swear I'm innocent. I was with you and Carly that whole time for the party, remember?"

Julia shook her head gently. "No, you weren't. You told me you had to take care of some details and sent Carly and me to wait for you by the elevator."

Josh dropped his jaw. "Julia, you don't believe that—"

"No, I don't think you are guilty." Julia took his hand. "But I can see that there was a narrow window of opportunity. The police need our help before they convince themselves that, as a suspect, you check all their boxes. They've already decided that you have a motive, at least in their eyes."

Josh's expression was grave. "How can I help?"

"For now, keep on the police about the GPS on Roger's cellphone; and maybe see if you can get more details from Pierre about whatever deal he and Roger had been discussing. Carly and I will track down Francesca, now that we have her address. I hope she will be able to answer questions about the mushroom tray, anyway. We'll go to her apartment tomorrow. For now, I'd like to put sleuthing aside and play tourist." She clapped her hands together.

"What do you have in mind?" Josh asked.

"I propose we try that tango lesson. If you're up to it, Josh."

"For our next visit to Monte Carlo? We had great fun dancing in the ballroom there." Josh winked at her over the top of his glass.

"You never know," said Julia, blushing at the recollection of her time with Josh when she'd first met him. She rummaged in her tote and found the scrap of paper with the details. "According to this, lessons start at seven-thirty.

Beginners go first. Partners aren't required." She looked up and grinned. "And the dance studio is nearby."

"It would take my mind off this police business for a couple of hours," said Josh.

Carly groaned. "Are you kidding? Tango lessons aren't going to help me. My husband has three left feet."

Josh laughed. "That would be a challenge, Carly. Let's do it for fun. I'll be glad to be a partner for both of you. You can take turns."

"That's sweet of you," said Julia, draining her glass. "We'll get there on time if we leave now."

Twenty minutes later, the three of them entered the dance studio, which was located on a street lined with storefronts. The building looked as though it had housed a larger business at some point in its history but had since been subdivided into smaller units. Julia noticed a bookstore and a clothing boutique on either side of the dance school.

They waited with a group of about twenty people, many of whom appeared to be paired up already. The studio was a large, unfurnished room with wooden floors. Mirrors lined the longer walls, where Julia noticed ballet barres. The lighting was dim, giving the overall effect of gloom. Or perhaps it was to simulate the atmosphere of a cabaret where one might dance the tango.

"What did you sign us up for, Julia?" asked Carly. "You said this would be a beginner's class. Why are all these people dressed in real dance clothes? And proper dance shoes, too."

"Keep smiling," Julia whispered. "And act like you know what you're doing."

"I'm leaving," said Carly. "That's what I'm doing." She turned and walked toward the doorway but was intercepted by a tall, slender male, black hair glistening.

"And where are you going, ma cherie?" the man asked,

showing beautiful white straight teeth. "The instructors are about ready to start teaching, and I need a partner."

Julia watched as Carly let herself be guided into position, pivoting to grin at her sister. Julia blew her a kiss as she and Josh stood in position, waiting for the dance lesson to begin.

The first ten minutes were all about posture and the "hold" or embrace. The basic steps were simple—slow, slow, quick, quick, slow—but remembering whether to go forward or back, and with which foot, became the challenge. Soon, however, Julia and Josh were dancing an amateurish tango, laughing as they tangled feet again and again until muscle memory kicked in.

The hour passed quickly. Julia was pleased that Josh had picked up the steps as easily as she had. She had always wanted to learn a ballroom dance or two, beyond the waltz that she'd learned from her father years before. He had been a decent dancer, having gone with a buddy to the Arthur Murray Dance Studio in Portland, Oregon. They had discovered that meeting women was difficult unless they knew how to dance, so they took lessons. Julia had enjoyed watching her parents dance on occasion in the family room. They had called it "fancy dancing."

Julia and Josh joined Carly at the side bench, where they gathered their belongings. Carly's dance partner waited quietly as the sisters chatted.

"Julia and Josh," said Carly, "this is my new friend, Antoine Richard. He comes here regularly to be partners for women who come alone. Like me." She glowed.

"Pleased to meet you," said Julia. "I couldn't help but notice your dancing. You're clearly not a beginner."

Antoine smiled, appearing relaxed. "No, mademoiselle. I get to dance for free as a partner for charming women like Carly." He kissed the back of her hand.

"Dancing the tango is more complicated than I expected,"

said Julia. "I'm afraid I'm not ready for *Dancing with the Stars* anytime soon."

"Julia," said Carly, "they dance six hours a day to look that good."

"Maybe we'll have to stay longer and take some more classes." Julia winked at her sister, who seemed to be enjoying Antoine's attention.

Antoine brightened at that idea. "*Mais oui*. Yes, Carly can stay in Paris with me, and I will give her private lessons."

Carly slid out of his embrace and stood next to Julia. "Antoine, thank you, but I have to go now."

Once outside, the three of them laughed all the way to the Metro station.

"Josh," asked Julia, "is Antoine what my mom would have called a gigolo?" She felt Carly's elbow in her rib and laughed some more.

Carly pretended to pout, but the smirk on her face gave her away. "I didn't fall for his line."

"Of course not, Carly. You have a way of attracting men that I couldn't begin to duplicate. Innocence and naiveté packaged in an adorable blonde. If they only knew."

Julia felt Carly's heel on her toes. "Ouch. I'm sorry."

∼

Sunday morning

Julia's palm itched the next morning. She couldn't remember what her mom used to say about which palm meant unexpected money found, versus lost. At the moment she just found it annoying. She and Carly were free to do as they wished for the day because Josh had made plans to meet a college friend who lived in Paris for lunch. He had offered to include the sisters, but Julia declined, thinking it would be awkward. They lounged on the settee while finishing their coffee, getting ready to plan the day's itinerary.

"Julia," said Carly, "doesn't it seem odd that Josh doesn't spend more private time with you? You said it was his idea to be in Paris together, but so far he has spent a grand total of maybe one hour alone with you. Where's the passionate kissing and flirting that I thought I would have to endure?"

"He's been preoccupied with Roger having died, of course. But he does seem distant." Julia sighed wistfully. "This surely isn't what he expected for the business part, and maybe not the vacation part either. It certainly hasn't felt romantic to me, although there have been a few moments that felt special." She smiled as though she had a secret.

"Do you think he resents me being here?" asked Carly.

"Heavens, no. I suspect he's glad you're here to keep me company. He'd probably feel guilty about leaving me alone otherwise." Julia patted her sister's knee. "And I'm happy you're here with me. Let's plan to stop by Francesca's today after doing our sightseeing." She consulted the "Top Ten Tourist Attractions" list that she'd gotten from the concierge the first day. "What about visiting Montmartre? The guidebook says it's 'Paris's highest hill and was once known as the home for starving artists and other bohemians.' There's a good view too, especially if we climb to the top of the Sacré-Coeur Basilica."

"How many steps?" Carly replied sleepily.

"Three hundred." Julia continued, "There's another bonus —the dance hall that we saw in Renoir's painting yesterday is a few blocks away. We'll see bona fide history. And it's not far to Francesca's from there."

"How will we get there? I bet it's too far to walk."

"We can take the Metro," said Julia. "I'll get directions from the concierge."

Dressed casually in bright colors that seemed to celebrate the warm spring day, Julia and Carly emerged from the Metro station a short walk away from the basilica. A beautiful blue April sky greeted them as they strolled down the ancient streets toward the church. Julia tried to imagine the streets filled with bohemian artists, poets, and the Moulin Rouge dancing girls of old. Tourists and pickpockets had replaced them, the guidebook had warned.

Inside Sacré-Coeur they found the entrance to the narrow stairway to the top of the dome. Julia found herself counting the steps as they climbed the claustrophobic spiral staircase. She was grateful for her athletic conditioning from her tap dance and gym sessions.

"Those stairs aren't for the faint of heart," said Carly, emerging at the top. She twirled on the landing, taking in all three hundred sixty degrees of the vista. "What an amazing view."

"I'm glad we decided to do this," said Julia. "It's too bad Josh isn't here with us."

"You'll see him later, sis," said Carly.

Julia smiled sadly as she turned to her sister. "I know. This hasn't been exactly what I imagined for our visit. I hope you're not disappointed, Carly."

"I've traveled with you before," she replied. "It never goes as expected. But I'm sorry you aren't having the romantic trip you expected, either."

Julia took a few photos of the surrounding landscape, trying unusual angles for interest. "If you're ready, it's time to go to Francesca's neighborhood before we go back to the hotel. It's not that far from here."

"How far is 'not far'?" countered Carly.

Julia checked the map. "A couple Metro-stops' worth. We'll get instructions from someone."

Carly led the way as they started the descent from the top. "I hope she has Sunday off from all those jobs."

With generous help from other Metro riders, Julia and Carly found themselves in the neighborhood known as the Marais. Julia recited the history of the area to Carly as they made their way to Francesca's apartment. They walked past art galleries and restaurants, fashion boutiques and Victor Hugo's house, now a museum. Carly declined the invitation to enter the Picasso Museum. To Julia's surprise, she announced that it was "too modern."

Francesca's apartment was in a small building with four units, each boasting names and buzzers. The buzzer for Francesca's unit didn't make any sound when Julia pressed it, so she knocked on the corresponding bright blue door. There was no response. Julia pressed her ear to the door when she heard music playing and determined that it was coming from inside the unit.

"It seems like she's home," said Julia. "Maybe she can't hear the knocking with the music on."

Carly knocked, louder this time. Thirty seconds passed. She tried the doorknob, finding it unlocked. She pushed the door open slowly, with Julia peeking into the room as she did so.

"Francesca, are you home?" Julia called from the doorway. She could hear the music coming from an inner room. "Let's go in, Carly."

Carly grabbed Julia's arm. "Wait. What if she's back there with a boyfriend or something?"

"That's a thought. Let's go back to the door and call her on her phone."

"I like that idea," said Carly.

Through a window in the door, they could see a phone lying on a small table in the short hallway. They let it ring ten times. No one came to answer. Julia ended the call and redialed. Still no response.

"We should go in, Carly," said Julia. "Something's wrong."

"You first," said Carly. "You're the detective."

The sisters slowly entered the tiny living room, peeking around the corner to the right into a quaint kitchen. The music emanated from a room to the left off the hallway. Julia tiptoed closer to peek in, expecting to see Francesca sleeping soundly, maybe with a guy. She gasped when she looked and motioned for Carly to join her.

Francesca lay in a pool of vomit on the floor of a miniscule bathroom adjoining a bedroom, clothes askew, curled up in fetal position. Julia shook her shoulder, asking "Francesca—are you okay?" She was unresponsive but alive. "Quick. Take my phone and call 112—the emergency number where they speak English—while I check her over." Julia automatically assessed her friend as any doctor would and found that Francesca's skin was flushed and dry, her pupils were dilated, and she moaned in response to stimulation. Her pulse was at least 120 and thready. Julia wished she had a pocket blood pressure cuff and stethoscope in her tote.

"The ambulance will be here in four or five minutes," Carly said as she re-entered the room. "What do you think happened?"

"I suspect Francesca has been poisoned like Roger. She has the signs of cholinergic toxicity like he did. I hope we got here in time."

The paramedics soon arrived. Carly waved them in and stepped aside as they swarmed into the apartment with their portable medical equipment. Julia gave a brief report of her assessment and explained that she suspected poisoning of some kind, which required immediate treatment. The lead paramedic handed Julia a business card with the name and address of the hospital where Francesca would be taken once they finished the initial treatment. They were ready to transport her within ten minutes and whisked her to the ambulance.

"Oh my gosh. What if we hadn't come by? She could have—" Carly covered her mouth with her hands and collapsed into the small sofa in the front room.

"We need to call the police, sis," said Julia.

"Yes, and what about calling Josh?"

"Him too, but police first. Will you look around and see if you notice anything out of the ordinary while I'm on the phone? And don't touch anything."

"That goes without saying, Detective Fairchild," said Carly.

Five minutes later, with the police on their way, Julia dialed Josh. "Hey. Carly and I stopped by to see Francesca on our way back from Montmartre." She explained the situation, then took a big breath. "An ambulance has just taken her and we've already called the police. Would you come over here right away? If you're done with your lunch date, that is."

"We're done. Give me an address and I'll have Vincent bring me over. I can be there in about twenty minutes."

"Okay. I hear more sirens up the street. It's probably the police this time. I expect a knock any moment."

Julia pocketed her cell and found Carly in the front room, where she was pointing to a brown briefcase in the corner.

"Do you suppose that's Roger's missing briefcase?" asked Carly. "It has monogram letters 'REW' on the outside of the case."

"Certainly looks that way," said Julia. "Have you looked inside?"

"No. I wanted to check with you."

"I'll use a tissue to prevent fingerprints and take a peek inside if it's not locked." Julia pressed the latch buttons, and the lid popped open. She gasped.

"What is it?"

"It looks like a packet of letters. No envelopes, but the one on top begins, 'Dear Roger.' And one of Josh's business cards." Julia's face fell as she held the briefcase up for Carly.

"That doesn't make sense. Are they from Josh?"

Julia snapped a photo with her camera before daring to touch anything. She gingerly picked up a letter and checked the signature. She let out a sigh. "No—they smell like perfume, and they're from Francesca."

"How did his briefcase and the letters get here?"

"I'm sure the police are going to be asking the same question," said Julia as she snapped it shut and put it back where Carly had found it.

Carly frowned. "Why would Francesca have Roger's briefcase?"

"And why the letters? Had he given them back to her for some reason?" Julia scanned the room. "I'm not seeing anything else that looks unusual. Do you suppose it was planted here?"

13

STILL SUNDAY AFTERNOON

Julia and Carly waited outside on the front steps for Josh while the police did their business. The first officers to arrive on the scene had asked a few questions, then excused the sisters while they searched the apartment.

"I have a feeling," said Julia, "that the police are going to reclassify Roger's death as not so accidental after all."

"Yeah. I'm having a 'déjà vu' moment. I can't help but wonder how you keep stumbling onto dead people." Carly glared at her sister. "Are you cursed or something?"

Julia managed a weak smile. "She's not dead, although someone apparently wanted her to be. I'm glad we stopped by when we did. Maybe there's some invisible force that is testing my ability to solve murder mysteries." She let out a long sigh. "I'd rather stick to my live patients and their medical problems."

Josh and Vincent arrived five minutes later in the gleaming limousine. It seemed out of place in the street that was otherwise lined with police cars and the small Renaults and Fiats that belonged to the street's residents.

Josh sprinted across the asphalt. "Julia. Carly. Are you

two all right?" He hugged Julia first, then put an arm around Carly.

"It's another day in the life of Julia Fairchild, amateur detective," said Carly drily.

"It's not like I go looking for trouble. You know that, Carly." Julia began giving Josh a brief version of what had happened. She fell silent when one of the policemen came out to the steps to talk.

"Bonjour. I am Detective Bouchard. Which one of you found the woman who had taken ill?"

Julia raised her hand. "I saw her first when I checked her bedroom. My sister was right behind me."

The detective looked at his notepad. "I know the other policeman asked you a few questions already, but for my own ears, why did you come by to see your friend?"

"We had a question about mushrooms that she brought to a cocktail party at the Marriott a few days ago," said Julia. "We tried calling her yesterday, but she didn't answer her phone. We were at Montmartre earlier and decided to stop by on our way back, hoping to catch her at home."

"We could hear music inside," said Carly. "We thought she didn't hear us knock so we tried the door. It was unlocked. She didn't hear the phone either when we tried calling. We could see it on the hallway table." She pointed past the detective, who looked in that direction.

He looked up, puzzled. "What mushrooms are you talking about?"

Julia explained about the mushrooms at the party, how Francesca had provided them, and about Roger dying, and the police investigation and autopsy report. Detective Bouchard wrote down some notes, then excused them while he went inside to telephone Detective Durand.

He returned a few minutes later and said to Julia, "I will make a report of our findings today and send it to the detectives in the Eighth District. I am told they know how to reach you. They will likely be talking with you tomorrow."

"Yes, officer. I'll do anything I can to help." She nodded as if to emphasize her offer. "Is there a chance I could take a look in her apartment and see if I notice anything?"

He looked at her thoughtfully, narrowing his eyes. "Yes, as long as you don't touch anything."

"May I look in the refrigerator?" Julia asked.

"Yes, but first check with the officer inside to be sure it's already been dusted for fingerprints."

Julia walked slowly through the small, neat apartment with her eyes open for anything that might explain why someone might try to murder Francesca. It seemed unlikely that she would have poisoned herself. Except for the briefcase, which had already been dusted for prints and taken by the police as evidence, she saw nothing in the small living room. The bedroom was also devoid of anything interesting. She opened the medicine cabinet in the tiny bathroom and found a partial bottle of eyedrops. They were unlabeled, which raised her curiosity because the medication was available by prescription only in the United States. Were they Francesca's? She took a couple of photos then used a tissue to pick up the bottle. If letters had been planted in the apartment, the unexplained eyedrops were also suspect. Everything else there appeared to be normal possessions for a young woman.

The kitchen was spotless. It was so clean that Julia wondered if Francesca ever cooked in her own home, considering her occupation. The refrigerator was almost empty. A partial bottle of chardonnay and a container of chocolate syrup stood as sentries amongst the fruit and cheeses. She opened the cupboards, which held the typical dinnerware and glassware as well as basic cooking staples. A collection of papers scattered on the miniature kitchen table was the solitary sign of anything out of order. Julia quickly shuffled through them. Some of them were printed on *Le Cordon Bleu* logo notepaper. She recognized some of them as recipes. The word "truffles" caught her eye, but the reprint article was in French, and she wasn't fluent enough in the language to know what it said. She took a picture with her camera with a plan to translate it later.

A lone policeman stood at the doorway, waiting for her to exit. Julia handed him the bottle of eyedrops. "These might be important. Will you please give them to the detective?"

He placed them in an evidence bag, acknowledged her with a polite nod, then closed and locked the door.

"Thank you," said Julia. "Merci."

∼

JULIA, Josh, and Carly sat in the sun at another of Paris's ubiquitous outdoor bistros. This time the umbrellas were red and black. The sisters had missed lunch and were famished. The simple lunch of deli meats, cheeses, and crackers with fresh fruit and a bowl of onion soup revived them. The pinot grigio helped too.

"You haven't told us if you found anything at Francesca's apartment," said Carly.

"There wasn't much to find," said Julia. "Except this." She pulled up the photos of the eyedrops.

"Eyedrops," said Carly. "Big deal. I've got eyedrops in my bathroom too."

"But these aren't ordinary eyedrops. This is a prescription medication that is more commonly used for conditions such as uveitis, which is an inflammation inside the eye, or to dilate the eye before an exam by the eye doctor."

"You can read medicine names in French?" asked Carly.

Julia smiled. "The chemical name is the same here as at home. Remember, I was a pharmacist before I was a doctor."

"That's helpful," said Josh. "But how do you know she didn't have that eye condition?"

"I don't, but I'm puzzled that there isn't a prescription label on it," said Julia. "This isn't an over-the-counter medication, so she had to have gotten it from a physician, or somehow managed to get it without a prescription."

"I still don't get why it's important," said Carly. "Maybe she borrowed it from someone, like her mom. Or maybe it was in a prescription bottle originally that she discarded."

"Or it may be one of the many medications that Europeans can get without a prescription from a pharmacist. Like antibiotics. For the moment it's an item that doesn't seem to fit the rest of the story." She scrolled to the picture of Josh's business card and the letters. "And there's this."

Josh's mouth dropped open. "Those were in Roger's briefcase?"

"Yes," said Julia. "It was otherwise empty."

"Roger and I often carry each other's cards when we meet with clients," said Josh. "But I don't know about those letters."

Julia nodded sadly. "My thought was that your card was planted there. Although it may have been stuck inside the pocket instead of being left in the briefcase intentionally."

Josh shuddered. "Someone may be trying to frame me, Julia. *You* know I was having lunch with my friend when this happened."

Julia eyed him. *I wonder if the friend is male or female*, she found herself thinking, then immediately banished the thought. He'd said it was an old college friend. She'd assumed it was a male. But was it? "We don't actually know when it happened," she remarked. "Though the vomit seemed pretty fresh."

Carly leaned back in the wrought-iron chair. "I saw an empty cup on the table in her living room. If she had company earlier, I would think there would have been two cups. Did you see anything in the kitchen, Julia?"

"I saw a French press coffeemaker on the counter. It was clean. And no dirty dishes in the sink."

"That would suggest that she either didn't have company today, or they didn't eat or drink while here."

"Or they cleaned up when they left," said Julia, her face grim.

"What's next?" asked Carly. "Are you going to let the police finish this investigation so we can be ordinary tourists?"

"That depends," she said, tilting her face upward to soak in the warm sun.

"On what?"

Julia sat forward with her elbows on the table, hands clasped. "Does anyone else find it curious that Kate and Becca became so friendly with Francesca after a couple of classes at the school that they would have her home address? Or that Francesca went out of her way to deliver that platter to the party?" She paused to sip her drink. "And we still don't know why Roger was in *your* bathroom, Josh, when he had a perfectly good one of his own."

"Don't forget that Simone told me that Alain visited Roger at the hospital," Carly added.

"And he seemed defensive about his meeting up with Troy," said Julia. "Then, seeing Pierre waiting for us at our hotel was a little spooky. I don't think he told the truth about the briefcase. And why did Francesca end up with it?"

"Pierre might have known she had it," said Carly. "He seems cagey to me."

Julia turned to Josh. "Did you ever catch up with Troy? I'd sure like to know his version of that encounter with Alain. You said that Clint Blackman was also based in London. Are he and Troy connected somehow?"

Josh slouched in his chair. "I guess I haven't done my part in this. I thought the police were on top of things and didn't need any help from us civilians, even though with my training as an attorney and security expert, I should know better. The police haven't arrested me yet, but I know they suspect me. And now they believe I have a motive as well as opportunity."

Carly reached out and patted his arm. "It's okay, Josh. Julia's like a bulldog when she senses something that doesn't fit the picture. It's in her DNA. And I love her for it." Carly glanced at Julia. "Most of the time."

Julia looked glumly at Josh. "The poison in Roger's stomach came from somewhere. If we can't find evidence of someone else having a motive and opportunity, the police may believe that they have to arrest you. We still have a few days to find out who that someone is."

Josh sat back as he shook his head. "I know you're right, and I know I'm innocent. What else can I do?"

"For tonight, nothing. I'll call and check on Francesca. Then perhaps we can at least enjoy the rest of the evening."

Julia was relieved to learn that Francesca was already responding to the treatment that had been initiated by the paramedics, though still unconscious. She promised the nurse that she would visit in the morning after being assured that her friend was stable for the time being.

Much more relaxed after the reassuring chat with the intensive care nurse, Julia proposed a visit to the Moulin Rouge. She was ready, as were her compadres, to enjoy some traditional tourist fare in the form of pure entertainment. Vincent dropped them off at the building with the landmark red windmill rooftop at the foot of the Montmartre hill.

She consulted the internet on her phone on the way and informed Carly and Josh that the Moulin Rouge, or "Red Windmill," had been a popular attraction in Paris since its opening in 1889. It was originally developed in the Jardin de Paris as a place where businessmen and the wealthy of Paris could "slum it" in the fashionable district of Montmartre. It was now best known as the birthplace of the modern form of the can-can dance, which found its roots in the dance known as the quadrille. The success of the Moulin Rouge and its entertainment inspired the evolution of cabarets across Europe.

Julia was mesmerized by the performance at the venue. The amazing production, *Féerie,* featured a troupe of eighty artists, including sixty "Doriss Girls," wearing fabulous costumes adorned with feathers, sequins, and rhinestones. They performed original dances and routines against a background of sumptuous sets in shimmering colors. The invigorating music had been recorded by a combination of eighty musicians and sixty chorus singers. There was, of course, a spectacular can-can dance. All in all, Julia was reminded of a performance by the Rockettes at Radio City Music Hall or a production by Cirque de Soleil.

"That was awesome," said Josh.

"That's what I picture when I think of Paris," said Carly.

Julia agreed. "I can't stop smiling," she said. "I wanted to get up on stage and dance with them."

Carly giggled. "I knew you wanted to be up there. It was way beyond what we do in our local cabaret production, for sure."

"I have an idea," said Julia. "What if we share some of these ideas when it's time to plan for our cabaret follies next year?"

The threesome maneuvered through the noisy crowd toward the taxi-stand. Josh had given Vincent the rest of the evening off while they enjoyed the show. Julia stopped and held her right hand out to alert Josh and Carly.

"What is it, Julia?" asked Josh.

"Look straight ahead, about thirty feet away." Julia tilted her head in the general direction. "I see Pierre and Laura getting into a taxi."

"Hmm. They look pretty chummy to me," said Carly.

"I didn't know they knew each other," said Josh.

"The plot thickens," said Julia. "What else do we not know about them?"

14

MONDAY MORNING

The sun shone bright and clear, promising a lovely day. Julia's first thought was that Laura had indicated she was leaving Paris sometime Monday. Even though Julia had promised to leave the official murder investigation to the police, she couldn't stop puzzling over the loose ends that eluded her. The biggest question in her mind had to do with Roger being in Josh's bathroom. Why was he there?

"Carly...didn't Simone say something to you about sensing something sinister about Alain when he left Roger's room at the hospital? Or am I imagining it?"

"She definitely said something to that effect. Why do you ask?"

"I was wondering what made her say that. Like maybe she has ESP."

"I'll ask her about it when we go shopping this morning," said Carly. "And I'll report her answer back to you later."

Josh called to see if Julia would join him for a meeting with Pierre later that morning.

"What about Laura?" Julia asked him. "Are you going to ask her to stay in Paris for a while longer while the police investigate the two poisonings?"

"That would be up to the police. So far they haven't seemed inclined to implicate Laura in this."

"I guess I'd have to agree," said Julia. "I have a gut feeling about it, but that's not evidence. And Carly's going to hang out with Simone this morning and do some shopping, so it'll be just the two of us meeting with Pierre."

"Perfect," said Josh. "I'm glad to see you by yourself."

"Would it be okay for Vincent to take me to the hospital to see Francesca before I come to meet you? I promised the ICU nurse I would come by."

"Of course. That's what doctors with good hearts do."

Julia sensed Josh smiling as she ended the call. She knew she was looking forward to seeing him without a chaperone for a change.

∽

Julia watched Carly get ready for her free time with Simone. Carly was certainly more of a free spirit than Julia, both in how she approached life and in her fashion style. She favored leggings and tunics, especially in bright colors. For her outing today she had chosen hot pink and black. Julia figured her sister would be able to hold her own in any crowd, with her honey blonde hair and her colorful clothes.

"Where did Simone say she was taking you today?" Julia asked as she got ready for her own outing.

"There's a fun shopping street around the corner from here," said Carly. "It's called Rue Cler, and it's full of food vendors, little bars and cafes, and other shops. She said it's a typical Paris neighborhood and that many locals buy their food there instead of at an American-style grocery store."

"Sounds like fun," said Julia. "If you find a good bar we can check it out for ourselves later."

"You bet. I'm going to meet her downstairs in five

minutes. I'll be back by three-thirty because all the shops close for a couple of hours from three to five."

"Will you bring back some cheese and bread and wine, please?" said Julia. "We can have a picnic later this afternoon."

Julia spent several extra minutes getting ready for her meeting. She decided to wear a turquoise cardigan over a white camisole, with black capris and black espadrilles. Dressing smartly, although not necessarily expensively, was part of her DNA—as much as solving mysteries. She figured it came from having to wear hand-me-downs all her growing-up years. She hadn't known as a child that not every family bought their clothes at rummage sales—today's garage sales—so she had never felt different from other kids. As an adult she marveled that her parents had managed to feed and clothe the family of two grownups and six children on what had probably been a borderline income.

She particularly remembered a pair of faded red pants in third grade that for some reason she had hated to wear. They mysteriously ended up in the "lost and found" box in her classroom coat closet at the end of the school year. She never claimed them as hers, despite repeated reminders by Mrs. Campbell for the students to check the box for missing items. Her mother finally stopped asking her if she knew where they had gone. *Such an odd memory to have stayed so vivid all these years,* she thought.

Vincent, sweetheart that he was, was waiting for her at the curb when she exited the hotel. He nodded and smiled with obvious approval of her look. "Bonjour, mademoiselle." He held the door open with a little flourish to his bow.

"Bonjour and merci, Vincent." She did a tiny curtsey. She was going to miss having a driver when she got home.

"Are you enjoying your visit to Paris, Miss Julia?" Vincent asked, observing her in the rearview mirror. "It is sad that you have had to worry about this murder while you are here."

"Yes, Vincent, I *am* enjoying my stay. It's kind of you to ask. Trying to figure out who killed Roger is something like figuring out what diseases my patients have at home. Except living patients can give me answers that dead ones can't. At least not directly."

"I see. Monsieur Larson has been smiling when he is with you." He winked in the mirror at Julia.

Julia felt her face redden. She winked back at Vincent, who she noticed was checking her reaction in the mirror.

"Monsieur Larson told me you are going to the Saint Antoine Hospital to see your friend Francesca before his meeting with Pierre. I hope your friend is going to be okay."

"Thank you, Vincent. That's very kind of you."

The late morning traffic was light, allowing Vincent to get to the hospital more quickly than Julia had expected. Once inside, she was grateful for her rusty French language skills because the signage was in French. A kind woman at the information desk called for permission for Julia to visit Francesca and directed her to the elevator.

Within a few minutes, Julia was escorted to the nurses' station, where an English- speaking Registered Nurse gave her an update. Julia had found that nurses were typically willing to share information freely once they knew that Julia a physician, even though she didn't have her stethoscope around her neck. Unfortunately, they had not yet identified what kind of toxin might have caused Francesca's collapse.

Julia stood by Francesca's bedside, noting the numbers on the monitors and observing her general appearance. Francesca remained intubated and looked peaceful. She didn't respond to Julia's voice, but the nurse had said her condition was definitely improving. Julia spent a few minutes talking to Francesca and telling her how much she was enjoying Paris. She told her about Carly shopping with Simone and ended with hopes for her recovery. She wiped a few tears from her eyes as she left the room and made her way back to the limo.

She sat silently in the limo, appreciating Vincent's respect for her need for silence.

Josh and Pierre were already seated at a small table in the light and airy Marriott lobby bar when she entered. Josh sneaked a kiss on her cheek as he helped her with a chair.

"Bonjour, Josh and Pierre," she said lightly. "Have you guys solved all the world's problems yet?"

Pierre's face darkened as he picked up his drink. Julia noticed his hand trembling as he raised his glass to acknowledge her.

Josh spoke first. "Pierre and I were chatting about the performance at the Moulin Rouge last evening. He said it was the first time he'd been to a live show there, even though he lives in Paris."

"That sounds typical," said Julia. "I live forty miles or so from the famous Mount Saint Helens volcano. It's a treat for me to go there when I have guests from another part of the country who want to see it. Did you enjoy it, Pierre?"

"Very much so," he replied.

Josh cleared his throat. "Pierre told me that Roger had promised to take Laura someday, but with his unexpected death, Pierre offered to escort her."

"That was kind of you, Pierre," said Julia. "I didn't realize Laura was planning to visit Paris while Roger was here."

"She wasn't," said Pierre. "This was something she had wanted to do some day, but never got the chance. They always put it off. With him gone, she wasn't going to get that chance again. I wanted to do something nice for her on Roger's behalf."

"Is she still leaving for home today then?" asked Julia.

She hoped Pierre didn't suspect she was digging for information, even though that's exactly what she was doing. She couldn't help herself.

Pierre checked his watch. "She should be heading to the airport within the hour."

The waiter was decked out in the restaurant's daytime uniform of black trousers, crisp white shirt with bow tie, and burgundy vest. He patiently took their orders while Julia formulated her next question.

Julia caught Josh's eye and gave him a half-nod before she asked Pierre, "Did Josh tell you that we found Roger's briefcase?"

Julia thought she saw the briefest widening of his eyes before Pierre answered, "No, he didn't. Where was it?"

"Francesca's apartment," she replied evenly, watching for his reaction.

"Really?" said Pierre, tilting his chin. "I wonder how it got there." He nervously sipped his wine.

"Hopefully we'll have more information after the police check it for fingerprints," she said nonchalantly.

Pierre choked on his wine. "Fingerprints? Why would they check it for fingerprints?"

Julia shrugged. "They usually do that kind of thing when there's attempted murder involved."

"B-but I thought the police decided that Roger's death was an accident, not a murder," Pierre sputtered.

"Not Roger," said Julia. "It looks like someone tried to kill Francesca."

∽

CARLY AND SIMONE wandered from one shop to another as they browsed through cheeses, wines, and expensive baby clothes before settling on the Café du Marché for lunch. The *plat du jour* of grilled fish with potatoes and fresh vegetables was priced right and sounded delicious to Carly. She and Simone toasted their friendship with the house white wine, which had been perfectly chilled. They relaxed and soaked in the sun's rays while waiting for the food to be served. Simone described the art therapy classes that she held for the children at the hospital while Carly people-watched the shoppers strolling by the café. She couldn't tell which of them were residents of the neighborhood buying food for that evening's meal versus visitors such as herself.

"Carly. You haven't heard a word I've said. You've been daydreaming."

Carly snapped out of her reverie. "I'm so sorry, Simone. I was wondering how to tell the locals from the tourists. *Everyone* has a shopping bag."

"Ah, but notice that the tourists are carrying bags with a shop's name. Most of the locals carry a nondescript bag that they use again and again."

"I see some baskets also," said Carly. "That seems very authentic for shopping in Paris, but it would look funny back home, except maybe at the farmers' market. At least I'm getting better about keeping reusable shopping bags in my car."

"Europeans have used their own shopping bags for many years. It is such a waste to have all that plastic to discard."

The food was delicious. Carly thought it amazing that such simple food could be so wonderfully prepared. Maybe it was the French names that made it taste better.

"Julia asked me to buy some cheese, bread, and wine to have a picnic later," said Carly. "I'll let you help me pick them out, if you don't mind."

"Let's head to the wine shop, my friend," said Simone, leading the way. "Wine Bacchus will have the perfect choice for you."

They tasted several whites and reds before settling on two bottles of each. Chattering to each other as they left the shop, they nearly bumped into Alain Marchand, who stood in the doorway.

"Mademoiselle Carly?" Alain said with a distinct slur. "I didn't know you were still in town."

"Hi, Alain," said Carly. "We're here until the weekend."

"Who's your friend?" He eyed Simone. "This isn't your sister."

"This is my friend Simone. She's helping me buy some food for a picnic later. Julia's at some meeting with Josh. She didn't need me tagging along."

Carly and Simone headed down the street toward the *fromagerie*, where cheese of all kinds and origins filled the shelves. Alain teetered as he walked with them, the smell of alcohol strong on his breath.

"Don't you live in Calais, Alain?" asked Carly. "What keeps you here in Paris? I thought your business meetings were all completed."

"I have some other contacts here, and a part-time girl-friend," he said. "The lady you saw me with at the Eiffel Tower. I'm going back later today by train. It's only a couple of hours of travel time."

"She's a pretty lady," said Carly, then added, "Well, nice seeing you" as Simone ushered her into the cheese shop.

"Ciao," said Alain. "Tell Josh I said hi."

Carly shivered. "He gives me the creeps," she admitted to Simone as they selected two kinds of cheese and a fresh loaf of artisan bread.

Simone's eyes followed Alain down the sidewalk. "He's sinister. I know it."

"I was supposed to ask you why you thought so. I forgot until we ran into him."

"It's his spirit," said Simone. "It's not a happy one."

15

MONDAY AFTERNOON, LATER

Julia and Josh told Pierre about finding Francesca. Julia watched Pierre's face closely as Josh related the story. She was surprised that he appeared to be genuinely shocked, without obvious traces of guilt. After a few more minutes he excused himself to meet with a client.

Julia and Josh found themselves alone again, which had happened rarely so far during the week, and enjoyed a second glass of wine.

"Josh, I know the police still have you as their favorite suspect." Julia reached across the table and took his hands in hers. "I don't believe you're guilty, but it does look bad."

Josh nodded, his face gloomy. "There's no way I would have or could have hurt Roger, and certainly not Francesca."

"I know you don't want to be involved in any more investigation, but I'd like to check out one more angle."

"What would that be?"

"What if someone from housekeeping saw someone going to Roger's room? If he *was* poisoned, maybe someone delivered something directly to him after our party. Maybe that's why he was saying the word 'mushroom.' Carly and I could go and ask."

"That doesn't seem too dangerous."

"And you were going to call Troy to see if he has anything to share about Roger or Clint. And ask the police about using GPS for Roger's cellphone."

"Oh, yeah. The detective said they'd have techs to check that today." Josh whipped out his phone to add a memo. "I'll make both calls when I get back to the room."

Julia checked her watch. "Carly should be back from her shopping about now. Is it okay if I send Vincent to pick her up and bring her back here to check out the housekeeping staff?"

"Sure. I don't need the limo for the time being. What's on the schedule for this evening? Do we get to have fun? Can you take time off from being a detective?"

"I would love to go out for an evening in Paris, Josh," said Julia. "I brought the perfect little black dress."

"Then let's do it. Shall we plan for seven o'clock? That will give you and Carly time to do the housekeeping thing and get dressed."

"Perfect," said Julia, finishing her glass.

They left the bar arm in arm, Julia exhilarated with the anticipation of a special evening. She pushed her concern about Josh's potential arrest to the back of her brain. But she couldn't help but wonder why he was so slow to make the few calls she'd asked him to make. Wasn't he as eager as she was to prove his innocence?

∽

JULIA AND CARLY scooted up to the sixth floor, hoping to find a housekeeper in the hallway. Julia knew it was possible that no one would remember if they had seen anyone visiting Roger or delivering mushrooms, now that it was a week after his death. She crossed her fingers.

A young Filipina wearing a housekeeper's uniform emerged from a room several doors down from Josh's room. The sisters hurried to intercept her before she could disappear into another room.

"Pardon, mademoiselle," said Julia, glancing at her name tag. "Bella, may I ask you a couple of questions?"

"Yes, of course," she replied, carefully placing her feather duster on her rolling cart.

"My name is Julia Fairchild, and I'm a friend of Mr. Larson in room 664. This is my sister, Carly."

The women exchanged polite smiles and nods.

"Do you remember the gentleman who was in suite number 668 last week? His name was Roger Westover."

"Oui, mademoiselle," she replied, nodding vigorously. "Yes, I remember him. He was American."

"Are you the person who discovered his room in a mess one morning?" Julia asked.

"Yes, that was me," she replied. "*Quelle surprise!* Because he always kept his room very neat."

"How late in the day do you work?" asked Julia. "I hope you remember if he had a visitor on the last day that you saw him."

"I work until two o'clock, but on that day I worked more because Cecilia, my manager, asked me to help. One of the afternoon housekeepers had called in sick. Same thing today." She scowled as she tossed a dirty rag into a plastic bag hanging on the side of the trolley.

Julia's heart fluttered. "Did he have a visitor that afternoon? That would be the day before you found his room such a mess."

Bella thought for a moment. "Ah, oui! I was working in the room across the hall and I heard him say, 'What a surprise to see you here. Did Laura know you were coming?' Then I heard his door shut and I went back to cleaning."

"Did you hear the visitor talk? Could you tell if it was a man or woman?" Julia asked.

"No, but I remember smelling perfume in his room when I did the evening service," said Bella. "It made me wonder if the visitor had been a woman."

"You didn't see her leave?"

"No, Ms. Fairchild," said Bella, slowly shaking her head. "I didn't hear or see any more. I'm sorry I cannot be of more help."

"Merci bien, Bella. Thank you. You've been extremely helpful." Julia found a business card in her bag and wrote down her hotel information. "Please leave a message for me if anything else comes to mind."

Back in the lobby bar, Julia and Carly sipped their drinks and munched on bar snacks of pistachios and pretzels.

"A woman…" said Julia. "Which woman could it have been? It obviously wasn't Laura, from what Bella said."

"Josh said Roger usually stays here when he's in Paris," said Carly. "Maybe he has other female friends from other visits that he arranged to meet while he was here." She wiggled her eyebrows with a sly grin on her face.

"It would have to be someone Laura knows," Julia said, nodding. "I suppose we should ask her."

Julia noticed Carly looking past her in the direction of the main lobby, gesturing to Julia at the same time. "What is it, Carly? What do you see?"

"I just saw Pierre and Alain walk across the lobby, all good-buddy-like. Now they're talking to the valet. I'm guessing they've asked for a taxi. Yep, the valet is motioning to the next cab." Carly paused to take a swallow. "When Simone and I saw him this morning, Alain said he was leaving Paris later today. It looks like he forgot to go."

Julia turned in time to witness the men get into a cab. "Unless Pierre is seeing him off at the train station. But he didn't have any luggage, did he? Finish your drink and let's go find out where they went."

"Julia. We're not going to follow them. Right?"

"Probably not, but it wouldn't hurt to know where they're headed. Hurry."

"I don't think this is a good idea," said Carly, shaking her head at her sister.

Julia flashed her sweetest smile at the valet and asked him where the handsome gentlemen were headed. He obliged her with the name of the restaurant. Julia was surprised that it was the same restaurant for which Roger had a telephone number—Café Hugo.

"That can't be a coincidence, Carly. I wonder what they're up to." She hesitated, frowning.

"I don't like what you're thinking, sis," said Carly.

"How do you know what I'm thinking?"

Carly put her hands on her hips. "You're thinking of following them to the café, but what will you do then? Interrogate them?"

"Probably not the best strategy, but I do want to be a fly on the wall." Julia grinned at the thought and whipped out her phone. "Maybe Josh can come up with some way to have an 'accidental' encounter."

Josh answered the call right away. "Hi, Julia. What are you and Carly up to?"

"We saw Pierre and Alain leaving the hotel together. The valet said they asked for a taxi to go to the Café Hugo, the one near Francesca's apartment."

"And?"

"That's the phone number that was in Roger's pocket, where Francesca worked. Doesn't that seem suspicious to you?"

"You mean as in 'probably not a coincidence therefore it must mean something' kind of suspicious?"

"Yes, something like that. And Alain said he was going to leave town a couple of days ago. So why is he still here?"

"I follow. Are you proposing to do something that might get you into trouble? That café is probably a small place. It would be awkward for you to show up there coincidentally."

"Yeah, I agree. So what if *you* call Pierre and tell him you thought of one more thing to discuss and offer to meet him? They probably wouldn't expect you to be in sleuthing mode. Maybe they'll accidentally drop a hint." Julia crossed her fingers.

"Always the detective, aren't you?" Josh chuckled. "Why would I meet him when I could tell him on the phone? And we already saw him earlier."

"Tell him it's complicated. And you don't want to talk about it on the phone."

"Hmm. I suppose I can do that to humor you, but I wouldn't count on learning anything new," he said. "In the meantime, I still plan to be at your hotel about seven. Think about where you want to go for dinner. We have a couple of evenings left to enjoy Paris, murder or no murder."

"Speaking of murder, the housekeeper at the Marriott told us she thought Roger had a woman visitor the last day he was alive."

"A woman? Why did she think it was a woman?"

Julia told him what they had learned from Bella. "It couldn't have been Laura, based on what he said. So who could it have been?"

"I'm sure I don't know, Miss Detective. You win. Maybe Pierre knows. I'll ask. See you about seven. And stay out of trouble."

"Roger that." When she realized what she had said, she giggled, and said "Oops" as she ended the call.

Noticing Julia's furrowed eyebrows, Carly asked "What's wrong?"

"Did it ever occur to you that Josh might be in on this?"

"Not really. What makes you think that?"

Julia sighed. "It seems to me that he's just going through the motions of identifying Roger's killer. As though Josh doesn't believe his partner actually *was* murdered. Or maybe it's that he doesn't care. But he has to be afraid that he's going to be arrested."

"Not everyone needs to get to the truth like you do, Julia. Most of us stay away from playing detective."

"And," Julia continued, "we can't be sure of his whereabouts between the party and going to his suite."

"Yeah. So…"

"Or just before we found Francesca. We only have his word that he 'took care of some details' or that he was having lunch with a college friend." Julia scowled. "It occurred to me that this 'friend' could have been a female. Oh, brother."

"But you're not telling the police, are you?"

"Of course not. I want to believe he's innocent. We just have to prove it." Julia paced for several steps. "I feel it in my gut that Roger's death and Francesca's poisoning are connected. Alain has something to do with it. I'm sure of it." She slapped her hand on her forehead. "What's the connection? I'm sure the doctors will have checked Francesca's stomach for poison. But 'who' and 'how' and even 'why' are still questions."

"I know you'll figure it out, sis," said Carly. "I don't doubt your skills for a moment."

Julia paused her pacing. "We talked about calling Kate and Becca." She checked her watch. "They should be out of class at the school by now. Are you game?"

Kate answered the phone after three rings. She volunteered that she and Becca had finished the first day of the bread-making class and were covered in flour. "There's a reason cooks dress in white hats and aprons, I've discovered," she said, laughing. "What's going on, Julia?"

"I'm not sure if you know, but Francesca was found unconscious in her apartment yesterday afternoon," said Julia.

"What? No!" said Kate. "They didn't tell us why she wasn't here today for our lesson. Is she okay? Do you know what happened?"

"Not exactly. I thought it looked like signs of poisoning."

"How would you know that? Did you see her yourself?"

"Yeah, we did. Carly and I stopped by her apartment after a visit to Montmartre. Fortunately, we were able to call for emergency help, and they were there in minutes. They took her to a hospital nearby." Julia pulled out the hospital card from her tote and read the name. "The police are investigating, of course."

"That's so sad."

"Part of the reason I called, Kate, is to ask if you or Becca knew anything more about Francesca, like having a boyfriend maybe? You two seemed to chat with her quite a lot."

"I don't recall her mentioning a boyfriend at all. Let me check with Becca in case she knows something." After a short pause, Kate said, "Becca says Francesca told her in no uncertain terms that she wasn't dating anyone. She supposedly had sworn off men."

Julia giggled. "I do that on a regular basis. Thanks, Kate. If you remember anything, you can reach me at the Hotel du Champs. I left the number at the Cordon Bleu also if you need it. Have fun tomorrow."

Julia plopped into a cushy wing chair in the lobby. "Nothing helpful there. Kate and Becca don't seem to be connected with Roger's dying. Why would they be? And I didn't think to ask if they knew whether Francesca had gone to his room. What am I missing?" She hit the arm of the chair with her fist. "Damn."

Carly stared at Julia. "You must be upset in a big way. I never hear you swear. Ever."

"I usually don't. It's not ladylike." She smirked. "But saying 'dadgummit' isn't strong enough for the frustration I'm feeling."

16

MONDAY EVENING

Julia and Carly took their time getting beautiful for the special evening out with Josh. Julia had brought the perfect sexy "little black dress" and tasteful costume jewelry. She touched up her makeup, adding eye shadow, liner, and blush. Carly looked sophisticated in sleek black pants and a black-and-white tunic with long flowing sleeves.

Even with the murder unsolved and Francesca still unconscious, Julia felt optimistic that they would have fun being normal tourists for a few hours. When she noticed that it was already seven-fifteen and she hadn't heard from Josh, however, she started to worry.

"What could be holding him up?" she asked, despite knowing that Carly wouldn't know the answer either.

"There's always the traffic issue. This is a normal workday for everyone except the tourists. Vincent is probably stuck at a red light somewhere." Carly deftly used the curling iron to create more drama in her hairdo. "Relax, Julia."

"I know you're probably right. But he's usually punctual. And he could have called to let us know he would be running late."

"He's a guy. I know my husband doesn't usually call if

he's behind schedule. He figures it would take more time to call and he'd be even later if he did." Carly admired herself in the mirror.

"That was before cellphones. Besides, this feels different." Julia started pacing the floor.

"You like to worry."

Another fifteen minutes passed before Julia's phone rang. She didn't recognize the number. "Hello. This is Julia."

"Miss Fairchild?" said a female voice with an accent.

"Yes. Who's calling?"

"This is Bella," said the vaguely familiar voice. "The housekeeper from the Marriott."

"Oh, yes. I'm surprised to hear from you, Bella." Julia widened her eyes toward Carly. "Do you have some more information about Mr. Westover?"

"I remembered that when I did the evening service, after he had the visitor, I saw a tray of mushrooms on the table. They were fancy ones—maybe truffles. There were pink rose petals in the center, and I remember thinking it was a strange decoration for a man."

"Okay. Did you notice if any of them were gone? Had some of them been eaten?"

"Yes, mademoiselle. The tray was about half empty."

"Do you remember what you did with the tray?" asked Julia. "Did you leave it in his room or maybe send it back to room service?"

"I left it there in case he was going to want to eat more later. It was gone when I went to his room in the morning. That is when I saw everything had been turned upside down. That is all I remember, Miss Fairchild."

"Thank you for calling, Bella. That is very helpful."

Julia shared the information with Carly. "We need to get that autopsy report somehow. It may identify the exact mushroom that was found in Roger's stomach. Maybe he ate some poisonous ones after all."

Julia placed a call to the police station and asked for a copy of the report. After she explained why it was important, the officer said he would leave a note for the detective in charge, who would contact her in the morning.

"I don't understand, Julia. We still won't know who delivered them."

"I know. But I've been thinking about the antidepressant, doxepin, that Laura said Roger had been taking," said Julia. "There are certain people who have a severe reaction, called an 'anticholinergic crisis,' when they accidentally eat certain foods or use other medications. I've seen a couple of cases of it in the intensive care unit. It's so uncommon that doctors don't usually consider it right away. What if someone knew how to cause that reaction and gave Roger the right kind of mushroom to trigger it?" Julia moved like a lawyer in front of a jury trying to make her case.

"That sounds premeditated to me. It would mean someone knew his medication ahead of time and also had to know about this potential interaction."

"Exactly," said Julia. "I'm wondering if Laura is an accomplice in all this."

"Instead of being the murderer? Why an accomplice?"

"She knew which medications he was on, which is important if I'm correct about this, but someone else could have played the lead role. I just don't know who. Yet." Julia touched up her lipstick while checking her watch yet again. She was startled when the phone rang, even though she had hoped it would. It was a Paris phone number but not one she recognized.

"This is Julia."

"Miss Julia," she heard Vincent say, "Mr. Larson was not

at the Café Hugo when I went to pick him up. He is not answering his phone. I called to see if you know where he is."

"No, Vincent," said Julia. "I've been expecting him here at my hotel for the last half hour or so. Something must have happened. He would have called me or you, I'm sure."

"Yes, he would call me," said Vincent. "Shall we go look for him?"

"Yes," said Julia. "Will you come to pick up Carly and me at our hotel?"

"Thirty minutes, Miss Fairchild. I will be there."

Julia held her phone reverently for a moment as her brain went wild considering possibilities. All with bad endings. "Carly, it looks like Josh has gone missing. Vincent is coming to pick us up."

"I'm changing clothes," said Carly. "I can't do proper detective work in this get-up. Your heels won't work either, I'm afraid."

∽

VINCENT'S FACE was drawn and his hands shook as he helped Julia and Carly into the limo. "What is your plan, Miss Julia?" he asked. "Where do we start?"

"We'll start where he must have been last seen—at Café Hugo." Julia held her crossed fingers up so Vincent could see them in the mirror. "Surely someone will have seen the three men together."

"Maybe their waiter overheard something," said Carly.

"At the very least, we should we able to find out if he left with Pierre or Alain, or both of them. It's not likely he left on his own. He would have called you, Vincent."

"But how will we know where to go after that?" asked Vincent.

"I don't know yet, to be honest," said Julia. "I have a bad feeling about this."

∼

Café Hugo was a lovely restaurant with a nice young vibe at the late evening hour. The dinner crowd was comprised of couples and small groups, many of them sitting in the covered outdoor area where Julia and Carly found the waiter who had served Josh.

"Yes, mademoiselle," said the long-haired young man. "I remember three gentlemen sitting right here. Two Frenchmen and an American," He indicated the still vacant table near the main entrance to the restaurant.

"Were you able to notice anything particular about them?" asked Julia. "Like tone of voice, or what they talked about?"

"Not exactly. At first their conversation seemed cordial, and then the taller man left."

That would have been Pierre, Julia thought, leaving Josh alone with Alain. "Did you hear any of the conversation of the two men who were still here?" she asked.

"The one who stayed seemed to be angry. He wanted the American to tell him where something was located. He kept saying 'I don't know where it is.'"

Julia and Carly looked at each other and nodded grimly.

"Did they leave together?" asked Julia.

"Oui, mademoiselle. They both looked upset. And as they were leaving I heard the American say that he needed to let his driver know the change in plans. The other man said something like 'He'll figure it out.'"

"I don't suppose they dropped any hint about where they were going?" Julia asked.

"No, mademoiselle," the young man replied. "I am sorry I

cannot help with that. I didn't see them get into an automobile."

"You've been very helpful." Julia handed the waiter a five-Euro note. "Thank you."

Julia and Carly retraced their steps to where Vincent waited with the limo. She didn't know whether Alain had a car—he had said he always took the train to Calais. But she kept her eyes on the lookout for Pierre's black Audi, though she knew it was unlikely it was anywhere nearby at this point.

Vincent asked eagerly, "Did you learn anything?"

Julia filled him in on what little they knew, ending with, "Dead end for now. I have a feeling we have to wait until we hear from them."

"What about talking to the police?" asked Carly.

"And tell them what?" said Julia. "That they should track down Josh and Alain on our say so?"

"You're right." Carly frowned. "By the way, I'm getting hungry. We missed dinner."

"Yes, we did." Julia's stomach growled as if in agreement. "Vincent, can you drop us off at our hotel, please?"

Julia and Carly wound their way back to Josh's favorite bistro near their own hotel. The gloom was palpable. Because of the late hour for their American appetites, they settled for soup and bread. Even the delicious French onion soup couldn't improve Julia's attitude.

"I wish I knew what Alain wants, and maybe Pierre too," said Julia, sipping the house red wine.

"It sure sounds like something to do with Roger that went wrong."

"Yes. It was very untimely for Roger to die and leave us with this mess." She sighed. "I feel so bad for Josh. He probably hates me right about now."

"I doubt that, Julia." Carly reached for a second baguette and slathered it with butter. "It's certainly not *your* fault that

Roger died or that Alain and Pierre are crooks. Or at least we think they are."

"True, but I still feel responsible somehow."

"That's your normal 'take charge' personality talking back to you." Carly slurped her soup. "And your need to know the truth."

Julia sat with her chin on her hands, elbows on the table, deep in thought. "Where does Francesca fit in all of this? Would she have delivered poisonous mushrooms personally to Roger? And if she did, why? Did someone pay her to do that?"

"And I bet that same person poisoned her," said Carly.

"Or arranged for it," said Julia. "The guys from London, Clint and Troy, seem to be involved with the legitimate end of this business deal."

"Although Troy had been a previous client, not a current one, according to Josh," said Carly.

"That's right. There seems to be an undercurrent of something shady going on backstage, so to speak. I wish I could put my finger on it."

Carly sat back in her chair, sipping on her wine. "We're going to the police station tomorrow to pick up that report on Roger's stomach contents. Wouldn't that be a good time to report this to that detective?"

"Yes, although I haven't been promised the report, and it's premature to report Josh's disappearance. On the news they always say to wait twenty-four hours to report someone missing."

"And he is a grownup. He could have left the café with Alain voluntarily."

"Except he would have notified Vincent," said Julia. "Or me."

"So you think he's been kidnapped? But if they are trying to frame Josh for Roger's murder, they won't want to hold him for ransom. What could Alain possibly be thinking?"

"I thought of something," said Julia. "What if they planned to take Josh to his hotel room to look for whatever seems to be missing? Like they did in Roger's room. After all, Roger was in Josh's room for some reason."

"That's not a bad idea, sis." Carly stood up to leave. "Shall we go over there?"

"I'll call Vincent. He'll want to help."

"There is one other possibility," Carly said, "though probably not one you will want to hear."

"What?"

"What if we have this all wrong? What if it's Josh who is angry with Alain, and maybe Pierre, for messing up the deal they had? What if Roger found whatever Josh was going to sell them and hid it so he couldn't? What if Josh killed Roger and is planning to continue the deal himself, but has to find whatever Roger hid? Maybe Pierre left the restaurant because he wants out, but Alain isn't sure? Or something like that. You have to admit, Josh hasn't been trying very hard to follow up on the investigations you've asked him for."

"You're right," said Julia.

"I am? Really?"

"Yes. You're right that I don't want to hear this. It's possible we have everything backwards and Josh is the guilty one. He has been acting strangely. But I have to listen to my instinct—and my gut is telling me that Josh is not a criminal or a killer—and is likely to be in danger. He may be hiding something, but he's no murderer."

Carly sighed. "I'm glad to hear you say that. We have to keep an open mind, of course. But let's call Vincent and go check Josh's hotel room."

VINCENT INSISTED on going into the hotel with the sisters in case they needed help. Julia's first response was a no, after which the older man pumped his biceps to demonstrate his strength. The three of them cautiously left the elevator and crept down the hall to Josh's room. Julia listened at the door. The room was quiet. There was no light visible under the door. She desperately wanted to search inside but didn't want to knock and alert anyone who might be in there.

Julia gestured to the others to follow her down the hall and around the corner. "I have an idea," she whispered. "I'll call room service and arrange for a bottle of wine to be delivered. When the server comes, I'll offer to take it in for him and get into the room."

"If Alain or Pierre is in there, they'll recognize you and know something's up," said Carly.

"Hmm. You're right. We need a Plan B," said Julia.

"I could pretend to be room service," said Vincent. "I'm wearing a uniform. I don't believe they have seen my face."

Julia smiled appreciatively. "Great idea, Vincent. I'll go buy some wine from the bar and you can deliver it. You're probably correct that they wouldn't recognize you."

Carly and Vincent waited out of sight while Julia hurried to the bar to get a bottle of wine and three glasses on a tray. She did some fast talking and flirting to convince the bartender that she needed the tray, promising to return it. She didn't have to promise her future first-born child, however.

Vincent looked every bit the part of an official server when Julia returned. Carly had borrowed some white linen from the housekeeping trolley in the hallway and created a realistic "apron."

Vincent knocked on the door. "Room service," he announced.

Julia watched surreptitiously from her post around the

corner. The door opened a crack, and she heard Alain say, "I didn't order anything."

Vincent cleverly placed the toe of his shoe against the doorjamb. "Mr. Larson ordered it to be delivered for his evening guests," he said, improvising on the spot.

"He's not here," said Alain.

"I can leave it on the table for him," said Vincent. He moved to enter the room.

Alain thrust out an arm to stop him, but then stepped aside.

After a short interval, Vincent emerged from the room and joined the sisters around the corner in the hall.

"I saw the one named Alain Marchand, I believe. The man who lives in Calais. He allowed me to set the tray on the coffee table. The room looked messy, but not torn apart. I could see through to the bedroom, where jackets and shirts had been strewn about on the bed. I asked, 'Is Mr. Larson packing tonight?' Mr. Marchand answered, 'I'm not sure what his plans are,' then handed me a ten-Euro note and escorted me to the door. I couldn't tell if anyone else was in the other room."

"Now what, Julia?" asked Carly.

"Why don't we wait for Alain to leave? He can't stay forever. Then we can knock on the door and see if Josh is there."

"That could work," said Carly.

"I don't know why we have to wait for Alain to leave," said Vincent. "I already said Mr. Larson was expecting guests. You two could knock now."

"That's true," said Julia. "I like that idea." She jumped when she heard a door open, then close, around the corner. "That could be Josh's room. Let's disappear for a moment." She led the trio around the corner away from the elevator.

Julia whispered to Vincent. "Why don't you walk down

the hall like you just delivered something to one of these rooms? Alain wouldn't be surprised to see you if that's him leaving now."

Vincent stepped around the corner, whistling softly as he sauntered toward the elevator. "Good evening, sir," he said to Alain as he pressed the button to go down. "I hope you are enjoying the evening."

Alain grunted in response, then quickly entered the elevator when it arrived. Vincent mocked a salute as the doors closed. Julia and Carly emerged from the adjoining hallway and hugged Vincent.

"Okay. Let's go check on Josh. I'm dying to hear his end of the story," said Julia.

They waited a long minute before Josh opened the door. His jacket was disheveled, his face pale. His jaw dropped when he saw his visitors. He motioned them in, closed the door, then enveloped Julia in a hug. She could feel him trembling.

Carly and Vincent joined in a group hug until Josh regained his composure.

"What's going on? Why was Alain here? Enlighten me, please," said Julia.

Josh fetched a fourth glass from the sitting room bar and poured four glasses of the wine Vincent had delivered. "Nice touch," he said with a ghost of a smile. "Find a seat and I'll tell you the story."

He waited until all were settled, then began. "You were right, Julia, when you suggested that Roger might be involved in something shady. Pierre admitted that he and Roger had worked out some kind of a deal to acquire software that they planned to pirate and repackage for the underground market. Roger hadn't delivered yet when he died. I told him I knew nothing about it, and Pierre left in a huff, telling Alain that it was a lost cause; there was no way Roger would have let me in on the deal. I think they were playing 'good cop-bad cop,' though, because after Pierre left, Alain was browbeating me to tell him where Roger hid the goods. I kept insisting I couldn't tell him because I don't know what Roger had or where he would have hidden 'the goods.'"

"Vincent said it looked like someone was searching in here," said Julia. "Is that why Alain was here?"

"Basically, yes. He didn't find anything because there's nothing to find in *my* room. They'd already searched Roger's room, as you know."

"What would he be searching for? Wouldn't it have been in the briefcase?"

"Probably at first. That's why someone took it, I'm sure. I would bet Roger had a thumb drive, which would be pretty easy to hide."

Julia nodded. "And it would fit in a safe deposit box."

"Or a jacket pocket," said Carly.

"Or almost anything," said Vincent.

They drank the wine in silence for a few moments.

"Maybe we can't find what Alain was looking for, but we can still try to find out what happened to Roger. I'll follow up on that report on the stomach contents in the morning." She looked at Josh. "I have a feeling you'll be hearing from Pierre or Alain again soon."

Josh shook his head. "I have no wish to see Alain ever again, deal or no deal. But I am supposed to meet with Pierre tomorrow to talk about a new potential investment. I don't know whether to trust him; but I need to do what I can to salvage our original deal on behalf of my company."

Julia knit her brows. "Just be sure to stay in a public place and keep your phone with you. And don't eat any mushrooms!"

17

TUESDAY MORNING

Julia got the promised call from Detective Durand. She explained her theory about Roger and Francesca's poisoning being connected. He was polite but firm that he was not able to release the autopsy report. She sat cross-legged in the comfy chair and shared the news with Carly. "Drat," she said. "There's got to be a way to get that information."

"Simone's husband works in the lab," said Carly. "Do you suppose he would help?"

Julia frowned. "He might not have access, if their hospital policy is anything like what we have in the States. But it wouldn't hurt to ask Simone, if you don't mind."

A few minutes later Carly grinned and bobbed her head as she ended her call. Simone had asked her husband, who said he could obtain the report without any jeopardy on his part. Julia and Carly danced a little jig and hurried to meet Vincent, who was waiting for them when they stepped out of the hotel.

"Where to, my ladies? Mr. Larson doesn't need me for a couple of hours. He said he will be meeting Mr. Dupont later this morning."

Julia buckled herself in. "Yes, he called a few minutes ago to let me know. I knew he'd hear from Pierre soon. Today we need to go the American Hospital, please, to do some serious sleuthing. Let's start by seeing what that report says about Roger's stomach contents."

Report in hand, they found an empty corner table in the hospital lobby. Vincent insisted on being in on the detecting after his successful ruse the evening before. Julia unfolded the three-page summary and began reading the medical terminology.

"Okay, sis," said Carly. "Please interpret all that gobbledygook for normal people like Vincent and me."

"Of course." Julia took a deep breath to calm herself as she skimmed the report. It was in French, but she was able to interpret much of it, thanks to her background with medical Latin and high school French. Vincent filled in when she floundered. "I'll skip over the details like acidity, color, and other unhelpful information." She quickly scanned the minutiae. "Here's something interesting: 'partially digested mushrooms of the *Agaricus bisporus* genus are present. There are also a few fragments of a second type of mushroom, specifically *Amanita phalloides,* identified in this specimen.'"

"Are those the good or bad kind?" asked Carly.

"Wait a second. There's more," said Julia. "'Present also are fragments of tablets, which are identified as *diphenhydramine.*' That would be common Benadryl, which I'm sure you both know is frequently used for allergies. And sometimes for sleep, like in Tylenol-PM." Julia looked up from the document. "Hmm. I wonder which problem he took that for. Laura should know. The doxepin would normally help him sleep, but there's no indication he had any of that in his stomach."

"We can call Laura and ask," said Carly. "And ask her

about Roger's visitor at the same time. Do you have her contact information?"

"Somewhere," said Julia. "I can always call Josh and get it. Don't let me forget to ask him."

Vincent said, "You didn't answer Carly about the mushrooms being good or bad."

Julia grimaced. "The first ones listed are a common grocery store mushroom, which you would recognize as a button-type. The *Amanita* mushrooms are a bad variety. I'll bet that's what was on the tray found in Roger's room." She put her head in her hands, elbows on her knees. "But they don't cause symptoms right away. It typically takes at least six hours. And we still have to figure out where they came from."

"Probably Francesca," said Carly, "considering Bella said they had rose petals like the tray she prepared for the party."

"That would be my first guess, but we can't ask her." Julia crossed her fingers and set the report down. "I hope she makes a full recovery. I'll call the hospital to check on her when we get done with this." She sighed, turning to her sister as she slid the report back in the envelope. "Seems we'll have to do some old-fashioned detective work, Carly, my dear. It's up to you and me to figure this out."

"Me, too," said Vincent. "I want to help."

"Of course, Vincent.," said Julia, winking at him. "And we'll definitely need your wheels as well. Let's head to the Marriott."

"How would a normal person go about buying poisonous mushrooms?" asked Carly. "Or is that something only the bad guys know?"

"Maybe they go collect them in the forest," said Vincent who was listening from the driver's seat. "My sister does that sometimes with other people. I've heard her talk about having to be careful about identification."

"That's a wonderful place to start," said Julia. "Could you call her and find out if there's any local place where people can buy them?"

"Yes, Miss Julia. I will do that right away after I get you to the hotel."

Julia and Carly made themselves comfortable in the lobby while Vincent made the phone call from the limo. Julia checked the time. "It's way too early to call the East Coast and track down Laura." Her phone rang with an unfamiliar local number on the screen. She frowned as she answered, "This is Julia."

"Bonjour, Miss Fairchild," said Pierre.

Julia turned toward Carly, mouth agape as she recognized the voice. "Hi, Pierre. What's new?"

"Nothing much," he said. "Have you talked with Josh today?"

"No, and I'm kinda mad because he stood me up last evening for our dinner," said Julia, crossing her fingers as she told the fib. "When I saw him yesterday, he was planning to call you to meet up and talk. Didn't you hear from him?"

"He did meet with Alain and me for a little while last night," said Pierre, "but I left, and he stayed with Alain to talk about some other business deal that didn't involve me."

"Oh," said Julia. "He must have gotten waylaid and forgot about the dinner. How can I help you?"

"He didn't answer his phone, so I was hoping he might be with you, or that you would know where he might be."

"I don't know, but I'll tell him you called when I see him."

"Thanks. Ciao."

"That was darned good acting on your part," said Carly, assuming a theatrical pose.

"Yes, but why would Pierre call me, looking for Josh?" Julia frowned. "Josh specifically told Vincent and me that he was going to be meeting with Pierre this morning, and it didn't sound as though that happened. I wonder where Josh went. Is he missing again?"

Carly nibbled on a fresh cookie she had grabbed from the platter by the coffee urn. "Probably just a mix-up in communications," she said. "My bet is that Alain is the bad boy here. Although Pierre isn't exactly the poster boy for truth and innocence either."

Vincent entered the lobby, beaming. "My sister says that the poison mushrooms grow in the forests near here. She knows of someone who collects them for their mystic store. It's called the Crystal Palace. She will call me again when she has that phone number. I will wait with the limo for Mr. Larson to call when he needs me."

"Ciao." Julia turned back to Carly. "Okay, that gives us a potential source. We can tell the police we know they are available for purchase *by anybody* if they know where to go."

"I thought of something," said Carly. "Wouldn't they look different from the usual mushroom? Can you stuff them?"

"I thought of that too and looked up a photo on my phone." Julia scrolled to the webpage. "Take a look. I bet that whoever brought them to Roger said something about them looking different because they're French. Maybe she told him they were truffles." She chuckled. "Even I don't know what those look like."

After comparing the mushroom photos Carly said, "Anything's possible. Roger's a guy. He'd believe they were something fancy."

Julia gasped. "Bella, the housekeeper, said she saw a tray of something she thought were truffles in Roger's room, remember? And I just remembered seeing the word 'truffles' on a piece of paper on Francesca's desk. She had several recipes and notes written on Cordon Bleu notepaper. Look—I have a photo on my phone." She showed it to Carly.

"That's definitely the word 'truffles,'" said Carly. "But maybe it's referring to the type of truffles we made in the chocolate class. Did you read the recipe?"

Julia's shoulders slumped. "I didn't think about there being other kinds of truffles, and no, I haven't even tried yet." She looked up and saw Josh as he exited the elevator. "There's Josh." She jumped up and waved her hand. "Josh. Over here!"

Josh bounded across the lobby to join them. He appeared freshly showered and was dressed in a suit and tie, like the typical businessman he was. He hugged Julia and patted Carly's shoulder. "I was hoping to catch you here. Vincent said he was going to take you to the police station this morning." He looked around. "Where is he?"

Vincent left a few minutes ago; he's waiting for your call in the limo," said Julia. "How was your meeting with Pierre?"

Josh glanced anxiously toward to exit. "Oh, fine," he answered. "How was your morning?"

Julia shot Carly a slight frown at Josh's evasive reply, but decided not to pursue it for now. "We went to the hospital instead of the police," she told him. "Do you want to see the official report on Roger's stomach contents?"

"Since it's probably in medical terms, I'll take a translation, please," he replied as he settled into one of the chairs.

Julia gave him the layman's version. "This proves that someone poisoned Roger. He couldn't have 'accidentally' eaten poisonous mushrooms. Someone had to provide them to him."

"Yes, but does it matter at this point?" said Josh. "If *you* haven't been able to figure it out, I don't expect the police are going to put a lot of effort into finding a guilty party other than me."

"I don't like loose ends," Julia admitted. "And I don't believe you're guilty."

Josh gave her a weak smile. "Thanks for that. Here's the deal. Vincent is driving me to a facility that Pierre told me about. He said it has investment potential and wants my opinion, so Pierre and I are meeting there. Vincent will be with me, so I think it's safe. I'll be back after lunch. What are your plans?"

"We need to check out this place where people can buy poisonous mushrooms," said Julia.

"What about checking Josh's bathroom again?" asked Carly. "Maybe we missed something in our quick search earlier."

Julia nodded slowly. "Good idea. If we knew what Roger was doing in there, we might be closer to finding the 'why' and 'who.'"

"Let's plan to do that when I get back from my tour of this place," said Josh. "Shall we plan for two o'clock or so?"

"Perfect." Julia blew him a kiss as he headed for the door to meet Vincent.

∼

THE CAB DRIVER made small talk as they rode through the city to the address of the Crystal Palace in the Marais neighborhood. Though Julia didn't expect to learn anything momentous, she hoped to establish that Roger's poisonous mushrooms could have been obtained by anyone who knew where to buy them. She was intrigued to discover that the shop wasn't far from Francesca's apartment.

The sisters entered the store and saw display cases filled with bowls of crystals and racks of books about healing using various natural elements and potions. Near the back of the shop Julia spotted what looked like a delicatessen counter. As she peered into the glass window, she saw a myriad of unusual specimens.

"Those look like maidenhead ferns, Carly," said Julia, pointing to a small plate near the front. "I watched a program recently about nature hunters collecting all kinds of edible wild plants."

"Even though we picked and ate wild berries in the woods as kids," said Carly, "I wouldn't want to eat most of what I see here."

"The point of the program was that you could make a healthy salad simply using what they collected, like wood sorrel, dandelions, chicory, and forget-me-nots."

"Not for me," said Carly as she scanned the display. "I'm not seeing mushrooms here."

"Me neither. Let's ask about them."

The proprietor spoke enough English to understand Julia's question. His face lit up when he heard the botanical name and he retreated behind a door. A moment later he returned with a handful of mushrooms.

He selected one and said sternly, "Must cook this to eat. Poisonous if not cooked. This is *Amanita pantherina.*" He picked a second one to show them. "This is *Amanita phalloides,* or 'Death Cap.' This is always poisonous. *Ne pas manger.* Do not eat."

"They look very similar to me," said Julia.

"Yes," he said. "People get sick and die every year because they mistake them in the forest."

"But you sell them both here?" asked Julia.

"Yes," he replied. "I always explain to customers about the danger."

"Why would people buy the poisonous ones?" asked Carly.

"The mystics use them in rituals, but not as food," the shop owner explained. "I have dried mushrooms also, but they often prefer to process them their own way."

"So anyone could buy them," said Julia.

"*Vraiment*—true," he admitted, "but I warn them about the poison."

"That's good," said Julia.

"Especially the Americans," he added.

"What do you mean?"

"Not many Americans come in here asking about the mushrooms. Mostly they ask about the crystals," he said. "But there was another American woman in here about a week ago. She asked a lot of questions. Like you." He narrowed his eyes as he scrutinized Julia.

Julia felt her pulse quicken. "Did she buy anything?"

"Not that day. She came back later."

"Do you remember what day that was?"

He held his hand to his forehead and squinted. "It was Tuesday." He paused. "Yes, Tuesday."

"Do you remember what she looked like?"

"Pretty. Long blonde hair. She wore sunglasses and a hat. It made me think of someone from Hollywood."

"Any guess as to her age?"

"About the same as you. Not very old but not a teenager either."

"I don't suppose she gave a name," said Julia.

"I didn't ask."

"Of course not. Well, merci, monsieur. You've been very helpful," said Julia as she and Carly left the quaint business.

"I can see how those could have been stuffed like the common mushroom and the average person wouldn't know they were being poisoned," said Carly.

"Or they could have been ground up and used in the stuffing of the common mushroom," said Julia. "And Francesca seems to be the most likely candidate to have done so. Could the American have been Laura?"

"Or Kate or Becca?" said Carly.

"It had to have been someone Roger knew," said Carly.

"The housekeeper said he knew the person who came to his door that day. And so did Laura."

"Who could that be?" Julia scowled. "I want to let Josh know what we found out."

"Are you going to call him?"

"I'll wait till we see him later today. He's probably still with Pierre." Julia turned to look at Carly, her face grim. "At least we think that's where he is."

18

TUESDAY LATER AFTERNOON

"You were going to call the hospital to check on Francesca," said Carly in the taxi on the return trip to the Marriott.

Julia thanked her sister for the reminder and dialed the ICU's direct number. "How is Mademoiselle Caron today?" she asked the English-speaking nurse after identifying herself.

"She is better today, Dr. Fairchild. Her sister Lesli arrived last evening, and Francesca seemed to be aware that her sister was in the room."

"That sounds good," said Julia. "Has she opened her eyes yet?"

"Not so much, but the doctor thinks she could be awakening soon. We all hope so."

"As do I. Would it be possible for me to talk with the sister if I come to the hospital? I have some questions for her."

"Oui, yes. I believe she would like that. Visiting hours are from four to six this afternoon if you can come then."

JULIA AND CARLY shared what they'd learned at the Crystal Palace shop when they met up with Josh after lunch. "I'm sure I could live on French soup, bread, cheese, and wine," said Julia after describing the strange selections of food to Josh.

"Add cookies and I'm in," teased Carly.

After a quick ride up the elevator to Josh's suite, Julia and Carly began their search of the bathroom while Josh prepared a report on the potential investment opportunity on his laptop.

"He keeps this room neat," said Carly.

"Maybe, but the housekeeper probably did most of it. We'd have to see the bathroom in his apartment to know the truth." Julia sat on the edge of the tub after she and Carly opened and closed every drawer and door. "If Roger hid something in here, he did a great job. It would help to know exactly what we were looking for."

"A thumb drive like we talked about wouldn't be very large," said Carly. "Or maybe we're looking for a paper document that he thought he needed to stash to show Josh later?"

Julia's face lit up and she pulled out the top drawer. "Let's look *under* the drawers. And behind them. Sometimes at home a piece of paper gets caught and slides out the back of the drawer in my desk at home." It took a minute to figure out the release mechanism to remove the first drawer. She found nothing of interest in the back of the cabinet or on the drawer's underside and turned her attention to the middle drawer. Still nothing, and the drawer was empty. The bottom drawer, also empty, was more resistant to being removed. Julia persisted and finally got it out and turned it over. She found a piece of tape hanging by one end. "Drat. Nothing except this piece of tape."

Carly peered over Julia's shoulder. "Look at the bottom of the cabinet. Isn't that a thumb drive?"

Julia squealed and picked up the small unit. "I bet this

was taped to the bottom of the drawer and fell off when I pulled it out." She used a tissue to carefully peel the tape off the drawer and pick up the thumb drive.

Josh looked up from his work when the sisters emerged with Cheshire cat grins on their faces. "I heard you squeal. Did you find a mouse?"

Julia opened her hand and showed him what they'd found.

Josh's mouth dropped open. "You mean it was here all along?"

Julia nodded. "Seems so. I bet this is why Roger was in there. He was hiding this. So what's on it that was worth dying for?"

∾

JULIA AND CARLY sat on either side of him while Josh inserted the thumb drive into the laptop, being careful to use a tissue to prevent adding more fingerprints. As soon as the program opened, he recognized it as proprietary software belonging to Alpha Gamma Security. Josh whistled and sat back on the settee.

"I'm guessing that Roger was planning to sell this software for a princely sum," said Julia.

"How do we know he didn't do that before he died?" asked Carly.

"This company would know through security breaches if it had been installed somewhere without proper access and verification," said Josh. "I haven't heard anything from my office about anything like that."

Julia's antennae twitched with excitement. "Maybe they didn't want to *install* the program. Perhaps somebody wanted to use it to build their own security software and then market it themselves."

"That's more likely," said Josh. "It would be hard to do anything with this directly. The company would shut down any illegitimate user almost as fast as they logged on."

"The real question is whether Roger was really planning to sell this information," said Julia. "And if he was willing to sell this software, why did someone kill him?"

"Maybe he changed his mind and backed out," offered Carly. "Or maybe Roger already got paid."

"Josh, are you able to check Roger's finances and see if he's had a major deposit recently?" Julia asked.

"Not exactly," said Josh. "I don't have authority for that. And it would be tricky to ask Laura about a big financial payoff. She could be in on it, for all we know."

"Considering that Roger brought the thumb drive to Paris," said Julia, "I'm willing to bet that one of the guys you've been meeting with was prepared to pay the big bucks."

Josh nodded. "Or they had a contact who was willing to buy it, like Troy. Maybe that's why he was here. And why he's avoiding my attempts to talk with him."

"Roger may have kept in touch with him even though he's not currently your company's client," said Julia.

"Then why did someone try to kill Francesca?" asked Carly. "She doesn't have big bucks."

"Maybe she knew someone," said Julia. "Or *something*."

"Oh," said Carly. "I forgot to tell you that Simone and I ran into Alain again on Monday morning, when we were at some wine store on Rue Cler. He was drunk again, or acting like it, anyway. We asked why he was still here, and not back in Calais, He mentioned business and a girlfriend. But I got the distinct impression he was following us." She paused. "Do you think he believes you and I know where Roger hid this thumb drive?" she asked Julia. "We do seem to be around whenever anything happens—like finding both Roger and Francesca."

"Or it could just have been a coincidence," Josh offered. "It wouldn't be unusual to find Alain near a wine store."

"Pierre and Alain have to be suspects," said Julia. "I wouldn't rule out Laura just yet either. She seemed pretty chummy with Pierre at the Moulin Rouge show."

~

STILL HUNKERED down in Josh's suite, Carly and Julia prepared a tray of cheese and thick slices of fresh artisan bread from Carly's shopping trip while Josh found the wine glasses and poured the drinks.

"Yum," said Julia. "It's not the picnic I'd planned, but we do have my three favorite food groups. Cheese, bread, and wine."

"Wine isn't a food group, sis," said Carly.

"If I count it as a fruit, it is," Julia countered. "Anyway, do you suppose the police are getting tired of us yet? We'll have to report the thumb drive to them, for sure. Unless we want to solve this murder ourselves."

Carly spoke up. "Yes, Julia. *Of course* you have to tell the police. I know what happens when you try to play detective all by yourself."

"So do I," said Josh. "I witnessed that scary boat chase in Amsterdam last year. We can go to the station tomorrow morning. Maybe they'll have information on the briefcase by then."

"I know. I know," said Julia as she waved her hand. "Did you call your office yet, Josh, about the thumb drive and any possible breach?"

Josh checked his watch. "It's morning office hours in

D.C. I should be able to catch the right person any time now." He sat back in his chair and tapped his fingers on the arm.

"What's wrong?" asked Julia. "You seem to be hesitant about making the call."

Josh shook his head. "This isn't something that I would have expected Roger to do. It's so out of character for him. He's 'Mr. Straight Arrow' through and through."

"Hmm," said Julia. "Here's a possibility. It occurred to me that Roger may have been the messenger, not the perpetrator. What if someone back at your office is in on this? What if you inadvertently tip someone's hand?"

Carly scoffed. "I thought people were innocent until proven guilty. You make it sound like everyone's guilty until proven innocent."

"We should operate on the premise that someone else may be involved for the time being," said Julia. "Josh and I should go to the police with this new information and see if they'll share what they have." She turned to Josh. "Is there any harm in waiting to call your office?"

He shook his head solemnly. "Let's drink this wine and enjoy the moment. There's always tomorrow."

∽

Wednesday morning

Julia dressed smartly for the visit to the police station. She was glad she had packed a summer dress and coordinating low heels, although her original plan had been to wear them for a special evening out. Josh and Vincent admired her "look" approvingly. They dropped Carly off at the American Hospital, where she was going to observe Simone teaching her children's art class. Julia felt confident that Carly would also be getting her hands on a paintbrush.

Julia and Josh paused outside the door to the police

station and met each other's eyes. Josh gave her a gentle squeeze as they each took a deep breath and stepped through the doorway. They were shown into the detective's office, where they waited briefly.

Detective Durand greeted them politely when he stepped into the bleak space. "My American friends return," he said. "I am told you have some information for me about Mr. Westover. Is that correct?"

"Yes, detective," said Josh. "You may recall that Mr. Westover was found in my bathroom at the hotel. Yesterday afternoon we found this thumb drive that had been taped under a drawer in my bathroom." Josh handed the envelope to the detective as he continued. "We suspect he had just finished hiding this when he collapsed."

Officer Durand opened the envelope, using care not to touch the sticky tape or device with his fingers. "Have you already checked to see what is on this?"

"Yes, sir," said Josh. "It's a proprietary software program that belongs to one of my company's clients."

"I see." Durand slipped the envelope and its contents into an evidence bag. "I will have it dusted for fingerprints while you wait, if you have time. The tape has fastened itself to the paper envelope, so we'll see about that. Give me five minutes."

"Thank you, detective. We'll be here." He turned to Julia. "Will he have an answer in five minutes?"

"No, Josh. They'll scan any prints they find into a database and compare them to known fingerprints. I'm afraid it takes longer than it does on television." She smiled ruefully. "And there might not be any matches in the system, if whoever has handled it other than Roger hasn't had reason to be fingerprinted."

"I hadn't considered that possibility," said Josh, shoulders slumping. "I was hoping for an easy answer."

"It's rarely the obvious one, I've found," said Julia.

True to his word, the detective returned shortly. "It will take some time to run the fingerprint program. Before you ask, yes, I have seen the recent reports about Mademoiselle Caron and the missing briefcase. There is a large backlog of requests for matching fingerprints, so I do not have more results for you yet. I am sorry. Is there anything else?"

Julia cleared her throat. "Well, yes, there is. I did some field research on poisonous mushrooms. We found a shop that sells them." She handed the shop's business card to the detective. "The owner told us that an American woman had been in to purchase some the previous week."

"Were you aware that Mr. Westover's autopsy report confirmed the presence of poisonous mushrooms?" He peered at Julia.

"Um, yes, sir." Julia felt her skin redden.

"I won't ask how you know this," he said with narrowed eyes.

"Yes, sir." She cleared her throat. "Once I knew the findings, I wanted to see if they were available for purchase by ordinary citizens. And they are."

"So I see." He studied the card. "I will send an officer to confirm your findings. This forces us to qualify this as a murder instead of an accidental death. I'm sure you would agree."

"And what about the attempted murder of Francesca Caron?" Julia asked. "It appears she was poisoned as well."

Detective Durand met her eyes. "An unfortunate situation, no doubt," he said. "I will tell you that for now, we are considering Miss Caron a possible suicide attempt."

"Suicide? Why would you think that?" Julia demanded.

"I am not at liberty to reveal too much of our reasoning," the detective replied evenly. "Suffice it to say that the letters we found in Mr. Westover's briefcase, all from Miss Caron, were of an, er, intimate nature. We believe she may have been in despair over his death, or perhaps guilt-ridden for having caused it. We know she prepared the mushroom appetizer. Of course she is not our only suspect." He fixed Josh with a steely gaze.

"Roger's briefcase and the thumb drive are company property," said Josh. "When can I expect their return? We wouldn't want the contents of either to fall into the wrong hands."

Detective Durand's expression remained inscrutable. "For now we will hold the items in a secure evidence room," he said. "They will be returned to you, or to Mr. Westover's widow, once the case is closed."

Julia shuddered and asked softly, "Is there anything else we can do to help you, detective? I have a couple more days here."

The detective cracked a smile. "That is kind of you to offer, Miss Fairchild, but we can take care of this investigation. I will let you know when I have more to tell you. Good day."

Josh had sent Vincent back to the hotel instead of waiting. It was another beautiful mid-spring day, so Julia and Josh decided to walk instead of hailing a cab. Strolling hand in hand, Julia found herself almost able to pretend there had never been a murder and this was a normal vacation in a beautiful city. She wished it were so.

"Josh, I know you don't want to pursue this any longer," said Julia, "but someone is guilty of murder, and I can't bear the thought of them getting away with it. Not to mention that you haven't been completely cleared yet."

"Yeah, I know," he replied. "I feel like I owe it to Roger to get to the truth. And I'd certainly like to have the police look at someone other than me. I didn't know he was having an affair with Francesca, but I can't say I'm surprised. I did get the sense things weren't going smoothly with Laura." He brushed his hair out of his eyes. "What do we do next, Julia?"

Julia flashed a smile at Josh, happy that he was willing to go ahead, at last. "First, we list all the people who may have benefited from having that thumb drive and would be willing to pay the price."

"And whom Roger may have been meeting on this trip," added Josh. "Including Francesca."

"Then we figure out Roger's movements from his arrival to his death, as best we can."

"He came a couple of days before I did. At the time I didn't think anything of it, but maybe it had to do with this other 'business.'"

"You've got the idea, Josh." Julia high-fived him. "We need to find out whether Clint was involved. I don't know him at all except from the party, but he does live in London and may have other connections to Troy."

"Right," said Josh. "I'll check that out."

"I know you checked with hotel security about video footage in the hallway, but what about security footage in the lobby or front door? We might see Roger talking with someone those couple of days he was here without you."

"You said you didn't see any mushrooms in Francesca's fridge."

Julia frowned. "No, although I was hoping to find some there. I did see some rose petals that were long past their prime. I wonder if they were her 'signature' at the cooking school." She thought for a moment. "Kate and Becca might know something. They seemed to want to get very friendly with Francesca. Now I'm wondering if they had an ulterior motive."

"Like what?" asked Josh.

"Like I don't know yet."

JULIA FOUND that Carly had finished her session with Simone at the hospital and was waiting for her and Josh in the lobby at the Marriott when they returned from the police station. Splotches of blue and yellow paint decorated Carly's arms.

"Did you have fun? It looks like you got to paint too."

"Some," said Carly, "but mostly I helped the kids with holding their paintbrush and naming colors and things like that. It felt good to be there. Some of them are there for long-term therapy, like for cancer, and others are in and out quickly. They all seem happy to be playing with colors and being kids for a little while."

"One of them may be a future Picasso or Monet," said Julia.

"What did you learn at the police station?"

"The letters in the briefcase turned out to be love letters to Roger from Francesca," Julia said.

Carly's eyes widened.

"Other than that, nothing new," said Josh. "We have to wait for fingerprints. The detective thanked us, then dismissed us, pretty much."

"He doesn't know the tenacity of 'Julia Fairchild, Detective,'" said Carly.

"Josh and I were talking about possible suspects on the walk back to the hotel." Julia gave Carly an update of their discussion. "We hadn't gotten to Alain or Pierre yet. And Laura fits in somewhere. She would have benefited financially from the sale of that software as Roger's spouse. Now widow."

"If she knew about it," said Josh.

"I have a gut feeling that she did," said Julia. "We're going to have to lure our murderer out somehow."

19

LATER WEDNESDAY MORNING

Josh and Julia formulated the idea that creating a dummy thumb drive would be the best way to lure the murderer out of hiding. Josh had called Alpha Gamma Security, who said they would go directly to work to create software that he would then upload onto a replica. Officer Durand was setting up a sting that he hoped would flush out the person who had already killed in an effort to obtain the software.

Vincent drove Julia and Carly to an office supply store, where they found a thumb drive that was similar enough to the real one for their purpose. Chances were good the prospective buyer had never seen the original anyway.

"Have I told you lately how much I appreciate you being my sister?" Julia gave Carly a sincere hug. "This has not been the romantic adventure I'd envisioned. I'm so glad you're here to fill in the gaps."

Carly chuckled. "You're going to owe me."

"I'll give you an IOU. Let's get back and get the fake data loaded onto the new thumb drive so we can get this show on the road."

PIERRE AND ALAIN ordered a second glass of wine while enjoying brunch at Café Hugo.

"What's your next idea, Pierre?" asked Alain. "Do you think Julia trusts you?"

He nodded. "She sounded cautious on the phone, but I believe I can coerce her to work with me."

"She seemed to take a liking to you at that party Josh had. She doesn't seem to like me much. But it could be my imagination." Alain swallowed a slug of his drink.

Pierre smirked. He suspected Alain's perpetual slur from his alcohol intake had a lot to do with Julia's hesitance, not to mention his breath. "I'm going to offer to help her find Roger's murderer. See if she bites. We need to find that thumb drive before Troy cancels his offer."

"What are you proposing?" asked Alain.

"I'll figure out something," said Pierre. "Trust me on that."

~

Later Wednesday morning

Josh wasn't waiting in the hotel lobby when Julia and Carly returned from the office supply store. After ringing his room and trying his cellphone, Julia said, "I don't remember him saying he had anything particular he had to do while we were gone."

"Maybe he finally called Troy and is on the phone and can't answer your call," said Carly.

"I bet not," said Julia, "but I'll give him the benefit of the doubt."

"Vincent was with us, so he can't be using the limo." Carly found the platter of fresh cookies for the guests.

Julia dropped into a leather chair next to the lobby fireplace. "It's almost as though he is leading a secret double life.

Where is he always disappearing to? Or maybe he doesn't want to create the fake thumb drive. Do you think this is an avoidance move?"

"Jumping to conclusions?" said Carly, waggling her finger. "Not 'innocent until proven guilty'?"

Julia smiled. "What if I call Pierre? He seems to want to help."

"Isn't he still one of your suspects?"

"He's not number one," said Julia. "And he's got wheels, so we wouldn't have to keep bugging Vincent to take us somewhere."

"Why do we need wheels?"

"I don't know," said Julia. "It seems like a good excuse to call him."

Carly shrugged. "I suppose it can't hurt to call Pierre looking for Josh—just the way Pierre called you yesterday. But I'd try Josh one more time first. Maybe he was tied up with something."

"Sure." Julia let the phone ring until it went to voicemail. "Call me when you can," she said tersely. "Men."

Carly smiled at her sister's annoyance.

"I am seriously beginning to wonder if Josh *is* in on this somehow, like you suggested," Julia lamented. "The thumb drive *was* in his bathroom. Maybe Josh and Roger are both guilty of whatever is going on."

Carly said softly, "You could drop the whole detective bit and not worry about whether or not he is guilty of something. Enjoy his company for our last couple of days here and chalk this up as an adventure."

Julia slouched down in the chair and looked at her sister. "I thought I had finally met someone who is fun to be with and isn't intimidated by my being a doctor."

"He seems comfortable around you," said Carly.

"Yeah, but is he totally honest?"

Julia started to call Pierre but hung up before she finished dialing. "Maybe we have this backwards. What if *Josh* hid the thumb drive in the first place, and Roger was retrieving it for whomever was buying it when he collapsed? Maybe they were both in on it. And Josh then had to figure out a cover story because we were there when Roger was found in his bathroom."

"I don't like that version," said Carly. "I want Josh to be innocent."

"So do I. In either case, what role did Francesca play that caused her to be poisoned?" Julia sipped her drink while checking her watch. "This should be a good time to call Laura and find out why Roger was taking the antihistamine."

"And who his visitor could have been," Carly added.

∽

Josh sat at the small café table on the patio, sipping a steaming mug of Irish coffee. He knew Julia had been trying to reach him, but he was ashamed to call her until he made the call he had promised her he would make. Steeling himself, he dialed Troy Ainsworth's number, almost wishing he wouldn't answer. He didn't want to have the conversation he was about to have.

"Josh. Good to hear from you. What's up?"

"Hey, Troy. How's business in London?"

"Very good. A little up and down with the stock market these days, but we're doing okay. What's on your mind?"

"I've been in Paris this past week with Roger Westover, my partner, meeting with a couple of our clients."

"Tell Roger I said hi," said Troy.

"I'll get back to Roger in a second. The reason I called is that I've seen a recent photo of you with Alain Marchand here in Paris. Roger mentioned that you might be considering hooking up with Alain for a new security program."

Troy hesitated, then said, "Go on."

"There could be some legal implications, considering that his client had you tied up with a five-year contract starting about a year ago." Josh's voice lowered a notch. "Before you transferred to the other firm."

Troy gave a nervous laugh. "We were brainstorming and bantering around some ideas, Josh. Nothing serious came out of the conversation."

"Good to know," said Josh.

"What were you going to tell me about Roger?"

"I'm sorry to tell you that Roger is dead," said Josh.

"What? Whatever happened?"

"Maybe an accidental death from food poisoning. The police are investigating the possibility of murder, but there's not much to go on."

"Murder? That's awful! I'm shocked to hear it." Troy paused, as if absorbing the news. "I'm sorry, Josh. I liked Roger a lot," he said. "I'm afraid I have to go now. Is there anything else?"

"Not right now. Thanks for your time."

~

"Hi, Laura," said Julia. "How are you doing? I know I said this before, but I am truly sorry about Roger."

"Thanks. I'm okay. Life goes on. I'm surprised to hear from you."

"I'm calling about Roger, actually. The pathologist found some Benadryl in his stomach. Do you know why he took that?"

"He carried it with him in case he needed it for allergies."

"Do you know what he was allergic to? Was it food or something like pollens?"

"A little of both. Pollen mostly, I'd say, as far as taking the allergy medicine," said Laura. "He hated to take it because he said it made him sleepy, but before he left for the trip he had mentioned that the pollen count might be high in Paris because of it being spring and all."

"Do you know which foods, by any chance? Mushrooms maybe?" Julia felt her pulse quicken.

"Hm, maybe," said Laura. "The police asked me that too. He never ate mushroom soup, although I think he just didn't like it. I know he loved stuffed mushrooms, so I don't think that would have been one of the foods. He also avoided strawberries. But I don't think his allergies were anything serious—not like people who collapse if they eat peanuts or anything like that."

"Interesting," said Julia. "I'm not sure if it means anything yet, Laura. Oh, one more thing. Do you know if any of Roger's friends from home were planning to visit him here in Paris?" She glanced at Carly and raised an eyebrow.

"Not that I know of. Why do you ask?"

"We were wondering because the housekeeper said she thought she heard him talking to someone from across the hall, where she was cleaning another room."

"I'm sure I wouldn't know anything about that. He didn't mention it to me."

"Okay. It was just a thought. Hey, I'll let you know if I find out anything about the Benadryl. In the meantime, take care."

"Thank you, Julia. Bye."

Julia shared Laura's answers with Carly. "So she denied knowing anything about a visitor. Interesting." Julia knit her brows. "The mushrooms are a puzzle. Hm." She crossed her legs. "What if it wasn't the mushroom itself, but what it was stuffed with?"

"And *that's* why Roger said mushroom," said Carly.

"I wish he had told us his visitor's name while he was at it."

"If he hadn't started seizing, I'm sure he would have."

"Darn it. Two steps forward and one step back. Who could have visited him at the hotel?"

Her phone rang. Julia narrowed her eyes and showed the screen to Carly. "Hi, Pierre. What's going on?"

"I was wondering if there's anything I can do to help the amateur detective. Josh seems pretty worried over the whole Roger thing."

"Hmm. I was getting the impression he wanted me to give it up and pretend nothing has happened."

"That's not what he told me, Julia. He's worried that the police are going to accuse him of murder."

"He's mentioned that, but there's no direct evidence so far."

"Look at it this way. What if you find evidence that definitely points in Josh's direction? I know you are friends; but you also seem honest. Would you be able to follow up on it?"

"I hope I would be impartial," said Julia. "But I've been looking for proof that it was somebody else. I don't see Josh as the murderer."

"Neither do I, but you have to admit that the circumstances don't look good for him."

"He hasn't been charged with anything, Pierre. But I get what you're saying."

"He's worried, Julia," Pierre repeated. "I'd like to help find out what happened to Roger. I like Josh."

"So do I," said Julia. "So do I. Thanks for calling. If an idea comes up, I'll get back to you."

Julia sat quietly in the chair, leaning back with her arms

stretched over her head. "I wonder what Pierre really wanted."

"Why? What did he say?" Carly sat on the settee while she touched up her fingernail polish. She held up her fingers and showed Julia. "I like this new color. It's called 'Paris Pink.'"

Julia smiled. "Yes, it's very French. Pierre was trying to convince me that my snooping around might be bad for Josh—that I might discover something that implicates him."

"Isn't he already 'implicated'?"

"He meant more convincing evidence than the police currently have." She sighed. "If only I could connect Francesca somehow. Could she have been trying to blackmail Roger with those letters? I can ask her sister, Lesli, if she knew anything about their relationship."

"Good idea," said Carly. "I overheard you tell the nurse you hoped to talk to Francesca's sister. Maybe she'll be there now."

"Right after I talk to Josh. Maybe he's free."

20

WEDNESDAY LATE AFTERNOON

"Hi, handsome. I have some news for you. Are you in your room?"

"Not at the moment," said Josh. "I'm waiting for Pierre to meet me in the lobby of his office building in a few minutes. He wants me to meet another potential client for Alpha Gamma Security group. Roger had been developing a relationship with the company. And—well, you know the rest of that story."

"Will this be a dinner, or drinks and talk?"

"Drinks and talk," said Josh. He chuckled. "I do still owe you a dinner."

"That would be lovely," said Julia, smiling as she thought of the possibility.

"What is it you want to tell me?"

"It'll keep till I see you," said Julia. "Good luck with your meeting."

~

JOSH HAD NEVER BEEN to Pierre's office because Roger had been the contact person for Pierre's business till now. The building was a starkly modern multilevel affair with reflective glass. The neighboring structures were much older and more traditional by French standards. The elevator took them to the sixth floor. Pierre's company occupied the entire level. The office itself had a comfortable feel, which was unexpected from the cold appearance of the building's exterior. The décor was done in soft, neutral tones with modern chairs and art. Late afternoon light streamed in through the windows, giving a sense of a connection with nature.

Josh sensed a tone of "all business" as he followed Pierre to a small conference room, where Clint sat waiting, drink already in hand. Josh noticed a wet bar on the far end. He nodded his acknowledgement to Clint as he sat down. "Is the other client going to be meeting us here?" Josh asked as Pierre poured a glass of Scotch for each of them.

Pierre shook his head. "Clint has a client that is very interested in the security system Roger was representing," he said.

"Do you mean Troy Ainsworth?" asked Josh.

"No," said Pierre, with a trace of annoyance. "Troy withdrew his offer once you informed him of Roger's death. And Alain seems to have dropped out as well. We have always had other possibilities, however. Clint's client is a large business with offices in both Paris and London. The potential financial benefit to you and your company is huge. Roger had expressed an interest in being in on the bottom floor of this investment with its potential rewards. I hope you might share some of his enthusiasm for the project."

"I'm not following you, Pierre," said Josh. "Does this client look at Alpha Gamma Security as a provider of a product for their businesses, or do you mean they wish to entertain a merger with them?"

"Think of it more as a joint venture involving software. If

we were to do this properly, we could share millions in profits."

Josh suddenly knew what the thumb drive was all about. The conspirators wanted to steal Alpha Gamma's system to create one of their own. And given that Pierre had brought both Clint and Alain to the table, Pierre also had to be involved in the data theft.

"I am not as familiar with your ideas as Roger was," Josh replied. "Perhaps you should be discussing this with Alpha Gamma Security directly, if this is simply to purchase their system. Roger and I would only be involved if you were interested in a merger deal of some sort."

Pierre tilted his head and looked out the window. "Funny thing. The security company didn't want to participate in my venture." He walked toward Josh. "But Roger did."

Josh checked his watch for the time. "I need a minute, if you'll excuse me while I touch base with Julia to firm up our dinner plans for tonight." He turned his back to Pierre and Clint and called Julia.

"Josh. What a surprise," said Julia.

"Hey, beautiful," he said. "I'm calling to confirm dinner with you at our favorite bistro. Can you meet me there at seven?"

"Of course," she replied, her voice conveying concern. "Are you with Pierre?"

"I'm having a very interesting meeting at Pierre's office with him and Clint," he replied. "I'll call you if we run late."

Josh pocketed his phone, leaving the line open. "What were you saying about Roger?" He hoped Julia got the hint and stayed on the line to listen.

"Perhaps we should continue this discussion when you're not distracted by dinner plans," said Pierre. He turned to Clint. "We can talk strategy in the morning. In the meantime, I'll deliver Josh back to his hotel."

Julia's sixth sense was on high alert after Josh's call. She had looked at the phone, noticed the line was still open, and heard the brief conversation that followed. Pierre was playing cat and mouse, she surmised, and Josh hadn't played his role properly. She left her end of the call open just in case the conversation continued in the car. She smiled in anticipation of learning what had transpired before Josh called her.

"I know that was Josh," said Carly who was checking email from her family, "but what did he say?"

"He'll meet us at seven at that bistro around the corner," said Julia. "Pierre must have said something about Roger before Josh called. He left the line open so I could listen but I didn't pick up anything useful." She checked her phone. "The call's been disconnected. We'll have to wait for Josh to fill in the blanks."

Julia's phone rang again. She recognized the number as belonging to the local police district station. "This is Dr. Fairchild."

"Good evening. This is Detective Durand. Is Mr. Larson with you? He's not answering his phone."

"No, sir. May I take a message?"

"I can tell you the results of the fingerprint testing if you wish, as I know who you are," the detective said.

Julia's pulse quickened and she motioned for Carly to get close to the phone to listen. "What can you tell me?"

"The briefcase had the fingerprints of at least three people —Pierre Dupont, Mademoiselle Francesca Caron, and an unidentified person. The thumb drive had the prints of only Mr. Roger Westover. We couldn't get anything definitive off the sticky tape."

"Does that mean that Mr. Larson is no longer under suspicion?" asked Julia.

"We have not been able to exclude him entirely yet. He may have purposely avoided leaving his prints while being in on this plan. Perhaps Ms. Caron will be able to help when… if…she regains consciousness."

"I spoke with her nurse earlier. She is apparently improving."

"We are monitoring her situation as well."

"Merci. Thank you," said Julia. "I will tell Mr. Larson that you called and share this information."

Julia shared the other half of the conversation with Carly, who said, "Wait till we tell Josh."

"He's not out of the woods yet, but all the evidence so far is circumstantial. We need to find the real murderer, or he'll need an excellent lawyer." Julia clasped her hands together and closed her eyes briefly. "This might be a good time to talk to Francesca's sister." She dialed the ICU number and asked for Lesli, who soon answered.

"Hello, Lesli. Thank you for taking the call. This is Julia Fairchild. I took cooking classes from your sister at the school. I'm so sorry that she is ill."

"Thank you. The nurse said you are a doctor?"

"Yes, I am. It's likely your sister was poisoned in a similar way as a partner of my friend Josh. His name was Roger Westover, and his wife found Francesca's name in his pants pocket. Do you know anything about a Roger?" Julia glanced at Carly as she crossed her fingers.

"Yes, a little." Lesli cleared her throat. "He was a lover, I guess you would say. Francesca said she broke it off with him because he got jealous about her other friends."

"Do you know when that happened?"

"She said it was the last time he was in Paris, about a month ago. He came regularly on business and would meet her at that café near her apartment."

Julia nodded for Carly's sake. "Café Hugo?"

"Yes. She worked there, so it was a convenient meeting place."

"Do you know if he tried to contact her again?"

"Not that she's mentioned. And she did usually let me know if he was going to be here—you know, so I wouldn't interrupt."

"Interesting," said Julia. "That means she might have been surprised to see him at the cocktail party. No wonder they were looking at each other so oddly."

"She certainly didn't mention to me that he would be coming," said Lesli.

"One more question. It seems they wrote letters back and forth. The police have her letters to Roger. But do you know where she might have kept his letter to her?"

"Letters?" Lesli broke into a trill of laughter. "My sister never wrote letters. She was famous for hating to write anything except recipe cards. She did everything by text, on her phone. There must have been some mistake."

"That's very helpful, Lesli. Thank you. Is Francesca awake yet? I forgot to ask the nurse."

"Not yet, but she's breathing on her own and fluttering her eyelids, so the doctors say she will be regaining consciousness soon."

"I certainly hope so. Is there anything I can do for you?"

"No, except to find out who did this to my sister."

"Of course. That's exactly what I'm trying to do. Ciao. Take care."

Julia shared Lesli's comments with Carly. "And look at this." She pulled up the photos she had taken at Francesca's apartment, of the recipe cards on the table and the letters in the briefcase. "The handwriting doesn't match at all."

"You mean—?"

"Right," said Julia. "Francesca didn't write those love

letters. They had to have been planted in the briefcase to make her look despondent over the end of the affair."

"So we now know for sure that Roger and Francesca had been having an affair," said Carly. "Who else knew that—other than Lesli, of course?"

Julia sat cross-legged on the chair. "Here's a possibility. What if Laura found out about Francesca and plotted to poison Roger?"

"What good would that do?" asked Carly. "She could have done that back home."

"Maybe she had someone who could help here and it would seem less likely that she was the guilty party that way."

"We don't know that she's the 'American' who bought those mushrooms."

"Right. We need to make a return visit there." Julia checked the time. "But it's too late today. Let's get ready to meet Josh for dinner instead."

21

WEDNESDAY EVENING

Julia and Carly walked to the bistro shortly before seven. Julia was thrilled to see that Josh was already there, his blue eyes shining and dimples showing with his smile, which she met with her own. Carly's loud, throat-clearing "harrumph" ended their exuberant reunion. Josh ordered a carafe of the red wine and a basket of fresh bread while Julia told him what she'd learned from Francesca's sister. Josh related the conversation with Pierre and Clint.

"Do you remember I told you that I'd heard that Roger and Pierre may have been having talks with a competitor of one of our clients?" said Josh.

Julia nodded assent. "Do you know who that is now?"

"Not yet," said Josh, "but I'm sure Clint is involved. I kept waiting for one of them to hint that Roger was bringing them 'something,' but neither of them went that far. Alain is the only one who has come right out and demanded it. But I got the impression that Pierre and Clint were trying to get me to say that I had found that 'something.' I wasn't about to reveal that we had found the thumb drive."

"What's next with those two?" asked Julia.

"They mentioned meeting tomorrow to talk strategy."

"That probably means finding a way to get you to admit that you have the thumb drive."

"And to get it away from me," Josh added. "So we are perfectly primed for me to say that I thought about it overnight and am ready to play ball—with the fake thumb drive, of course."

Carly nudged Julia. "Are you going to tell Josh about the call from Detective Durand?"

Josh arched an eyebrow. "There's news?"

"He said he'd tried calling you first, but trusted me to share the results with you," said Julia.

The waiter arrived with their wine and to take their dinner orders. Josh waited impatiently as the young man quickly took care of business. "Okay, go on."

"Do you want to guess whose fingerprints were on the briefcase?" Julia teased.

"Roger's?"

"Yes, of course, but also Pierre's," Julia said triumphantly. "I guess he 'forgot' that he'd handled it when Carly and I asked him about it a few days ago and he said he'd never seen it."

"Interesting," said Josh. "What else did you learn?"

"They also found Francesca's prints and an unidentified person's."

"Hmm," said Josh. "Of course, since we found it at Francesca's apartment, her prints make sense. More so than Pierre's."

"The thumb drive had Roger's prints on it but not yours, thanks to your using a tissue when you handled it," said Julia. "Nothing on the tape."

Josh let out a big sigh. "I am so glad they didn't find anything else that ties me to this mess."

"The detective admitted that they don't have conclusive evidence, but that you're not totally off the hook." Julia met

Josh's eyes. "They still believe you could have been complicit with Roger's plan, even without your prints being present."

Josh's face fell.

"So we still need to find the person who poisoned Roger and Francesca."

"Right," said Josh. "Now what, Detective Fairchild?"

"You'll have to go ahead with the sting and catch the bad guys who want that thumb drive. Has it occurred to you that Roger may have been planting the thumb drive in your bathroom to implicate you? Maybe even blackmail you?"

"The person or persons also could get away with a murder," Carly added.

Josh exhaled slowly. "It crossed my mind that Pierre and Clint might try extortion if I don't make some offer to them."

"Exactly," said Julia. "Now that we know that only Roger handled the drive, we can assume the potential bad guys don't know what it actually looks like. You can easily pass off the dummy we bought earlier as the real thing, once you load it with the 'fake' software from Alpha Gamma."

Josh nodded. "We'll have to confirm with Detective Durand that we'll go for an old-fashioned 'sting' and arrange to meet Pierre or whomever with the thumb drive. After a proper exchange of money, of course."

Carly grinned. "They might give us fake money for the fake thumb drive."

"They won't know it's fake until they try to use it," said Julia.

"Right," said Josh. "But they won't get to try the dummy at all if this goes well."

"I'll bet that's why Roger's briefcase was taken when they trashed his room," said Julia. "They expected to find the thumb drive."

"And when they didn't get their hands on it," added Carly,

"they had to go to Plan B." She sat back in her chair, arms crossed. "What about those letters?" She spoke to Josh. "Turns out Francesca probably didn't write them."

"Likely planted to make Francesca look guilty," said Julia. "We'll have to ask Durand to have the letters checked for prints as well. They were probably all written by the same person at the same time."

"But why?" asked Josh.

"I suspect the timing of Roger's death was unintended," said Julia. "The mushrooms normally don't cause death right way. It doesn't make sense to kill him off before the bad guys got what they wanted. Something went wrong with the master plan."

"What's that old adage about 'best-laid plans of mice and men' going wrong?" Josh asked.

Julia smiled. "Notice it doesn't mention women's plans." She held her hands in front of her face as Josh pretended to throw a hunk of bread at her.

"Unfortunately, when Roger collapsed, they had to figure out something different. That's probably why Francesca had to be eliminated," said Julia. "She had to have known something about the mushrooms and couldn't be trusted to keep her mouth shut. Plus it served as a backup plan. If the murderer couldn't hang Roger's death on you, Josh, they could make it seem that Francesca poisoned him, and then poisoned herself. Luckily, it seems that Plan B has backfired as well. The nurse at the hospital said that Francesca is likely to wake up soon."

A moment of silence hung in the air. Josh said solemnly, "Let's finish our dinner and give our friendly police a call."

Wednesday after dinner

Back at the Marriott, Julia placed a call to the police while Carly helped Josh with the uploading of data to the dummy drive.

"The police will be ready anytime we can set this up, Josh," said Julia. "Detective Durand suggested meeting at one of the kiosks in front of the Eiffel Tower. He will have plenty of men stationed to keep eyes on the transaction. He said a sting would be safer with pedestrians around."

"I'm expecting to hear from Pierre in the morning," said Josh. "I'll admit that I've had the thumb drive all along and offer it to him for a price. I'll tell him that we learned tonight that the police have decided to call pin Roger's death on Francesca as a murder-suicide, so I am now free of suspicion and can proceed with the deal."

"Great," said Julia. "Good thinking. How much will you ask for?"

"A million euros doesn't sound like enough for this sophisticated software," said Carly.

"I heartily agree," said Josh. "This is worth millions and millions of euros in the business world. But I don't want to be greedy. Let's say a good price would be ten million euros."

Julia pursed her lips. "They'll probably counter with a smaller number, or they may say something about Roger's price being less than that."

"But we don't know what Roger was asking," said Josh.

"It doesn't really matter," said Julia. "Negotiating the price will be part of the sting."

Josh accompanied Julia and Carly in the limo back to their hotel. After Josh and Vincent had driven away, Julia and Carly sat in the lobby, both feeling glum.

"Will Josh be able to play his part on the phone with Pierre tomorrow?" asked Carly. "I know lawyers learn how to debate cases in their training, but I'm not sure about acting."

"He'll do fine," said Julia. "He wants to be out from

under suspicion. I'm worried about the transaction itself. There's a lot of money involved. And Pierre could be suspicious about Josh having 'suddenly' decided to go for the deal."

"If the software is as valuable as Josh says it is, Pierre should be happy just to get it in his hands," said Carly. "He'll have to know that Josh could have continued to deny its existence and go back to D.C. instead of trading it for the payoff."

"My hope is that Pierre is greedy enough to fall for the trade and not realize that Josh may be working with the law," said Julia. "It's not over till tomorrow."

Thursday morning

Julia didn't sleep well. While it was unlikely that someone would break into their room at night, searching for the thumb drive to avoid paying off Josh, Julia's senses were on full alert. The April morning sun streamed into the room before she was ready to bounce out of bed, but at least she had finally slept a few hours from pure exhaustion.

Julia and Carly decided to ditch anything that labeled them as tourists, preferring to blend in with the locals as much as possible.

"I'll be glad when this sting thing is all over," said Carly.

"Me too," said Julia. "Maybe we'll still have a little time to enjoy Paris. But Josh isn't totally safe as long as he has even the dummy in his possession."

Josh had slept fitfully and needed a double espresso to get started that morning. He frowned at his phone when it buzzed and saw Laura's name on the screen. *Why would she be calling me?*

"Hey, Laura," he said. "What's going on?"

"I wanted to call to thank you for all you did for Roger and me last week."

"No problem," said Josh. "Roger was my partner, and I was happy to do what little I could."

"It was nice to have someone there that I knew," Laura purred. "I can't imagine having to go through that routine in a foreign country without a familiar face around."

"Glad to help," Josh said. "What are you doing now?"

"I'm getting ready to join my sister's family in Cape Cod for a few days. My niece is getting married next week, so I'll be able to see the rest of the clan for a happy occasion. That will be nice after having the funeral last weekend."

"I'm sorry I couldn't be there," said Josh. "I didn't realize you had family on Cape Cod."

"I grew up near Boston. My mother's father has had property on the Cape as long as the Kennedys have," she said proudly.

"Why are you up so early? It's, what four o'clock in the morning there?"

"Oh, um, I'm flying out at six a.m. I'm on my way to the airport."

"Well, I'm glad you have a joyous event to look forward to. Take care now." Josh hung up, puzzled by her call. He and Roger hadn't had a social relationship, beyond the office and the rare beer at a local pub when one of the guys announced a deal closing or other momentous event. He shook his head and returned to reading a briefing on behalf of a client interested in investing in real estate in southern France.

Two more double espressos later, at almost ten a.m., he finally got a call from Pierre.

"Have you thought anymore about the investment opportunity I mentioned yesterday?" Pierre asked right away.

"Some, but what you've said is too vague for me to be able to make a decision." Josh wished he had a way to record the call. He grabbed a pen and paper to take notes.

"Let me give it to you straight," said Pierre. "Roger had some software for sale. He stood to make a ton of money by investing in this side venture with Alain, Clint, and others. All he had to provide was the software, for which he would be paid a substantial down payment, plus royalties later."

"Roger? Mr. Straight Arrow?" Josh laid it on thick. "No way would he do that."

"It seems his wife had a gambling problem, and the bad guys were knocking on his door for payment."

"Laura said he was talking with some banks to help him with a money issue, but I can't believe he would do something like you're suggesting."

"Laura still has the money issue, and Roger's gone," said Pierre. "This would help her out."

"What do you want from me?" asked Josh.

"Roger had the software on a thumb drive. It wasn't in his briefcase, and we couldn't find it anywhere in his room."

"*You* trashed his room?" said Josh.

"Not me. I didn't want my fingerprints in there," said Pierre, sneering. "Perhaps you and your girlfriend found it."

"What did you say this was worth to you and your investors?" asked Josh.

"A lot more than the five million we were going to pay Roger," said Pierre.

"So if I were to find this elusive device, you're willing to pay me and leave it at that? Everyone walks away and nobody says anything?"

"That's the deal," said Pierre, "although I hope Laura gets a big piece of it. Roger was doing it for her, you know."

"Understood. Let me get back to you."

Josh called Julia immediately and gave her Pierre's story. "You'd have been proud of me, Julia. I didn't let on that I knew about the device, much less that we found it."

"How are you going to convince him that you're ready to play ball?" asked Julia.

"I'll tell him what we decided last night—that now that the police have cleared me of Roger's murder and are ready to blame Francesca, I feel I can safely proceed with the deal, and I've had the thumb drive all along."

"Perfect," said Julia. "Go ahead and set up a time and place with Pierre, and then we can notify Detective Durand. And while you are at it, let's remind him to dust the letters in Roger's briefcase for prints. I'll be they won't find Francesca's. But maybe they will find they match the third person who handled the briefcase—the one they haven't identified yet."

22

THURSDAY EARLY AFTERNOON

Julia and Carly mingled with the usual afternoon crowd that milled about the grounds in front of the Eiffel Tower. Julia noticed young couples holding hands as they strolled through the landscaped park. She saw small families with one of the parents, usually the mom, pushing a stroller, enjoying the sun and fresh air. Teenagers in groups of three and four chatted loudly as they talked about whatever teens talk about amongst themselves. She watched the jovial crowd check out the miniature Eiffel towers, French flags, berets, and all sorts of cheap jewelry available to purchase in the souvenir shops.

Her heart raced as she thought of the possibilities of the transfer between Josh and Pierre going south. She hoped that she was well-enough disguised with her straw hat and sunglasses to avoid detection by Pierre. She felt somewhat reassured by the presence of one of the undercover cops who waited within fifteen feet of her. Standing some thirty feet away, closer to the shops, Carly wore a floppy black straw hat and retro-style white-framed sunglasses. She had borrowed an outfit from Simone that completely changed her look. Even Josh hadn't recognized her at first glance when they had reconnoitered at the sisters' hotel earlier. He had told her that the detective would be unhappy if he found out she and Carly were planning to lurk in the crowd. Julia wasn't about to be deterred.

She turned to look at Josh, standing about fifty feet away. He leaned casually against the corner of a kiosk, looking every bit the bored boyfriend waiting for his girlfriend to appear. Every now and then he glanced at his watch, then scanned the shops and shook his head.

Bells chimed the hour from a church somewhere nearby. The din of the crowd seemed to soften momentarily as they listened to the bells ring once, twice, three times. Pierre was to meet Josh at ten past the hour, which seemed like an eternity of waiting.

Julia had turned to look in Josh's direction one more time when she felt an arm around her waist. She jumped and felt her heart stop when she turned to see Pierre.

"Walk with me, Julia, and don't try anything smart," he whispered gruffly as he pushed her forward. "We're going to surprise your boyfriend."

Julia walked as slowly as possible while her brain raced to come up with a plan.

Josh clenched his jaw and narrowed his eyes when Pierre and Julia stood in front of him. "This isn't part of the plan, Pierre. You can let her go."

"She's my insurance policy," Pierre said with a smirk. "Not that I shouldn't trust you, but I don't trust you."

"I've got the thumb drive, Pierre," said Josh. "I don't want the money. I'll trade it for Julia."

Carly had noticed Julia walking with Pierre and sidled closer to the undercover policeman standing a few feet away. He talked quietly into his shoulder mic when he saw what was happening.

"She comes with me," said Pierre. "I'll release her after

I've checked the software. In case you've tried something funny."

"It's all good, Pierre. Let her go."

"Not so fast, Josh. I'll take the thumb drive and you can walk away." Pierre pulled Julia a little more tightly to his side.

"You know I can't do that," Josh replied.

"Oh, I believe you can," said Pierre. "Or Clint is ready to put a bullet in Julia's chest." He glanced to his right, where Clint stood with his right hand hidden under his jacket.

Josh stared at Clint, who smirked and shrugged a shoulder. Josh handed the thumb drive to Pierre, making sure it was visible in the window of the envelope. "You're not going to get away with it, you know."

Pierre pocketed the small package and moved toward the street, pushing Julia ahead of him. Clint followed, keeping an eye on Josh as he stepped in behind Pierre.

Julia's thoughts went wild as she considered various ways to escape, discarding them as quickly as they came to mind. Clint's gun was a strong deterrent. She was unable to see if anyone was following them. As they approached the street, she saw Pierre's black Audi idling at the curb with Laura at the wheel. Clint went to the far side of the car behind Laura, while Pierre reached for the rear passenger door.

Once Pierre pulled the door open enough and started to push Julia into the car, she stomped on his foot with the heel of her shoe, whirled around, and brought her clenched fist up under his chin. Pierre yelled at Clint to shoot, but he was unable to get a good shot at Julia from inside the car as she was swallowed up by the crowd.

Pierre jumped into the car, and Laura sped off. Julia ran as fast as she could, grateful for her regular walking routine and gym sessions at the YMCA. She collapsed into Josh's arms when he met her about halfway back to the kiosk.

"The police are already on the chase," said Josh. "They won't get far. I am thankful you're not hurt."

"I'm not sure how good a shot Clint is, but I wasn't going to stop running until I was far enough away from the car," Julia said, trembling, thankful that Josh was holding her up. "I didn't think he would shoot into a crowd. Laura was driving the getaway car, in case you didn't see the driver."

"So much for the grieving widow," said Josh.

"Let's go back and get Carly," said Julia. "She's probably frantic if she didn't see that I got away."

Carly was waving her arms and sobbing when she spotted Julia and Josh walking toward the kiosk. After a long hug she asked, "What happened? How did you get away?"

"I remembered a couple of defensive maneuvers from the class I had to take at work; they arranged it for the whole staff at the hospital," said Julia. "I'll be able to report back that the training worked fine." She grinned and pumped her biceps.

"For which I'm very glad," said Carly. "Now what?"

Josh said, "Let's go back and talk to the police. I don't care about the thumb drive, of course, but there's still a charge of attempted extortion."

"And murder," added Julia.

∽

BACK AT THE Marriott a few hours later, Julia, Josh, and Carly put their heads together over a carafe of pinot grigio, accompanied by a platter of buttery crackers with brie cheese and fresh grapes.

"Our sting didn't turn out like it does in the movies," said Carly, "but nobody got shot or killed."

"Cheers to that," said Josh. "Unfortunately, the police told me they lost sight of the car in the heavy traffic. They'll be watching for it all over the city. They've alerted the British police as well in case they decide to head for England and drive through the Chunnel."

Julia clapped her hands. "I just remembered. Carly, did you happen to see Kate? She was standing near the souvenir stand with the flags lined up at the top."

"No, I missed her," said Carly. "What would she have been doing there?"

"Who is Kate?" Josh asked. "Have I met her?"

"No," said Julia. "Kate and Becca were the other two Americans in the cooking class. It seems quite a coincidence that Kate would be hanging out here—and by herself."

"Yeah," said Carly. "They both should have been heading back to Cape Cod by now, wouldn't they?"

Josh looked up. "Cape Cod? As in Massachusetts?"

"Uh huh," said Carly. "Kate's dad owns a restaurant there that Becca wants to jazz up with some French dishes."

"And to beef up their catering business," Julia added. "Why?"

"This may be another of those coincidences," said Josh, "but Laura called me this morning and mentioned that she would be going to Cape Cod for a family wedding. I thought she was calling from the States."

Julia's eyes widened and her pulse increased. "Do you suppose Laura knows Kate and Becca?"

"Somehow, I wouldn't be surprised," said Josh, "although Cape Cod is a large area."

Julia sipped her wine and was quiet for a moment, deep in thought. "What if Kate and Becca and Laura were all here at the same time on purpose? Maybe Laura planned for Roger to die right after he sold the thumb drive to Pierre, but things got screwed up when he crashed in Josh's bathroom."

Josh nodded. "And when they didn't find it in his room, she had to come up with a different plan."

"I wonder if he had a change of heart," said Julia, "and

decided to hide the unit in Josh's room instead of selling it." She looked at Josh. "You said he was Mr. Straight Arrow and wouldn't have done something like this."

Josh nodded. "I'm guessing he had planned to make the transfer the afternoon of the party, because that was the last meeting scheduled for this group. He must have gotten waylaid in the process. Or changed his mind, and that's why he was in my bathroom." He paused. "If that's true, how do those poison mushrooms that were found in his stomach at autopsy fit in?"

"Let's say that Roger was supposed to have exchanged the thumb drive for the money right after the party. Laura would have assumed that had happened. She arranged for Kate or Becca to deliver a tray of special mushrooms—maybe she called them truffles—to Roger in his room. And he was supposed to get very sick but not die right away. That mushroom causes liver failure if you eat enough but doesn't cause people to die right away."

"What makes you think it was Kate or Becca?" asked Josh.

"Bella, the housekeeper, mentioned that Roger seemed to know his visitor. It wouldn't have been Laura, based on what Bella reported, but if Kate or Becca is a friend of Laura's, he may have been surprised to see her, but would have known her," said Julia. "And she mentioned the perfume in the room, so that fits our theory that it was a woman."

"It still doesn't make sense to me. If it wasn't those mushrooms, then what else made him so sick, Julia?" asked Carly.

"The antihistamine he took for allergies could have reacted with his antidepressant at about the time he was hiding the thumb drive in Josh's room. It would have caught him unaware. The mushrooms probably didn't cause the immediate reaction that we saw."

"Is that what caused him to die?" asked Carly.

"Not right away, but in his impaired state, the poison may have been what tipped him over the edge," said Julia. "Or Alain may have been doing something when he was in Roger's hospital room."

Josh waved his hand. "Explain, please, so I can understand what you're talking about."

"Sorry," said Julia. "My doctor brain doesn't always remember that normal people use a different vocabulary." She took another swallow of her wine, then launched into the explanation.

"Roger was taking an antidepressant that can interact with other medications as well as certain foods. I remember Laura mentioned that he was on doxepin, which is in that specific chemical class. The autopsy showed he had taken Benadryl, perhaps for the spring pollen in the air here. That combination can cause a condition called anticholinergic syndrome, where the body's nervous system is revved up. The heart races, temperature goes very high, the victim gets confused and can die. Like what happened to Roger."

"Can't it be treated?" asked Josh.

"Yes," said Julia, "but the physician would have to include that possibility in the differential diagnosis and start the antidote right away. It's not a common situation, although I've seen a couple of cases of it myself. In Roger's case, the physicians had no idea he was on the antidepressant and wouldn't have known that he had taken an antihistamine. When they first brought him in, they didn't even know about the mushrooms. A recipe for disaster."

"Or, more accurately," said Carly, "a *prescription* for disaster."

"What did you mean about Alain maybe doing something in Roger's room?" asked Josh.

"Do you remember that I found some eyedrops in Francesca's apartment?" said Julia.

Josh and Carly nodded in reply.

"Here's a possibility: Francesca or Alain may have had some background in pharmacy or chemistry. The eyedrops were a medication called homatropine, which is used for various conditions. It is also one of the drugs that can interact with Roger's antidepressant and cause that severe reaction."

"Are you thinking that because Roger didn't die right away, they decided to help him along?" asked Carly.

"Something like that," said Julia. "Simone said she saw Alain go into Roger's room. It would only have taken a moment for him to squeeze some eyedrops into his eyes without the nurse noticing."

Josh rested his chin in his hand. "Sounds plausible. Now how do we prove it?"

Carly added, "And how do we work Francesca's poisoning into all of this?"

23

THURSDAY EVENING

Still later that evening after the failed sting, Julia, Carly, and Josh met at what they now called "Josh's favorite" bistro. Bolstered by the appetizers they had enjoyed at the Marriott, they opted for a light dinner of mini-quiches and salad, and another carafe of wine. Then, as the sun's final rays melted into the darkening sky, they relaxed over a dessert of juicy nectarines with rich vanilla ice cream.

"Okay, Miss Amateur Detective," said Josh, "how do you propose we go about identifying Francesca's poisoner? I know you're not going to give this up until you've figured it out, so I've decided I may as well go on playing Watson to your Sherlock Holmes." He held up his wine in mock salute. "Not to mention that I haven't been fully exonerated yet."

"Thank you, Josh," said Julia, holding up her own glass.

"Here come our assignments," Carly announced, turning to Josh.

Julia tossed her brunette bob out of her eyes, happy with their willingness to continue the search. "With our newfound knowledge that Laura has family in Cape Cod and may well know Kate or Becca, we should put some pressure on them."

"How?" asked Carly. "We don't even know where they're staying."

"I keep going back to the little man at the mystic shop. He mentioned that an American woman had come in and asked questions about the poisonous mushrooms."

"Do you suppose he would recognize a photo?" asked Josh.

"Probably," said Julia. "Except we don't have any of Laura or Kate or Becca."

"Too bad we didn't take a group photo of us at Le Cordon Bleu," said Carly. "That would have helped."

"True, but I have another idea that might work." Julia grinned devilishly. "What if we can lure them to the shop somehow and see if the shop owner will identify the woman for us?"

"And how are you going to accomplish that?" asked Josh.

"I thought maybe we could offer a prize that she won as a customer and has to pick it up at a certain time," said Julia.

"I wouldn't bite on that one, sis. Try something else." Carly licked her spoon, enjoying every last dollop of her ice cream.

"What about finding a way to get the shop owner to wherever Laura is?" Josh suggested. "He could tell us if she was the woman. If it wasn't Laura, it would have had to be Kate or Becca." He leaned back, looking pleased with himself for the idea.

"That would be asking too much of the shopkeeper," said Julia, shaking her head. "There's got to be a way to do this." She rested her head on her hands as if they could transmit more ideas into her brain.

"I love the cheese here," said Carly. "I wish we could take a supply of it home with us."

"It tastes better knowing you're in Paris," said Josh. "Trust me on that."

"I could take cookies home instead," she countered. "I bet they would taste delicious no matter where I ate them."

Julia interrupted the bantering with a sudden hand slap on the tabletop. "What if we asked the police to have Laura come in one more time for a final sign-off, or some such, and they take her photo for the official file, and then we can take it to the shop owner to review?"

"I don't want to tell the police what to do," said Josh. "This is *their* murder investigation, after all."

"Hmm. It would certainly be helpful if one of us had a photo of her," said Julia. She thought for a moment, then asked, "Josh, do you suppose there's a photo of her somewhere in your office files, like from a Christmas party or something?"

"There's probably one on Roger's desk. His secretary could scan it and send it to me." Josh checked his watch for the time and calculated the time difference from Paris. "Sharon won't be in the office for another six hours or so. But your question triggered something." He grinned like a bingo winner. "I have several photos that were taken at a function a few weeks ago in D.C. It was a big deal because Roger got an award for signing the biggest contract with a new client the previous quarter. Laura was there for the dinner. She was all dolled up and happy to pose for the camera. I know I have one in here." He scrolled through his photo gallery until he found what he was looking for. "Voila!" He showed the image to Julia and Carly. Laura wore a beautiful cranberry-red sleeveless dress that complimented her significant cleavage. Her jewelry was elegant and looked expensive enough to insure separately.

Josh asked, "Should we go to the Crystal Palace first or to the police with this?"

"I say we should confirm the photo with the shop owner first, because if Laura isn't the woman he saw, we would

214

have to eat some crow at the police station." Julia scrunched up her face. "I don't want to have to do that. And if it wasn't her, we can describe Kate and Becca."

"Let me call Vincent, and we'll go now to check it out. Ready, ladies?"

"Whoa, Watson," said Carly. "Do I have to point out that the mushroom shop would be closed by now?"

"You're right," said Josh. "I got carried away for a moment. We'll plan a visit in the morning. For now, let's finish this wine and I'll escort you lovely ladies home."

∽

Friday morning

Julia and Carly chatted about the flowers in bloom along the route back to the Marais neighborhood. Window boxes spilling with impatiens, calibrachoa, dianthus, and petunias adorned many of the windows of the small houses. Spring-blooming roses and azaleas dotted the yards, which tended to be smaller than in Julia's own town, but were well tended. Parisians obviously enjoyed beautifying their surroundings with the colorful landscaping. Julia found herself making mental notes to reconsider growing roses. She hadn't had great success with them in the past.

The trio entered the Crystal Palace shortly after it opened at 9:30 a.m. Julia had a moment of panic when she realized that there might be more than one person who worked in the store, and the shopkeeper they'd spoken with last time might not be there. She unconsciously held her breath until the familiar short man emerged smiling from the back room.

"More mushrooms?" he asked.

Julia breathed more normally, replying, "No, monsieur, not this time." She held up Josh's phone with Laura's picture. "Do you remember seeing this woman? You mentioned that another American woman had been here a few days before us, who also bought mushrooms. Is this the one you saw?"

The proprietor squinted as he leaned in closer to examine the photo. "She is beautiful," he said, turning to Julia. "Oui. Yes. That is the woman I saw. Is she a friend of yours?"

Julia, Carly, and Josh looked at each other with thin smiles on their faces. "We know her, yes," Julia replied.

"She came twice, actually."

"To buy more mushrooms?" asked Julia.

"No, mademoiselle. She wanted to buy foxglove."

"Foxglove? As in digitalis?" asked Julia.

"Oui. That's what you call it in America."

∼

DETECTIVE DURAND LISTENED ATTENTIVELY to Julia's narration of how she believed Roger had been murdered. She explained that he might have died accidentally from the combination of the antidepressant and the antihistamine, but when the poisonous mushrooms had been added to the mix, it became lethal. She also told him how digitalis could have been added to coffee or tea without Francesca's knowledge. Or added to stuffed mushrooms. "She'll be able to tell us as soon as she is fully conscious."

When Julia was finished, he said, "Thank you. I will ask the hospital about a toxicology screen on Ms. Caron. Do you happen to know where Mrs. Westover is at this time? We have not seen her or Mr. Dupont since the episode yesterday at the Eiffel Tower."

"We also saw Kate there, who we met at Le Cordon Bleu. And don't forget about Clint Blackman. He was there too."

"As were you, Miss Fairchild." The detective glowered. "You could have been shot, or gotten an innocent bystander shot."

"I know; I am truly sorry," said Julia.

Durand raised an eyebrow, clearly dubious. "We have been monitoring the airport as well as the highways," he told her. "Does Mrs. Westover have other friends here?"

"Besides Pierre? Possibly Kate and Becca," Julia replied.

Josh said, "If I were Laura, I would be headed out of Paris as soon as possible. She could have used an assumed name, I suppose. Although that would be tricky with passports and all."

"The railway system would be easier to use to get away," said Julia. "What about that?"

The detective got up from his desk. "Wait here, please, while I have someone make some calls."

When he was out of earshot, Julia said, "Maybe he'll let us go with them to the airport, if that's where she is."

Josh said, "I hardly think so. The police probably don't want innocent civilians in the way of their work." He cocked his head toward Julia. "He was pretty upset that you were there yesterday."

"I know. I apologized several times already," said Julia.

"Laura's probably still with Pierre," said Carly. "Gloating over getting the thumb drive."

"What will happen when they try it, Josh?" asked Julia. "Will it be obvious that it's a fake?"

Josh shook his head. "Not right away. The IT tech at Alpha Gamma Security said it would look and work as an authentic program until they try to execute certain commands. Pierre isn't likely to get that far into it. He's probably going to pass it off to someone who would know how to use the material. That's when they'll discover it's a dummy."

"And by that time, the police will have Laura, and maybe Pierre and Clint, in custody," said Julia. "We hope."

Detective Durand returned after a few minutes and sat on the corner of his desk. "Mrs. Westover is scheduled to fly out of Charles De Gaulle Airport this afternoon at one-forty p.m. If Mr. Larson will be so kind as to forward that photo to me, we will be able to identify her more easily." He handed his business card with an email address on it to Josh.

"Yes, of course," said Josh, quickly entering the information to share the photo.

"Miss Fairchild," he continued, "I know how much you would like to witness Mrs. Westover being taken into custody. While I can't allow you to be present for that, I can have you come to the station tomorrow morning at eight. We will be ready to press charges at that time. I will give you special permission to be in the gallery when my officers are taking her statement."

"Thank you, detective," said Julia. "I can do that."

The threesome left the station and convened outside near the limo. "I want to see Laura's face when the police approach her," said Julia.

"The detective said we couldn't be there," said Carly. "I hope you're not planning to do anything you'll regret."

"Who? Me?" Julia teased.

"Laura could be at the airport already," said Josh, checking his watch. "She'll be killing time until her flight. She's probably already cleared security as well."

Julia nodded. "Yes, if she's like most of us; but she could be one of those people who show up at the last minute, like one of my friends back home."

"What are you suggesting, Josh?" asked Carly. "That we should go to the airport and hang out and hope to see her?"

"I guess not," he said. "We can't take the risk of tipping her off and spoiling the whole police plan."

"I'm stuck at the fact that we still don't know how Kate and Becca fit into this," said Julia. "I wonder if it would hurt to call Kate and ask about that platter of mushrooms that got delivered to Roger."

"What if she gets suspicious and calls Laura right away?" asked Carly.

"If we wait till Laura's scheduled flight time, we should be safe."

"What if Laura doesn't get arrested? What if something goes wrong at the airport?" asked Josh. "She could have made a reservation for a flight she doesn't take."

"Have faith," said Julia. "The bad guys get caught sooner or later. All we can do is wait for the police to make their move."

24

SATURDAY MORNING

Julia's alarm pierced the air, startling her awake after a fitful night. She jumped out of bed, showered quickly, and got dressed, all the while anticipating the showdown at the police station.

"How about I go down to the lobby and grab a couple of coffees and pastries while you get ready?" Julia asked as Carly dragged herself out of bed. "Josh said he would be here no later than seven-fifteen, and it's already six forty-five."

"Sure. I'll need a big cup of coffee. Thanks."

Julia almost skipped down the hallway and on to the reception area, where the coffee urn and pastries sat on a side table. She breathed in the wonderful aroma of freshly brewed coffee and reached for two mugs. She felt a heavy hand on her arm and turned. "Pierre. What are you doing here?"

He gripped her arm firmly and pulled her into his side. "We're going for a little drive. You and me," he whispered. "You've caused me enough grief for a while."

Julia looked around but didn't see the desk clerk. She opened her mouth to scream but Pierre covered it with his large hand. She tried to hold her ground, but she was no match for Pierre's size and strength. He was built like a pro football player, and she was more like a long-distance runner. He pushed her in front of him to his Audi, which was idling at the curb with Kate standing at the open door of the back seat. He shoved her roughly into the car. Kate jumped in next to her and quickly bound Julia's wrists together behind her back, securing them with plastic zip ties. As Pierre sped away from the curb, Kate pushed Julia's head down and tied a cloth blindfold over her eyes.

Julia wriggled her wrists but was unable to get any leverage to loosen them. She could barely see a glimmer of light at the bottom edge of the blindfold. "I don't suppose you're going to tell me where we're going," she said, more confidently than she felt.

"You guessed right on that, Julia," said Pierre. "There's a tourist attraction in Paris that most people don't put on their top ten list. I happen to believe it's a must-see." He laughed maliciously. "Don't you agree, Kate?"

"Yes, unless you have claustrophobia," she replied.

Julia tried to recall the "top ten tourist attractions" in Paris from her guide but couldn't remember more than eight. Pierre had to be referring to something more obscure than the usual hot spots. "How do you know I haven't been there already? Carly and I have been seeing a lot of Paris while Josh has been busy."

"I'm sure you didn't go there," Pierre said. "Josh would have mentioned it."

"Only if we remembered to tell him," said Julia. "I didn't tell him everything."

Pierre laughed again. "In my experience women blab about everything they do, sooner or later."

They drove for about fifteen minutes, stopping for traffic signals now and then. Kate whispered to Pierre a couple of times, but Julia couldn't make out what she was saying. She sensed the car slowing down as it went around a corner, then came to a stop. One of her captors—she guessed it was Kate, judging by the whiff she got of her perfume—opened the right-side back door and pulled on her arm. She felt the blindfold slide a little way down the back of her head, allowing her to glimpse buildings in what appeared to be an older part of town. They looked like old warehouses with spray-painted graffiti on the walls. She didn't see or hear any sign of pedestrian traffic.

"Where are we?" she asked, more afraid and wary. *How will Josh and Carly find me?* She dearly wished she'd taken her phone with her to the lobby, although Pierre would probably have confiscated it anyway.

Kate readjusted the blindfold, then took one arm while Pierre grabbed the other. They walked her down what Julia assumed was a sidewalk and stopped after a short distance. Julia heard the sound of metal jangling, then the loud screeching of a door being opened. It creaked noisily, as if complaining about being disturbed. Pierre pulled her into a space that was much darker than inside the car or on the sidewalk. She heard the telltale switch of a flashlight and could sense its beam through her blindfold.

Kate pushed her forward from behind, and Pierre gripped her arm. The three of them moved slowly along in darkness. Then Julia felt herself being half-dragged down a long flight of stairs to a lower level. Shivering in the cool, damp air, she wished she was wearing a jacket.

They walked for about ten minutes, Julia noting numerous twists and turns along the route before they finally stopped. "Welcome to the catacombs of Paris," Pierre said wickedly. "Normally tourists come here with a guide to lead them in and out. This is a one-way trip for you, unless Josh gives me the original thumb drive. My IT specialist tested the first one he gave me and found it to be fake. You'd better hope he loves you. Or you will have to find your own way out."

Julia shivered in her lightweight clothing. She wasn't about to tell him that the police had the thumb drive, or Pierre would surely kill her then and there.

"Kate," said Julia. "Are you going to be part of this murderous plot and leave me here to die?"

"You're the detective, Julia," said Kate. "Show us how good you are at getting out of here. I'm so sorry I don't have any breadcrumbs with me. Not that you could see them in the dark anyway. You're on your own, I guess."

Pierre said to Kate, "It's time to meet up with Josh. Then we can make our way to the train, *cherie*. I know a lovely restaurant in Lyon where we can have lunch." He moved away, and Julia's surroundings became pitch black. She heard Pierre call, "Good-bye, Julia. And *bon chance!* Good luck!" Their laughter and footsteps faded quickly as they hurried down the passageway.

Julia rubbed her head against the rough stone, causing the bandana to slide down to her neck. She peered into the darkness to see which way Pierre and Kate had gone. She saw a whisper of light off to her left for a moment, but then it was black again, presumably after they went around one of the turns in the tunnel. She leaned forward into a crouched position and stepped backward through her bound hands, one leg at a time. She used her teeth on the zip tie lock, concentrating on the area closest to the slide itself. She made slow progress but finally was able to chew through the plastic and force the tie open.

Shaking her numb hands to get the feeling back, she walked in the same direction Pierre had gone, lightly gliding her hand along the cold wall to give her some guidance in the inky blackness. She took deep breaths and told herself to stay calm. She knew Josh and Carly were already looking for her. She said a silent prayer to St. Anthony, hoping her plea would work for lost people as well as when she misplaced her keys.

As she moved as quickly as she dared on the rough surface under her feet, she felt her step tracker buzz on her wrist, advising her that she had met her goal of 250 steps for the hour. She tried to recall how many steps she'd noticed the last time she had checked her watch. She could use that information as a rough estimate of how far she'd come into the tunnel. She guessed it had been around 1,000 steps when Pierre grabbed her in the lobby. She now had close to 4,000, which should mean that she was about 3,000 steps away from the entrance, minus the 250 she'd just walked.

She took another calming breath and kept moving. Every heartbeat and breath echoed in the silence. She felt a trickle of water under her fingers now and then as she moved her hand along the wall. She held back tears as she felt her way in the blackness, hoping that she would be one of the lucky ones to find her way out.

∽

Carly emerged from the shower, refreshed and finally fully awake. She called out to Julia. "Hey, sis. Where's my coffee?" Failing to hear a reply, she stepped out of the bathroom and checked the room. No Julia. "Hmm. Wonder what's taking her so long," she said aloud.

Ten minutes later Julia still hadn't shown her face, and it was nearly time to meet Josh. Carly grabbed her bag as well as Julia's tote to save an extra trip back to the room. Maybe Julia had to wait for the coffee to be made, she thought.

A few hotel guests stood around the coffee bar, but Julia wasn't one of them. Carly went to the desk clerk and asked, "Have you seen Ms. Fairchild? She came down about twenty minutes ago to get coffee and forgot to come back to the room."

He smiled cheerfully. "Yes, mademoiselle. She left with a

gentleman at least fifteen minutes ago. I saw her as she was getting into a car at the curb."

"Are you sure you know who I mean? She was supposed to come back and get me."

"Yes, I'm sure." He smiled thinly and turned his attention back to his computer.

Josh entered the lobby the moment that Carly pulled out her phone to call her sister. He looked around and asked, "Where's Julia?"

Carly said, "I was hoping she was with you."

"Me? Why? Am I late?" He checked his watch.

"The desk clerk said she was here—she was supposed to be getting our coffee—and left with a gentleman. I assumed it was you."

Josh shook his head. "Not me, and probably not a gentleman either." He went to question the desk clerk.

"I can't be certain, but it sounds as if she was taken again by Pierre Dupont," he said on his return. "There was a woman by the car with him as well."

Carly's eyes brimmed with tears. "I'll call her." Julia's phone began ringing from inside the tote. Carly gasped and gripped Josh's arm. "She doesn't even have her phone. We need to call the police."

∽

DETECTIVE DURAND AROSE from his industrial-style chair when he saw Josh and Carly at the counter. "I've put out an APB for Pierre Dupont's car. You may wait in my office until we hear something. I will hold off on questioning Mrs. Westover for the time being. We detained her at the airport, as expected."

The clerk brought a couple of coffees with the obligatory powdered creamer and sugar. Carly dutifully stirred the dry powder into her coffee after blowing her nose again with a wad of tissues.

"If Laura is here, who was the woman with Pierre?" Carly asked.

Josh's phone rang before he could venture a reply. He showed the detective Pierre's number on the screen before answering. "Where is Julia?" he demanded.

Pierre sneered. "I can tell you where to find her after you give me the *real* thumb drive. Where would you like to meet?"

"Same place as last time. I can be there in about twenty minutes." Josh looked at the detective, who nodded his affirmation of the plan. "Can you do that?"

"Of course. You bring the thumb drive. I'll take care of Julia."

~

JULIA MOVED STEADILY but carefully along the chilly tunnel. The floor was uneven and invited a fall if she stumbled. She felt colder than she'd ever felt skiing and longed for a warm down jacket. She came to a place where the path turned sharply to the right. She took a couple of steps toward where she thought the opposite wall would be. Running her hand along the wall in the dark, she discovered that the tunnel split into two directions. She fought back tears as she willed herself to intuit which route would lead her out. She didn't want to be found as a pile of bones years later.

She jumped when she felt the Fitbit vibrate on her wrist with a message that she'd reached her daily goal of active minutes. Her breath caught as an idea came to her: *I wonder if I can use Strava to get me out of here*. She'd tried to use the fitness app before, because it was so popular with runners and cyclists, but she'd had trouble synchronizing it to her cellphone. She paused and scrolled through the apps until she found Strava. When she pressed the icon, a message popped up to remind her to sync it to the mobile app on her phone. She sighed, crossed her fingers, and followed the tunnel that veered to the right.

~

JOSH WAITED in front of the kiosk with his hands in his pockets. Undercover cops mingled in the noisy crowd on the grounds of the Eiffel Tower. Pierre strolled up from the sidewalk, whistling a tune that Josh didn't recognize. Over Pierre's shoulder Josh saw one of the policemen approach Pierre's gleaming Audi, where a woman sat at the wheel, engine running. Pierre joined Josh and held out his hand.

"I don't see Julia."

Pierre sneered. "I'll take the thumb drive."

"Where's Julia?"

"Give me the thumb drive first; then I'll tell you."

Josh pulled his empty hands out of his pockets. "Sorry, Pierre. The police confiscated it as evidence."

Pierre reached out to grab Josh as two of the plainclothes officers rushed to overpower Pierre. He struggled but was handcuffed instantly.

"Where's Julia?" Josh demanded.

"Find her yourself," Pierre yelled before turning to look behind him when he heard Kate sobbing, handcuffed between two more cops.

Throughout the next anxious and frustrating minutes, Kate refused to say anything, despite desperate pleas from Josh and warnings from the police. She remained silent until the senior officer informed her she would be charged as an accomplice to Roger's murder and the attempted murder of Francesca and Julia, as well as Julia's kidnapping. "You are looking at a very long prison sentence. Cooperate and it will go easier on you."

Kate broke down into hysterical tears. "Okay, I'll tell you. We left her in the catacombs. But I don't know Paris so I can't tell you exactly where we were."

The police assured Josh they would find Julia, but the look in the senior officer's eyes didn't offer the promise that his words implied.

Carly jumped out of the unmarked police car where she had been waiting. She searched Josh's and the detective's eyes for signs of hope. Josh ushered her back into the car and filled her in. The officer who was driving followed the patrol cars carrying Pierre and Kate back to the station, where Josh would file charges and talk with Detective Durand.

Josh and Carly waited again in the detective's office while he fetched coffee. Carly's eyes brimmed with tears with the realization that they had no substantial clue to locate Julia. "How will we find her?" she sobbed. "*Will* we find her?"

"Frankly, she could be anywhere," Josh admitted. He stopped his pacing and looked down at Carly, realizing his own feeling of fear and helplessness. "Paris is a huge city to get lost in. I wonder how Pierre thought he was going to get away with this." He sat next to Carly with his elbows on his knees, hands together and fingers interlaced. "So much for one last romantic day in Paris."

Carly managed a tiny smile and reached over to pat Josh's shoulder. "It's certainly not *your* fault. Julia has a certain propensity for finding trouble, even when she's not looking for it."

Josh appreciated her attempt to comfort him, but Carly's eyes reflected her anxiety over her sister. He sighed and put a protective arm around her. "She does indeed." He checked his watch when he heard nearby bells ring. "It's already been over two hours since Pierre took her."

Julia's phone chimed with a message. Carly read the screen. "Your weekly Fitbit report," she said aloud. "Julia's Fitbit!" she shouted and held the phone up for Josh. "She was telling me about all the neat features on her new Fitbit, like tracking her route when she walks around the lake. Doesn't that mean it has a GPS built in? She showed me how she even gets text messages on it. Could we use it to find her?"

"Maybe. Let's check her phone apps and see."

"Okay. Here's the Fitbit app." Carly handed him the phone. "I don't know how to use it to track someone. Can you figure it out?"

Josh scrolled through the menu items and found the option to "follow" someone using the Strava app, which Julia had installed on her phone. In another minute or so, he "found" her and showed Carly the red tracing that followed her route that day. They hurried to find Detective Durand, and Josh quickly explained their discovery. In another few minutes, the three of them were in a police cruiser with lights flashing and sirens sounding, as the detective sped through the city.

The police car pulled up to the last location noted on the screen. Josh and Carly looked around at the many old brick warehouses in the industrial area. "Now what?" said Carly. "Where are the catacombs? Where do we start?"

The detective said, "Please, may I see the cellphone?" He studied the track on the screen. "Her trail stops ten meters down the sidewalk, where there is an unmarked entrance to the tunnels beneath the city. Follow me."

They walked about thirty feet down the street to a rusted gate-like door with graffiti tags on the walls on either side of it. "There's a myriad of entrances to the catacombs, in addition to the authorized one near the Metro stop for the Montparnasse Tower. The police try to stop the locals from making illegal entries, but it takes constant surveillance to find the latest 'new' entrance and lock it up. Looks like this is one of them."

"I don't know if a signal will reach Julia's step tracker, but it might be worth trying to send her a text and let her know we're nearby," said Carly.

Detective Durand said, "It's worth a try, though I have my doubts about it penetrating the layers of rock between us and Ms. Fairchild. The trail stopped right here as you noticed from the Strava app. It tracked her until she entered the catacombs. Her step counter would still work, but that's not helpful to us. We'll have to go in and look for her. I know my way around a little. I was one of those young people who explored the tunnels," he admitted, with a sheepish look on his face. He called for backup and pulled out a flashlight from his car. "Let's go."

The bright LED light pierced through the intense blackness of the underground stairs. Carly gasped when she first saw the long staircase that led to the passageway. "How will we ever find her?"

"I doubt she's very far down the tunnel. Mr. Dupont wouldn't want to waste too much time here. He would be more interested in getting away from Paris." He bellowed into the darkness ahead. "Julia! This is Officer Durand." Only silence in response.

"Miss Pedersen, please send her a text to walk toward my voice if she can hear me. We can only hope that it will work down here. Otherwise, she might be afraid that I'm Pierre."

Carly immediately sent the text message as they continued along the passageway. "This is a creepy, spooky place. Why would anyone come down here on purpose?" She turned to the detective. "Why did *you* come down here?"

"You want to know why I explored the catacombs?" He chuckled. "Because I could. It was a rite of passage in my youth. I finally wised up and stopped when one of my friends got seriously lost overnight. That was an eye-opener; we never came back after that."

"I just got a 'failed message' note." Carly sighed. "Texting doesn't work down here."

⁓

Julia continued her slow walk through the blackness, checking her step total every couple of minutes. She shivered in the damp cold and wished for a drink of water. She felt something furry run over her foot and shrieked. She pressed her back against the wall, hoping to give the furry creatures wider berth, and held her hand to her chest as she regained her composure before she resumed walking, now a little faster. She tripped on a hard object and caught herself, relieved she hadn't twisted an ankle or fallen to the stony floor. She swore under her breath, then gave a little prayer of thanks that she was not injured. She slowed her pace and used her foot like a blind person would use a cane to search for unseen obstacles.

She checked her step count again—6,700. She sighed and hoped she'd made the right choice at the turn of the tunnel.

⁓

Carly stopped walking. "Did you hear that? I heard a voice screaming in the distance. It has to be Julia." She yelled as loud as she could, "Julia! We're coming!"

Julia heard a voice call and saw a faint light in the distance. "Help!" she shouted. Then she clapped her hand over the mouth. *It could be Pierre waiting for me. To hurt or kill me.*

Carly said, "That *is* Julia's voice. Can we hurry?"

"Julia! It's me, Josh," he called loudly through the cold air.

"I can hear you," she yelled in reply. "I can see your light. Thank God!"

A long five minutes later, Officer Durand's flashlight shone on Julia. She and Carly collapsed in each other's arms, sobbing and hugging. Carly had worn a jacket for the cool morning outing. She took it off and wrapped it around her trembling sister.

"I am so glad to see you," Julia said between sniffles. "I was beyond scared. And there are rats down here."

Officer Durand chuckled at Julia's accurate observation.

"Seeing the catacombs was *not* on my bucket list, I'll have you know."

25

SATURDAY AFTERNOON

Julia scrubbed her body and washed her hair in the shower, trying to rid herself of the mustiness of the catacombs. She donned her go-to outfit of white capris and long-sleeved navy-blue-and-white-striped t-shirt for a fashionably late lunch with Carly and Josh, with a visit to the police station afterwards. She scurried to the lobby, where her sister and Josh had waited while she made herself presentable. Josh, still in the khaki pants and button-down-collar blue plaid shirt he'd worn for his meeting with Pierre, met her midway across the room and greeted her with a warm embrace and kiss.

"I'm starving," said Julia. "For a while, when I was stranded in that dungeon, I was sure I would never have another chance to eat."

"You weren't down there long enough to miss a meal," Carly said. "You couldn't have been hungry yet."

Julia made a face. "I didn't get breakfast, remember? Pierre grabbed me before I even had a sip of coffee."

"If it makes you feel any better," said Carly, "I didn't have time to eat either."

Josh took Julia's hand and led the way to the lobby exit. "I'll treat for lunch. I missed breakfast too."

Vincent stood next to the limo. He grinned broadly when he saw Julia and hugged her tightly. He kissed her on the forehead and winked as she entered the car. "You are like Cinderella going to the ball."

The April afternoon weather was perfect for a sidewalk lunch at the nearby bistro. The crisp white tablecloth and dark blue napkins added a touch of polish to the otherwise simple café. A carafe of chilled pinot grigio was an ideal complement to the fresh green salad and fruit plate that accompanied the succulent grilled shrimp and scallops dripping with garlic butter. The waiter brought a basket of freshly baked French brioches, still warm from the oven. Julia slathered one with jam.

"Yum." Julia closed her eyes in a moment of food ecstasy. "I could live on fresh bread, cheese, wine, and fruit."

"You forgot to include dessert," said Carly. "I'm stuffed, but I left a little room for something sweet, like a fruit tart."

Julia smiled. "Of course you did. I'm almost surprised you didn't order it first." Julia moved away as Carly pretended to punch her.

"I'm ready to hear your explanation of how Pierre and Laura and Kate did their dastardly deeds," said Josh.

Julia breathed in the fresh air, ever so grateful to be in the light instead of blackness. "You know, I thought Laura was at the bottom of all this, and I was right." She shook her bangs out of her eyes. "Pierre was obviously deep in it also, but it wasn't until I heard that Laura adamantly denied going to the mystic shop that I realized that Kate or Becca had to be involved."

"But the shop owner identified Laura," said Carly. "What about that?"

Julia bobbed her head as she finished swallowing a sip of

her wine. "In retrospect, I realized how closely he held the photo to his eyes. He was probably very near-sighted and didn't have his glasses on. Kate and Laura both have long blonde hair, and he simply misidentified her."

"I see," said Josh. "Are you saying *Kate* is the guilty party who delivered the poisonous mushrooms to Roger at the hotel? But why?"

"Roger and Laura were in a financial mess. Laura said they had been unable to borrow enough money against their assets. Let's assume Roger came up with the scheme of selling proprietary software to a competing company and used Pierre as the 'agent,' so to speak. At some point, Roger must have changed his mind and told Pierre. Maybe that final morning before the party, because you had said that was the final official day of meetings. Pierre probably called Laura immediately to tell her, and maybe to see if she could change Roger's mind."

Julia paused to taste one of the desserts that Carly had ordered—a mini-eclair. "This is delicious. Anyway, Laura had planned to have Kate, whom she knew from the restaurant on Cape Cod, deliver the tray of mushrooms to Roger. She had been suspicious that Roger was having an affair while on his trips to Paris and decided to kill him and keep all the money from the deal for herself. What she didn't know is that Roger had hidden the thumb drive in Josh's room after he retrieved it from the hotel safe."

"That explains why Pierre took the briefcase then," said Josh. "They assumed he'd hidden it in the lining or something."

"Or something is right," said Julia. "They didn't expect Roger to collapse. I suspect that was a reaction to the combination of his antidepressant and antihistamine, combined with the poisonous mushrooms. They would have worked much more slowly otherwise, and the murder might never have been detected. And ultimately the eyedrops might have finished him off."

"But how did Francesca fit into all of this?" asked Carly. "Laura acted like the name 'Francesca' was new to her."

"'Acting' is the operative word. Remember the note that Laura said she had found in Roger's pocket at the hospital? She probably found it some time ago, before this trip, and did some research on her own. She checked out the cooking school and persuaded her friend Kate to take classes there as a way of learning more about Francesca. She only showed us the note to cast suspicion on Francesca. The tray of mushrooms that Francesca brought to the party was to impress Roger, not us. They were probably innocent, normal stuffed mushrooms. Then Laura arranged for Kate to deliver a similar tray to Roger in his room, styled as Francesca had done at the school. The difference is that hers had dried poisonous mushrooms in the stuffing."

Carly said, "So that explains why Roger said something about being surprised to see Kate. He would have known her from the restaurant in Cape Cod but wouldn't expect to see her in Paris."

"Right," said Julia.

Josh had been quiet but had a puzzled look on his face. "You're implying that it was Laura's plan all along to have Roger die."

"Yes," said Julia, "but not before she had her hands on the money that she would inherit as his widow. Once Roger collapsed without revealing the location of the thumb drive, she had to figure out a Plan B. She still needed that thumb drive. But she and Pierre were probably worried Roger might wake up and accuse them, so they made sure he died, by adding the eyedrops. Pierre must have gotten them somehow. It may well have been Pierre, not Alain at all, who slipped the drops into Roger's eyes while he was unconscious."

Josh nodded his head slowly. "But the data was still missing. That explains why first Roger's room, then my room, was searched. And why Pierre grilled me about the thumb drive, not knowing I hadn't found it yet. And later got Alain to do the same."

"Yes, they would have found Roger's briefcase in his room, and his cellphone as well. They probably destroyed the contents of the briefcase and dismantled the phone when neither one held any clue as to where they could find the thumb drive."

Carly licked her fingers, enjoying the crumbs from the last tartlet on the tray. "I don't get how Francesca hooked up with Kate and Becca. And why was she poisoned?"

Julia nodded. "I suspect Kate and Becca arrived a few days before we started cooking classes. Remember that we commented on how chummy they seemed to be with Francesca from day one?" Carly nodded. "Kate probably asked the school to put her in touch with an instructor ahead of time. And asked for Francesca."

"But why try to kill her?" Josh repeated Carly's question.

"The time-honored reason of knowing too much," said Julia. "With Laura's spousal jealousy thrown in. Kate wrote the letters and hid them in the briefcase to make it appear that Francesca killed Roger over a lover's quarrel—a scorned woman. On reflection, I recognized the perfume on the letters. Remember the maid said the woman who delivered the poisoned mushrooms to Roger's room was wearing perfume?"

Carly asked, "What about Alain? I thought he was kinda cute—even though Simone sensed that he was sinister the first time she met him."

Julia winced. "Alcoholics are not my kind of 'cute.' My guess is that he looked up to Pierre and was willing to do anything he was asked to do. But he didn't take direct action to kill anyone."

"You haven't explained how Kate and Pierre ended up together," said Carly.

Josh said, "I can answer that. Roger hosted meetings at Kate's family's inn on occasion. It was convenient because Laura's family is from there, and it's a nice change from Washington D.C. for business purposes. I recall him mentioning that Pierre had been there at some point and he would have met Kate then."

"Here's what I think happened, based on what you just said," said Julia. "Okay, Kate has taken up with Pierre. She's a young, pretty girl, and he's a suave French guy. Let's assume that Laura doesn't know anything about that. Laura tells Kate about Roger's betrayal with Francesca and asks Kate to help with her scheme to keep all the money from the software gig. Laura offers to pay Kate a lot for her help.

"Kate tells Pierre, who is also pleased to get rid of Roger, who would have been the tie between the stolen software and himself. And then Kate and Pierre decide to get rid of Francesca, who might have squealed on them if she suspected they had played a role in killing her former lover. My guess is that Kate brought more mushrooms to Francesca's on the pretext of showing off her newly learned cooking skills to her Cordon Bleu teacher. The digitalis in the form of foxglove could easily have been added to the stuffing. Of course, Francesca would have had to sample the appetizers that Kate brought for her approval. Remember, Francesca went home right after our party, so she didn't even know that Roger had taken ill, much less died. So she had no reason to fear eating Kate's mushrooms."

Julia took a long swallow of her wine. "Or Kate could have just brought her some special tea or coffee, laced with dried foxglove, as a 'thank you.' That would explain the

French coffee press we saw sitting on the counter. Kate would have left the briefcase at Francesca's while she was there, empty except for the letters and business card she thought would help frame Josh for both murders—Roger's and Francesca's—or barring that, the letters would throw suspicion on Francesca as a murder-suicide. Either way would have been okay with her. Except we found Francesca in time, so it's only attempted murder in her case."

"And the letters would have connected Roger and Francesca," Carly added. "But why bother with the eyedrops?"

"Laura probably gave them to Kate, telling her to leave them in Francesca's bathroom, just in case that angle was ever noticed. Knowing Laura, she probably managed to arrange to preserve Pierre's fingerprints on the bottle—we know they were found on the briefcase. This would be insurance in case Pierre ever turned on her." Julia paused and sipped her wine.

"Becca was an innocent bystander, it appears. She had gone back to the Cape, just as we expected, while Kate stayed on. She was shocked to learn of Kate's involvement in murder and kidnapping."

"'What a tangled web we weave when first we practice to deceive.' I'm not sure if that's Shakespeare or someone else," said Josh. "I remember it from a class in first year law. It helps remind me that it pays to be honest." He looked into Julia's eyes, then quickly away.

"Honesty is always the right policy," said Julia while Josh poured the last of the wine into the three glasses. "Once we finish this, we need to make one last visit to the police station. Then we can be normal tourists for our last evening in Paris."

"That'll be the day," said Carly.

26

SATURDAY AFTERNOON

Julia and Carly met first with Detective Durand to debrief him and answer questions he still had about Roger's murder and Francesca's attempted murder. The detective explained that they were working to assign the proper level of involvement to each of the players in the game. When the detective was satisfied that he understood what had happened, he excused the sisters. Josh then gave his statement, which corroborated with the evidence, after which he was formally exonerated and excused.

~

JULIA SELECTED the sexy backless black dress with a deep V-neck that she'd brought to wear for her last evening in Paris, certain that finally there wouldn't be any more sleuthing to interfere with a romantic dinner. She added dazzling earrings and a matching necklace to complete the look. She checked her hair one last time, touched up her lipstick, and twirled in front of the mirror, smiling wistfully at her image. Her vacation had been hijacked by a senseless murder and a misguided attempt at another. She hoped her time with Josh this one night would make up for the missed dinners and time together that she had envisioned when he had first proposed that she join him in Paris.

Simone had invited Carly to an artist's opening at a prominent gallery, promising plenty of food and fun. Adorned in colorful garb and bling, they had already been gone a half hour.

Julia entered the lobby of her hotel at the same moment that Josh, cutting a dashing figure in a navy blazer and charcoal slacks, stepped in from the street. He handed her a small bouquet of delicate blossoms and bowed gallantly as she curtsied. Josh offered his arm and off they went to the sound of applause from the desk clerk and several other couples in the lobby.

Vincent, spiffy in his chauffeur's uniform, stood at the door of the limousine. His attempt at a straight face was betrayed by little upturns of his lips, then a full grin. He broke protocol when he hugged Julia before helping her into the "chariot." He whispered that he had a vase in the front seat for her flowers before she scooted across the leather seat.

Josh slipped in beside her. "You amaze me, Julia. Earlier today you held your cool in the catacombs, and now you look ready to meet royalty. Do they teach that in medical school?"

"Holding my cool or looking good?" she replied coyly.

Josh laughed. "Both. Either."

"Definitely we learned how to 'keep cool' in the face of any adversity or emergency or uncertainty. I'm not sure anyone actually looks good enough in scrubs to meet royalty."

"How do you learn that—taking care of emergencies, I mean?" Josh asked seriously. "It seems like there's a lot of medical stuff you'd have to remember, and you can't pull out a book or manual. You have to act immediately."

"Practice, training, and teamwork. And a lot of algorithms

that are easier to remember than pages of instructions." Julia turned to Josh. "It gets stuck in our DNA and becomes automatic. I'm sure the same thing happens with your legal education."

The limousine slowed as Vincent encountered heavy traffic on the Rue de Rivoli in the Marais area of Paris. "Where are we?" Julia asked. She didn't recognize the buildings from any of her daytime excursions.

"I still owe you that special dinner, so tonight we will be dining at a restaurant known for its exceptional food and elegance. L'Ambroisie is supposed to be romantic as well. Or so I've heard." Josh squeezed her hand. "We're here," he told her as Vincent stopped at the curb.

The maître d' escorted the couple to a table for two near a gigantic painting that covered an entire wall. The table was so close to the wall Julia almost felt as if she was part of the battle scene depicted by the artist. She gazed at the magnificence of the room, taking in the crystal chandeliers and high ceilings. "This has to be the fanciest restaurant I've ever been in," she murmured to Josh.

"Only the best for you, Miss Julia," he replied. He ordered wine and the chef's special for the meal after listening to the waiter's recommendations.

The meal of perfectly prepared lamb and scallops served with roasted asparagus was heaven to her taste buds. Julia was grateful for the small servings of the rich food, especially when the waiter insisted that they have a dessert "on the house." He brought several delicious morsels to accompany the after-dinner espresso.

After the wonderful meal, the evening air was still warm enough for a stroll along the adjacent Place de Voges. Julia breathed in the air of freedom. She shuddered when she recalled the early part of the day. It was hard to believe that so much could change in a matter of a few hours.

"Thank you, Josh, for a delightful evening. I couldn't ask for a better ending to this crazy vacation."

"My pleasure. It isn't exactly how I'd planned to spend our time in Paris, but it has been plenty exciting."

"I'll grant you that," said Julia. "I'm sorry about Roger."

"That was a stunner. It's sad to see what some people will do for money."

"I thought those crooks were confined to television and the movies," said Julia. "I'm still shocked that the crook was someone you actually work with."

They wandered along the park's perimeter. When they came to a corner and turned to the right, Julia stopped. "Josh. Look." She pointed to a café sign at the end of the block. "There's Café Hugo. That's the place that got all this started in the first place."

"What do you mean?"

"The piece of paper that Laura found in Roger's pocket had the café's phone number and Francesca's name on it. How ironic." She sighed, bemused. "It's as though we've come full circle."

∽

Sunday morning

The morning sun glowed through the morning haze as Julia and Carly waited on the sidewalk in front of their hotel, luggage ready to load when Vincent and Josh arrived. Once in the limo, Carly was high on adrenalin and regaled them with a detailed description of the crazy modern art she and Simone had seen at the gallery the evening before. She mimicked the art expert's accent and tone as she talked.

The ride to the airport was otherwise quiet. Josh was somber; Julia was meditative.

While Vincent took care of the luggage, Josh took Julia's

hand and led her a few feet away. "Julia," said Josh. "I need to tell you something that I should have said sooner."

Julia felt her heart skip a few beats.

He took her hands in his and held them to his chest. "In the six months since we saw each other last fall in Amsterdam, I've met someone. We've been seeing each other since February." He searched Julia's eyes. "She reminds me a lot of you. Smart, pretty, quick on her feet."

"And she lives a lot closer."

"That too." Josh stared across the street, then turned back to Julia. "I considered canceling out on meeting you this trip, but I wanted to see you again, and Retha, that's her name, encouraged me to follow through. Right now, I don't know if anything serious will happen."

Julia felt her eyes start to well up as she nodded. "I understand. A long-distance relationship is a challenge. Let alone my being a doctor."

"I love that you're a doctor, even if I'm not so hot on solving murders every time I run into you." Josh hugged her. "If we lived closer, even within a couple of hours of each other, I would want to see if something could develop."

Julia found a tissue in her pocket, dabbed her eyes, and blew her nose. "And here I thought I'd finally met someone who could be my match. I know how hard it is for the typical guy to have a meaningful relationship with a lady doctor." She looked up into his deep blue eyes. "I had a feeling you were distracted, but I hoped it was the Roger incident and your business."

"I know I haven't spent much time with you. A lot of it *was* dealing with the police and the ongoing investigation," he said, moving his hands to her shoulders. "And I'll admit that I still wanted to show you Paris like we'd talked about."

"Even if your heart wasn't in it anymore," said Julia

sadly. "I have a question. Did you really meet a college friend the other day for lunch or was it...her?"

Josh met her blue eyes again. "It was a college friend. I promise. Right now I feel like a first-class cad."

Julia shook her head, smiling. "No, you're not a cad or a bad guy. I think you're quite the romantic soul who hates hurting anyone's feelings. And I understand how hard it is for you to tell me that you've met someone."

Josh nodded, his dimples flat.

"She must be pretty special, and she's lucky to be seeing you."

"Thanks for understanding, Julia." Josh kissed her cheek gently. "And thank you for figuring out the rest of the story about Roger and Francesca. I've heard bad things about jails." He shivered involuntarily.

"The risk management attorney warns us when he lectures that no one looks good in orange. Carly may be the exception," said Julia, trying to smile, knowing it was her sister's favorite color.

Josh chuckled.

Julia brightened. "That reminds me. I talked to Francesca's nurse this morning. She's awake and talking and is going to be all right. I'm so glad of that. And she's giving her statement to the police to clear up details. It seems she thought she was just helping Kate and didn't have any idea what she was up to. Lesli asked me to stay in touch because Carly and I saved Francesca's life. Someday I'll come back to Paris to see them and enjoy more of the city, like the Louvre, which we didn't get to see this time." Julia wrinkled her nose. "I'm sure I won't go on a guided tour of the catacombs, however."

Josh hugged Julia one last time and held her close for a moment before she turned to follow Carly and enter the line to go through security. He watched her with misty eyes as she snaked through the line, glancing back at him a few times.

Julia felt Josh's eyes follow her. Her heart felt leaden and her eyes welled with tears as she turned one last time to meet his gaze. She waved and blew one final kiss, whispering, "Ciao, my friend."

THE END

sadly. "I have a question. Did you really meet a college friend the other day for lunch or was it…her?"

Josh met her blue eyes again. "It was a college friend. I promise. Right now I feel like a first-class cad."

Julia shook her head, smiling. "No, you're not a cad or a bad guy. I think you're quite the romantic soul who hates hurting anyone's feelings. And I understand how hard it is for you to tell me that you've met someone."

Josh nodded, his dimples flat.

"She must be pretty special, and she's lucky to be seeing you."

"Thanks for understanding, Julia." Josh kissed her cheek gently. "And thank you for figuring out the rest of the story about Roger and Francesca. I've heard bad things about jails." He shivered involuntarily.

"The risk management attorney warns us when he lectures that no one looks good in orange. Carly may be the exception," said Julia, trying to smile, knowing it was her sister's favorite color.

Josh chuckled.

Julia brightened. "That reminds me. I talked to Francesca's nurse this morning. She's awake and talking and is going to be all right. I'm so glad of that. And she's giving her statement to the police to clear up details. It seems she thought she was just helping Kate and didn't have any idea what she was up to. Lesli asked me to stay in touch because Carly and I saved Francesca's life. Someday I'll come back to Paris to see them and enjoy more of the city, like the Louvre, which we didn't get to see this time." Julia wrinkled her nose. "I'm sure I won't go on a guided tour of the catacombs, however."

Josh hugged Julia one last time and held her close for a moment before she turned to follow Carly and enter the line to go through security. He watched her with misty eyes as she snaked through the line, glancing back at him a few times.

Julia felt Josh's eyes follow her. Her heart felt leaden and her eyes welled with tears as she turned one last time to meet his gaze. She waved and blew one final kiss, whispering, "Ciao, my friend."

THE END

ACKNOWLEDGMENTS

Many thanks go to my brilliant editors, Carol Gaskin and Sandra Haven, who made my story better than when I started. Although I've been to southern France, I have yet to visit Paris to see the wonderful "City of Lights" for myself. (As of this writing, my scheduled trip has been canceled three times due to COVID.) I relied on Carol for her expertise with the details that make the French setting more accurate and realistic. And I've memorized Rick Steves' map from his Paris guidebook.

Thank you to my Ace reader, Angela Thompson, my Beta reader friends, my Rabble Writers Facebook group (I love you!), and my husband Steve for letting me ramble on whenever I had a new idea to test. A special thanks goes to my real-life younger sister, Carleen (depicted as "Carly," if you didn't guess), for allowing me to put her in all these pretend situations. I might have to really send her to Paris someday.

And thanks to YOU for reading my books and for the positive reviews. It makes my day.

PJ Peterson
   www.pjpetersonauthor.com

ABOUT THE AUTHOR

PJ Peterson

PJ is a retired internist who enjoyed the diagnostic part of practicing medicine as well as creating long-lasting relationships with her patients. As a child she wanted to be a doctor so she could "help people." She now volunteers at the local Free Medical Clinic to satisfy that need to help.

She loved to read from a young age and read all the Trixie Belden and Nancy Drew books she could find. It wasn't until she was an adult that she wrote anything longer than short stories for English classes and term papers in others. Writing mysteries only makes sense given her early exposure to that genre. Sprinkling in a little medical mystique makes it all the more fun.

If you enjoy reading this third book in the Julia Fairchild Mystery series, feel free to visit her website at www.pjpetersonauthor.com.

CPSIA information can be obtained
at www.ICGtesting.com
Printed in the USA
LVHW010105310122
709792LV00001B/183

9 781733 567565